THE DISCIPLE

ERNESTO MORALES-RAMOS

The Disciple

by Ernesto Morales-Ramos

First edition published in English

Published by: TecnoTur Publishing

Internal images designed by: Robert Carrero

Editing and internal layout: Allan Tépper

Cover design: Andreína Ascanio Toro

ISBN of the paperback: 979-8-9934183-8-4

ISBN of the electronic version (ebook): 979-8-9934183-9-1

ISBN of the audiobook: 979-8-9988687-9-5

EDITOR'S NOTE

All conversations that took place between the protagonist (Becky, aka Rebeca) and other Puerto Rican characters happened in their native tongue (Castilian), except when they involved foreigners who didn't speak or understand it.

In those special cases, they all spoke English unless otherwise indicated.

पृथ्वी

Earth

1

Bhutan, Himalayan Mountains, 8th Century

The snow fell in near perfect silence.

At twenty thousand feet, sound itself seemed to freeze. The mountain peaks rose like the teeth of some ancient god, tearing at the belly of heaven. Between two of these granite fangs, hidden from all but the most determined seekers, a dark cavern entrance yawned—dark, forbidding, impossibly remote.

The Cavern

Inside, butter lanterns flickered against walls of living stone.

Eleven figures knelt in a semicircle, their voices rising and falling in rhythmic prayer:

«Om ah hum vajra guru pema sid-dhi hum.»

The chant echoed through chambers carved not by human hands but by geological time itself. Behind them, pressed into the granite wall like a fossil from some spiritual prehistory, was the body imprint of Guru Padmasambhava—an enlightened being whose physical form had somehow left its mark on solid rock.

The effect was unsettling. Even in this age of miracles, it suggested powers beyond comprehension.

Yeshe Tsogyal moved among her disciples with the grace of smoke. Beautiful, ageless, she seemed to float rather than walk. Her eyes held each of theirs in turn—warm, knowing, terrible in their intensity. This was a teacher who could see through flesh and bone to the trembling soul beneath.

One by one, objects materialized in her hands.

For the first disciple: a wooden chest, ancient beyond measure. Inside, golden scrolls appeared as if written by invisible hands, characters forming in languages that predated Sanskrit itself.

For the second: a piece of granite. Yeshe squeezed it, leaving the impression of her fingers in the hard stone as if it were made of clay.

For the third: a bronze statuette of Guru Padmasambhava, gleaming in the lamplight.

Each object appeared, was acknowledged, then vanished with a strange blue luminescence that left afterimages on the retina.

Finally, Yeshe reached her youngest disciple.

Tashi Chidren was barely fifteen, beautiful in the way of mountain flowers—delicate, unlikely, destined for a short bloom. Her face was flushed as she fought back tears. She understood what this ceremony meant. Goodbye. Perhaps forever.

The object that materialized for her was a phurba—a three-edged dagger, a ritual implement with the faces of three deities at the top of the handle. The metal caught the lamplight and threw it back in strange patterns.

Tashi bowed low. The dagger vanished with that same eerie blue glow.

A single tear escaped down her cheek. Yeshe Tsogyal caught it on one finger with impossible gentleness. She touched the tear to the stone floor.

A blue flower sprouted instantly, impossibly, where the tear had touched the ground.

Tashi felt a shiver shoot up her spine, electric and warm, spreading through her entire body, her back straightened, her eyes opened wide as she witnessed yet another miracle performed by her guru with the same ease as merely taking a breath.

2

San Germán, Puerto Rico, Present Day

A bunch of beautiful, blue flowers swayed in the tropical breeze. Smash! The claw of a mechanical excavator destroyed them in an instant, lifting a mound of earth as the rusty machine tore into the ground, spun around and dumped its contents into a pile behind it.

Under the dawn's sunlight, the excavator's silhouette resembled a huge scorpion.

Jiménez, the machine's operator, face creased and sunburnt sweated over his controls in an endless ballet of digging, spinning, and spitting soil.

As he dropped another bucketful into the pile, something caught the sunlight.

The excavator's engine died without warning.

Jiménez swore in his native language of Puerto Rico, then English, then a hybrid of both that would have impressed linguists if any had been present to hear it. He was alone on this godforsaken spit of land, three miles from anything resembling civilization, and his Caterpillar tractor had just decided to quit.

At sixty, Jiménez had made peace with machinery's treachery. Equipment failed. That was the nature of things. But the *timing* of this particular failure bothered him.

He'd just hit something different. Something that had no place in that terrain.

Not rock—he knew the feel of rock through the excavator's controls like a surgeon knows bone through scalpel. This had been different. Hollow. Deliberate.

Unnatural.

Jiménez climbed down from the cab, his knees and back crackling, protesting the descent. The afternoon sun hammered down on his neck as he approached the mound of earth his excavator had just vomited onto the muddy mound.

Something caught the light.

A stone slab.

He pulled it free from the mud, his fingers finding purchase on carved edges. It was rectangular, about the size of a small computer monitor but much thicker and definitely heavier. As the dirt fell away, he saw writing—characters like nothing he had ever seen—definitely not Castilian, or even *Taíno*.

The stone was warm to the touch. Unnaturally warm.

Jiménez looked around, suddenly aware of how isolated he was. The wild blue flowers he'd destroyed with his first pass appeared sprinkled over the earth mound, many more than he thought he had uprooted, scattering in all directions in the breeze.

For a moment, he became aware that there seemed to be no sound, the usual chirp of birds and swaying trees were silent.

As Jiménez surveyed the stone slab a thought came to mind—this could be a significant archeological find. That idea posed a problem and an opportunity, his dig could be stopped by the government's cultural protection authorities but, on the other hand, it could mean some cash.

The laborer gently placed the stone next to his excavator and ran to the front of his machine to examine the recently-dug hole. He sifted the humid earth with his hands, burying them deep, up to his elbows, frantically searching for more treasure.

Nothing.

He looked back at the stone and climbed out of the hole wiping his muddied hands on his jeans. He walked to the back of his excavator, fetched a blue, plastic tarp and a nylon rope. He wrapped the stone with the tarp.

The engine turned over on its own.

Jiménez jumped back, startled, dropped the stone, laughing nervously. The package landed with a thud that seemed too heavy for its size.

The excavator's engine rumbled at idle, patient, waiting.

«*Mierda,*» he muttered.

His hands were shaking. «Just a short in the electrical system», he told himself. «Happens all the time. Nothing strange about machinery acting up. Nothing strange at all.»

He retrieved the stone, tied the tarp tightly around it with the rope, and strapped it behind the seat. The engine purred like it had never quit.

Jiménez kicked the excavator's huge, worn tires as he cursed at it. He climbed back to his seat.

He continued working until sunset, but his mind wasn't on the job. His mind was on the stone, wrapped and waiting behind him, thinking this could be the treasure that would make his retirement possible, his life finally easy.

That night, Jiménez climbed the cinder-block steps to his humble home. It was small, with wooden walls and a zinc roof, the kind that dotted the oldest parts of the town of San Germán.

He was holding the wrapped stone under one arm and a bag of groceries in the other. The old door squeaked loudly when he opened it. The even older wooden floors groaned as he walked in. He shut the door, kicked off his muddy boots at the entrance, and turned on the lights.

He plopped the stone on the sofa, went into the kitchen and came back gulping down a beer. He dragged a chair to face the stone and brought a floor lamp closer. After surveying his setup, he returned to the kitchen and came back out chugging his second beer.

Jiménez turned on the floor lamp, pointed it towards the wrapped stone. He thought for a second, then moved one of the side tables to the front of the sofa and propped his mobile phone, looking for the perfect angle for recording his find.

This would gold on social media, he thought, proof that he'd found something genuinely valuable.

He turned on the phone's video camera and unwrapped the stone.

The lights went out

«*Carajo*,» he muttered. «Another blackout?»

But that wasn't right. Through the window, he could see the street lamp outside, glowing steadily. Just his house, then just his lights.

Except the street lamp was flickering now. Blue light, pulsing like a heartbeat, throwing impossible shadows across his walls.

Jiménez quickly grabbed his phone. Dead. He ran into the kitchen, tried the flashlight he kept there. Dead.

The darkness pressed in like something physical.

His hands found the candle he kept for blackouts—the kind with the Virgin Mary printed on the glass jar. The match flared, and in that moment of light, he saw the stone clearly.

The characters seemed to move in the candlelight, rearranging themselves into patterns that hurt to look at.

The front door squeaked.

Jiménez spun around, nearly dropping the candle. «Who's there?»

The floor groaned—old wood announcing the presence of weight it hadn't been designed to bear.

A figure stepped from the darkness. Hooded, moving with the fluid precision of a trained killer. The candlelight caught the edge of a face —South Asian, young, utterly without mercy.

«Out of my house!» Jiménez tried to sound commanding. It came out as a plea.

He didn't see the first blow. He only felt it—a strike to his throat that turned his breath to broken glass in his lungs. The candle fell from his nerveless fingers and rolled across the floor. The second blow put him down.

Through failing vision, Jiménez saw the hooded figure—Bhatua, a former *Gurkha*, the most feared special forces soldiers in the world, wrapping the tarp with lightning precision.

The lights came back on.

Bhatua quickly turned off the lights manually, picked up the still-burning candle, and methodically set fire to the curtains.

He pulled out a combat knife, tore into the couch's cushions, pulled out the stuffing and set it on fire.

Then he continued with anything else that would burn.

Bhatua moved through the smoke with practiced efficiency, the wrapped stone tucked under his arm like a football. He burst through the front door and sprinted to a waiting SUV—a black Mercedes G-Class with tinted windows, the kind of vehicle that screamed money and menace in equal measure. The back door swung open and he dove inside.

Mohammed sat behind the wheel, a mountain of a man whose bulk made the luxury vehicle seem smaller than it was. South Asian, burly, with the dead eyes of someone who'd seen too much and felt too little. He gunned the engine before Bhatua had even closed the door.

The SUV accelerated smoothly away from the burning house.

Bhatua allowed himself a smile as he looked through the rear windshield. Flames were already visible through the windows, orange light dancing against the gathering darkness. In the distance, he could hear sirens beginning to wail.

Too late for Jiménez. Too late by far.

A phone rang—not the cheap burner Bhatua carried, but Mohammed's encrypted sat-phone, the one they only used for *him*. Mohammed handed it back without a word.

The screen showed an incoming video call.

Bhatua answered it, and the face that appeared made him straighten involuntarily, a reflex borne of years of military discipline.

Druk Dorji looked like money and power condensed into human form. Oriental, mid-forties, with black hair slicked back from a high forehead and a goatee trimmed with the precision of a surgeon's scalpel. He wore what appeared to be an expensive shirt—Italian, probably—and behind him, Bhatua could see the edge of floor-to-ceiling windows overlooking mountain peaks.

Bhutan. The master was calling from Bhutan.

When Dorji spoke, it was in Dzongkha, the language of their homeland. Bhatua had grown up speaking it in the mountain villages before the military recruited him, before he'd learned to kill efficiently and without question.

«You found it, yes?» Dorji's voice was smooth, cultured, but underneath ran a current of something ancient and wrong.

Bhatua nodded, not trusting his voice. He held up the wrapped stone.

«As the oracle predicted,» Dorji continued, his eyes fixed on the bundle, «the last disciple will awaken there soon.»

«Can you see who it is, Master?» Bhatua asked. The question had been burning in him since they'd located the stone. If the oracle could predict where, surely it could predict who.

«Not yet.» Something flickered across Dorji's face—frustration, perhaps, or hunger. «We will return to that island soon to find him. For now, just bring me the stone.»

«Your will be done, Guruji.»

Outside the SUV, a firetruck screamed past, its red lights painting the interior in bloody flashes. Mohammed didn't slow down. The Mercedes ate up the distance between the working-class neighborhood and the expressway that would lead them to the airport where they would begin their days-long journey back to Bhutan.

On the phone screen, Dorji's face remained impassive, but Bhatua knew that look. The master was pleased.

The call ended without further ceremony.

Bhatua looked down at the wrapped stone in his lap. It felt warm through the tarp, almost alive. Whatever this thing was, it had been worth killing for.

And if the master was right—if the last disciple was somewhere on this island, living an ordinary life, as yet unaware of their true nature —then it would be worth killing for again.

Behind them, smoke rose into the Puerto Rican night sky.

Inside the house, Jiménez woke inside an inferno. The smoke blinded him, choked him. The flames jumped towards him, setting his clothes on fire, scorching his skin, burning his lungs.

Jimenez screamed.

New York City

Becky Torres screamed.

She opened her eyes wide with fright.

Her arms flailed, knocking a vase from the corner table.

The wilted blue flowers inside scattered across the floor in a spreading pool of water. For a moment, she couldn't remember where she was. The dream had been so vivid—fire, screaming, the smell of burning flesh.

«Becky?» Sylvia Chang's face swam into focus above her. «What happened? You okay?»

The apartment crystallized around her. New York. Winter. Safe. She was safe.

«Shit,» Becky managed. Her body was drenched in sweat despite her shivering from the cold.

Sylvia tried to wrap her arms around her, but Becky shrugged her off and stumbled toward the thermostat. Sixty-two degrees Fahrenheit (around 17 Celsius). She cranked it up, hearing the heater kick on with a wheeze.

«Hey, take it easy!» Sylvia called after her. «You just went through a hell of a trip!»

Becky ignored her, slipping on the spilled water and nearly going down. She caught herself on the bathroom doorframe, grabbed a towel, threw it over the mess. Her hands were shaking.

In the kitchen, she found her prescription bottle—Kava extract, the label said. Natural anxiety relief. She gulped one down dry, wincing.

«What are you doing?» Sylvia appeared at her elbow. «Your body's still pumped up with ayahuasca!»

But Becky wasn't listening. She was staring out the window at the bleak New York winter—bare trees, dirty snow, people hunched against the cold.

Everything was gray and dying.

Becky's phone buzzed. Sylvia grabbed it, looked at the screen.

«It's your sister. Do you want me to—?»

«No, that's okay, I'll take it,» Becky answered, still dazed. She took the mobile phone from Sylvia's hand and answered. Her sister, Isabel's, voice was unintelligible, high and frantic.

«Shit,» Becky said.

Isabel's volume increased but her words remained garbled by emotion.

«Okay, calm down,» Becky said. «I'll fly down in a couple of days.»

More frantic noise.

«What ticket? My email? Hold on.»

Becky found her laptop, opened her email. There it was—a flight confirmation. Departing today. This afternoon.

«It's for this afternoon? What the fuck, Isa? No way! I don't have any time to—okay, sorry, calm down, I get it! Yeah, you do what you gotta do, we'll talk tonight. Love you too.»

She hung up and stared at the laptop screen.

«Everything okay?» Sylvia asked.

«Yeah. No. Not really.» Becky's voice was flat, distant. «I gotta get back home. I mean, to the Island.»

«What happened?»

«My father just died.»

The thing about ayahuasca, Becky thought as she entered her bedroom, throwing clothes into a backpack, is that it strips away all the comfortable lies you tell yourself. For twelve hours, you see the world without filters. Every shadow hides a demon. Every pattern reveals a truth.

The problem is figuring out which truths are real and which are just the drug talking.

Her father was dead. That was real.

Her nightmares were getting worse. Also real.

And something else, something she couldn't quite articulate: the feeling that all of this was connected. The dreams, her father's death, even that weird vision during the trip of blue flowers and ancient stones.

«Listen,» Sylvia said, appearing in the bedroom doorway. «Since you're going down there, I'd like you to reach out to a friend of mine. He's an astrologer.»

Becky looked up from her packing. «Oh God, no. How about giving me a break?»

«Just in case. My friend Roberto is the real deal. He's an expert in Eastern philosophy. He might help you better than I can.»

«I swear, you've had me do voodoo, Santería, reiki, rebirthing, everything there is, like shopping at a spiritual Walmart. If there were goat yoga in the city, you'd have those smelly animals climbing all over my ass.»

Sylvia smiled. «I can see your brain is back to normal—if there is such a thing with you. I'm just looking out for you. This... event... is major, it can trigger things. I'm giving you a safety net.»

Becky felt her resistance crumbling. Sylvia had been there for her through everything. The least she could do was keep an open mind.

«Fine.» She zipped the backpack closed. «Send me his contact information.»

Sylvia pulled her into a hug. «Really sorry about your dad. Have a safe trip.»

After Sylvia left, Becky stood in the middle of her small apartment and let the silence settle around her.

The ayahuasca was still in her system, making everything sharp and strange. She could see the dust motes in the winter light, each one a tiny universe. She could feel her heartbeat in her fingertips.

Most of all, she could feel the weight of what was waiting for her back home.

The island. Her family. Her father's corpse.

And something else. Something old and patient and terribly wrong, coiled like a snake in the foundation of her life.

She grabbed her backpack and left.

3

Germany, Black Forest, 1632

The forest was older than Christianity.

The mist clung to everything—the massive trunks of fir and pine, the faces of the six women who chanted behind her, the clearing where their bonfire burned against the gathering darkness.

«*Om Ah Hung, Benzra Guru Jnanasagara bam ha ri ni sa siddhi Hum.*»

The words weren't German. They weren't Latin, either, though the priests who hunted them assumed anything foreign must be the devil's tongue. Juliane, barely seventeen years old, had learned them from her teacher, who had learned them from hers, in a chain that stretched back centuries to a time when the Buddha's wisdom had walked west along the Silk Road.

She stood tall as she led the chant, her posture commanding despite her youth.

The other women—farmers' wives, merchants' daughters, widows—looked to her for guidance. In a world that gave women few choices beyond marriage or the convent, Juliane had found a third path.

Then she saw it.

At the edge of the clearing, barely visible through the mist, a figure floated among the trees. Translucent, glowing, unmistakably female.

Lady Yeshe Tsogyal.

Juliane's breath caught. The stories spoke of her appearing to the faithful in times of great need. She broke from the circle, clasped her hands in prayer, and ran toward the apparition.

A tree root caught her foot.

She went down hard, the breath knocked from her lungs. When she looked up, expecting to see the vision vanished, she instead saw something impossible.

Blue flowers grew where none had been a moment before.

And nestled among them, gleaming in the firelight, was the same bronze statuette of Guru Padmasambhava that had been shown to a disciple in a cave in Bhutan centuries before.

Juliane reached for it. The metal was warm to the touch, as if it had been held in living hands.

Tears filled Juliane's eyes. She understood what this meant. After years of study, of secret practices, of risking everything to walk the Buddha's path in a land that burned heretics— she realized she was one of them—one of Yeshe Tsogyal's original disciples, reincarnated.

Behind her, a young girl's voice, in German, shattered the moment.

«Run! The bad men, they're coming!»

Juliane spun around, clutching the statuette to her chest. A woman—

strong, tall, blond haired—stood at the edge of the clearing, her face twisted with terror.

Then came the sound that haunted nightmares: hoofbeats. Dozens of them.

The horsemen materialized from the forest like demons from hell itself, their armor catching the firelight, their faces hidden behind steel. Foot soldiers followed, carrying torches and swords. They surrounded the clearing with the efficiency of men who had done this before.

The women huddled together, their chanting forgotten.

One horseman approached slowly, his mount's hooves making no sound on the soft earth. The others parted for him with deference due to rank. When he flipped open his visor, Juliane found herself looking into a face she would never forget.

Druk Dorji, with his Asian features which were incongruous under a German soldier's helmet. His visage was exactly as we had seen him on Bhatua's sat-phone screen, in Becky's dreams.

His eyes seemed to see through flesh to the trembling soul beneath him.

«Who are you, sire?» Juliane kept her voice steady. «What do you want with us?»

«I seek justice.» His German was perfect, unaccented.

«We are doing nothing illegal nor sinful, sire.»

«Your very existence is sinful.»

His eyes changed then. The brown irises flared red—not the red of reflected firelight, but something internal, something wrong.

The women froze, transfixed.

All except Juliane, who held the statuette tighter and lifted her chin.

Druk Dorji gestured to his soldiers.

What followed was butchery dressed in righteousness.

The soldiers fell upon the women with systematic brutality. Screams echoed through the ancient forest. Juliane tried to run, tried to help, tried to do something, but a red-bearded soldier wrenched the statuette from her hands and carried it to his master.

Dorji examined it with the care of a collector appraising a rare piece. Then his eyes found Juliane's again.

She smiled at him. Not with fear, not with hatred, but with the compassion she had spent years cultivating.

«All life is precious,» she said.

Dorji spurred his horse. The animal leaped over the bonfire in a single bound, impossibly high, impossibly fast. Before Juliane could draw another breath, his sword sang through the air.

Her head separated from her body with surgical precision.

The bonfire exploded, sparks and flames shooting into the night sky. And through it all, Druk Dorji's laughter boomed across the clearing, inhuman and terrible.

Somewhere Over the Atlantic,
Present Day

Booming laughter woke Becky.

She jolted upright in her airplane seat, sending her tray table flying and an ice-filled cup tumbling into the aisle. Her hands flew to her throat, expecting to find—what? A wound? Blood?

Nothing. Just skin and the rapid pulse of her carotid artery.

«I'm so sorry, miss!» The flight attendant materialized beside her, concern written across her features. For just a moment, in the dim cabin lighting, her face looked like someone else—The lady she saw floating like a glowing, transparent apparition among the woods in her dream.

Becky's breath came in short gasps. «I was—I was dreaming.»

«A bad one, I'm guessing.» The attendant's voice was kind. Professional kindness, but kindness nonetheless. «Let me help you clean that up.»

Across the aisle, a passenger exploded with laughter at whatever he was watching on his tablet. Becky flinched with fear, her body remembering the sound from the dream her mind was desperate to forget.

The attendant dealt with the spill efficiently, courteously informed the passenger to lower his voice, turned back to Becky, then leaned in close. «Is there anything else I can get you?»

«No. Thanks. I'm fine.»

«Okay. Just buzz me if you need anything. We'll be landing soon.»

Becky nodded and turned to the window, lifting the shade.

Below, a scatter of lights marked some city on the coast. Civilization. Safety. The modern world where swords and horses and burning forests were safely confined to history books.

So why did the dream feel more real than the airplane around her?

She pressed her forehead against the cool plastic of the window and tried to slow her breathing. The techniques Sylvia had taught her—count to four breathing in, hold for four, out for four.

Simple. Mechanical.

It didn't help.

The dreams were getting worse. More vivid. More detailed. And always, always, that same horrifying figure with the red eyes and the terrible laughter that had her shivering with fright well after waking up.

Puerto Rico

The Uber wound through San Juan's streets, through the modern hotel district, and eventually into the quieter suburbs where old money lived. Becky watched it all through the window with a feeling of dislocation. This was supposed to be home, but it felt like somewhere she'd only read about in tourist magazines.

The car pulled up in front of her family's house—a sprawling, modern structure that screamed wealth without quite tipping into vulgarity. Her father had always been careful about that. Appearance mattered in his circles. Lawyers, judges, politicians—they all had to project the right image.

Becky thanked the driver and approached the front door dragging her feet with all the enthusiasm of a prisoner returning to her prison cell.

Inside, chaos reigned.

Her sister Isabel paced back and forth in the living room, gesturing wildly as she yelled into her wireless earbuds in rapid-fire bursts. She was beautiful in that high-maintenance way that required daily trips to the salon, monthly trips to the spa, and a wardrobe budget that exceeded most people's annual income.

«What part don't you understand? The people aren't going to fit! We need more space!»

An elegant black woman in business attire—Ana Ramos, according to the nameplate on her briefcase—was shuffling through documents on the coffee table. When she saw Becky, she stood and extended her hand.

«Hi, Rebecca. How are you? I'm Ana Ramos, from your father's law firm. I'm very sorry for your loss.»

«Just call me Becky.» She ignored the offered hand. «What's going on?»

Isabel interrupted her call with a dramatic jab at her earbuds. «Becky!» She rushed over for a hug, tears already forming. «I'm a ball of nerves! Give me a second.»

She pressed her earbuds again. «Hello? No, you still don't get it...»

Becky gestured to Ana and headed for the kitchen, needing distance from her sister's drama.

In the kitchen's relative quiet, Ana tried again. «I was saying how sorry I am about your dad. I admired him very much.»

Becky found a beer in the fridge, opened it, and downed it in one long swallow. She burped, then offered one to Ana.

«No, thank you.»

Becky shrugged and grabbed another. «What happened?»

«I think it's better that Isabel tells you.»

«I'm asking you.»

Ana cleared her throat, clearly uncomfortable. «As I understand it, your mom, along with your sister and your father, were celebrating his birthday at a restaurant, and your father suffered a massive heart attack. Right there during dinner.»

«Oh.» Becky paused. «I didn't even remember.»

«Pardon?»

«His birthday. I forgot it was his birthday.»

Ana shifted her weight, and Becky could see her recalculating, trying to figure out what kind of daughter forgets her father's birthday, even a dead father's.

The kind who spent her whole life trying to forget him, Becky thought. The kind who moved three thousand miles away and changed her phone number twice.

«When's the funeral?» she asked.

«Next Friday afternoon, if all goes well with Forensic Sciences.»

«Wait, what? I can't stay that long. I have to get back!»

She stormed back into the living room, beer in hand, ready for a fight.

Isabel had just ended her call. She slumped onto the sofa, worn out, on the verge of a breakdown.

«What's with having the funeral next Friday?» Becky demanded. «That's crazy, Isa. I can't afford to stay that long!»

Isabel took the beer from Becky's hand and drank, ignoring her sister's rant, «I'm going crazy! The governor wanted a state funeral, mom insisted on something intimate—which, of course, means two hundred people—and I'm the sandwich in between!»

Ana appeared in the doorway, tucking her documents into her briefcase with practiced efficiency. «I better retire so you two can be alone. We're still waiting on the State Revenue Service to schedule the inspection of the safety deposit boxes. As soon as I have any news, I'll call you.»

«What inspection?» Becky asked.

«The State Revenue Service requires an inspection of the boxes in front of all the heirs before we can file the deceased's tax return.»

«What? The dead pay fucking taxes?»

«Becky, please.» Isabel's voice carried a warning.

«In most cases nothing is actually paid,» Ana continued smoothly, as if profanity when dealing with family law was perfectly normal. «It's almost a formality. But the three of you have to be present.»

«Wait.» Becky set down her beer. «You don't expect me to just hang out here until the tax people decide to show up, do you?»

«Given your father's standing with the government, we're confident this will take a couple of days at most.»

«But why do I have to be there?»

Ana shifted into full lawyer mode, her voice taking on the patient tone of someone explaining basic concepts to a child. «Your mother, being the widow, gets half of all the assets accumulated during the marriage. The other half is divided equally between the two of you. That's why you must all be present to witness the inventory.»

«I don't care about any of it.»

«Once all the goods are calculated and divided, you can dispose of your assets as you like.»

«Fuck me!» Becky grabbed her empty beer bottle. «This is a fucking nightmare!»

Isabel elbowed her sister, scolding her. Ana's expression remained professionally neutral.

«I apologize for this inconvenience, but it's the law.»

Isabel stood, smoothing her designer dress. «No need to apologize. You've been nothing but professional and very helpful to me—to all of us.»

Becky looked at her sister quizzically. Correcting herself after «to me» had been odd. Pointed, even.

«Thank you,» Ana said. «Nice meeting you, Becky. Have a nice evening.»

«I'll walk you to the door,» Isabel said quickly.

Becky waited until they'd left, then tiptoed after them, curiosity overcoming her exhaustion. She positioned herself by one of the living room windows that overlooked the front entrance.

Outside, Isabel looked around carefully—checking for witnesses, for neighbors, for anyone watching. Then she pulled Ana close and kissed her. Not a friendly peck. A real kiss, deep and lingering.

Becky smiled despite herself.

By the time Isabel returned, Becky was walking out of the kitchen back onto the sofa, fresh beer in hand, a picture of innocence.

«Have a nice evening?» Becky mimicked Ana's professional tone. «Really?»

Isabel's face flushed. «Give her a break. Like I said, she's doing a wonderful job.»

«And what job is that, exactly? Because she's sure as hell giving you a lot more than legal advice.»

Isabel's embarrassment deepened. «Hey, we're both on our own, and we love each other. Is that a problem?»

«It's not a problem for me.»

«So why the attitude?»

Becky shrugged. «I'm just a little surprised, that's all. I'm supposed to be the black sheep of the family, and suddenly you—the perfect daughter—are walking on the wild side?»

«Well, I guess things change.»

«Are you happy?»

«With her, yes. Very happy.»

Becky studied her sister. Isabel had been through hell with her ex-husband—the kind of marriage that left scars. «As long as you take care of yourself, I'm cool with whatever you do. You went through a nasty divorce with a fucked-up guy, and the last thing I want is for you to get hurt again.»

Isabel's eyes began to water. She sat down next to Becky and snatched the beer out of her sister's hands. . «That was a thousand years ago. Ana's the best thing that's ever happened in my life.»

«I'm glad you're happy.»

They sat in silence for a moment, sisters connected by shared history and separate pain.

«Why'd you get me out here today?» Becky asked quietly. «Why not right before his funeral? I mean, he's not going anywhere.»

Isabel shook her head, scowling at Becky, obviously hurt by her sister's crass sarcasm. But she understood where it came from, the years of anger, pain, and, eventually detachment. She wiped her eyes. «What do you want me to say? It's been a crazy couple of days and I've been handling all this by myself—»

«She didn't want me here, did she?»

«What? No! What are you saying? Of course she wanted you here!»

«What the fuck for? Appearances?» Becky's voice hardened. «Come on, you're the one who called me. Does she even know I'm here?»

Isabel's tears welled up. She closed her eyes, trembling, and turned her face away.

«Of course she knows. She spent all day preparing your room. Well, you know, supervising Juliana who did all the work.»

Becky softened. «Good old Juliana. I miss her.»

«She misses you too. So, believe it or not, mom does want you here.

And yes, I need you here too. You know I'm not strong like you. All of this is really hard for me.»

«How's she holding up?»

Isabel made a drinking gesture.

Becky shook her head. Some things never changed.

«So, how have you been?» Isabel asked, clearly eager to change the subject.

«Same old shit. The nightmares are just getting worse. But I'm working with a friend in her healing practice. Her name's Sylvia. I've learned quite a few things about reiki, body work, chakras, ayahuasca, that sort of thing.»

Isabel laughed. «So you've finally come out as a witch. I knew it.»

They both laughed, needing the release. Then silence fell again, heavier this time.

«I just have this feeling all the time,» Becky continued, «like I was meant for more. I know it sounds like a cliché, but it's like I can't believe this is all there is to it, you know?»

«I'm here for you, you know that, right?»

Becky nodded.

«I know you're probably going to tell me to go to hell,» Isabel ventured, «but why haven't you considered studying law? I know you'd be great at it.»

«You're so right, I'm going to.»

Isabel perked up. «Really?»

«Yeah! Gonna tell you to go to hell!»

Isabel smiled, then leaned forward to embrace her sister. She wrinkled her nose and pulled back. «Whoa, forgive me, but when was the last time you bathed?»

«You bitch! You made me run to get on a plane like a fucking nut! It's a miracle I grabbed two panties and a toothbrush.»

They laughed again, easier this time.

«Are you gonna be okay?» Becky asked.

«I'll be a lot better once you take a bath.»

«Well, I'm going to take a leisurely two-hour bath in your honor. Back in the States all I have is a shitty little shower with a window that won't lock and lets all the fucking cold in.»

«That's horrible! I don't know why you're not living in a nice apartment instead of that pigsty.»

«Because I pay for that pigsty out of my own pocket without the help of mommy and daddy.» Becky paused. «I do miss my bathtub, though.»

«Your bathtub misses you.»

«You're a bitch!»

Becky grabbed a cushion and gently smacked her sister with it, then got up and planted a kiss on Isabel's forehead.

Becky's bedroom

Her room was not exactly as she last remembered seeing it.

It had been somewhat fixed as a guest bedroom, for guests that never came. Expensive furniture, expensive linens, expensive everything. The room that once belonged to a girl who'd had every material advantage and none of the things that actually mattered was now a cold space for catering to overnight visitors that never really felt welcomed to stay.

After her bath, Becky felt almost human again. She wrapped herself in a luxurious towel and surveyed the dresser drawers, looking for space to unpack her few things.

The first drawers were empty, space allotted for those guests that never stayed there, enough for her to stuff her belongings.

She emptied her backpack filling the drawers with a few random cosmetics, sanitary napkins, her bottle of pills, and the very few items of clothing she brought for what she thought would be a very short trip.

She opened the bottom drawers and found expensive lingerie she'd left behind—silk and lace pieces that now seemed like artifacts from someone else's life.

She posed with a few items in front of the mirror, smirking and shaking her head at her past vanity, then tossed them back carelessly.

In another drawer, she discovered an old photo album.

Her hand hesitated over it. She almost closed the drawer without looking. But something made her open it.

Photos of herself as a child stared back. Carefully posed.

Becky looked at the images with something approaching hatred. She threw the album into the trash can.

A knock at the door made her jump.

«Yeah, come in.»

Her mother entered—Evelyn Torres, seventy-three, a stately matri-arch whose hollow eyes spoke of grief and alcohol in equal measure. She held a drink.

«Oh,» Becky said. «I thought you were Isabel.»

«Sorry to disappoint.»

Becky tensed, anticipating drama. «It's good to see you, mom.»

Evelyn stopped in her tracks, staring. «You... you look so different.»

«It's been a long time.»

«Yes it has.» Evelyn's gaze fell on the photo album in the trash. She retrieved it. «What's this doing here?»

«You know I fucking hate photos.»

Evelyn leafed through the album, her fingers lingering on certain pages. «This is not yours to dispose of.»

«Fine. Whatever.»

Evelyn stopped at one particular photo, running her fingers over it softly. «You were such a beautiful girl.»

«I was? Not anymore?»

«You were a beautiful girl. Now you're a beautiful woman.»

Evelyn stumbled as she moved to sit on the bed—the alcohol making itself known.

«I almost just killed myself!» she laughed bitterly. «That'd be a joke. Two for the price of one!»

«You should throw that shit away,» Becky said, gesturing at the album.

«This is mine, not yours, and I want to keep it.» Evelyn held up the album defensively. «I just don't understand what you have against photos.»

«They piss me off. I don't let anyone take my picture. You don't know how fucked up it is nowadays when everyone's walking around with their mobile phones taking pictures of every damn thing.»

«When you were little, there were no cameras on mobile phones. Your dad had a real professional camera. He even had equipment to develop pictures down in the basement. He'd spend hours tinkering with that stuff.» Evelyn's voice grew distant with memory. «Most of them are here, his beautiful pictures.»

She kept shuffling through the album. «He was always taking photos of you when you were a little girl. Don't you remember? God bless him. He was crazy about you. It all stopped when you grew older.»

«What, I stopped being a pretty girl?»

Evelyn frowned and took a big sip of her drink. «You stopped being nice to him.»

Evelyn found a particular photo—young Becky, maybe seven, sitting on her father's lap. The little girl wore a frilly white embroidered dress with a large blue flower-shaped bow on her waist.

Evelyn placed the album on the bed in front of Becky. Her expression grew darker, sadder. «You guys used to be so happy together. Then, I don't know why, you grew rebellious. A passing phase, I thought, like all teenagers. But you never grew out of it. So sad.»

Becky glanced at the photo, shivered uncomfortably, closed the album abruptly and moved around the room, putting distance between herself and her mother.

«Just so you know,» she said dryly, «I'm flying back home as soon as the service is over.»

Evelyn downed her drink. «Well, even that short time is much more than anyone's seen of you in years.»

«Isabel's come to see me.»

Evelyn got up unsteadily. «Yeah, well, you know I don't feel safe visiting that godforsaken slum where you live. I know you live there just to spite me! Your father hated that place too.»

«Yeah, well, it's mine and I didn't need anything from you two to live there.»

«Your father always provided for us and protected you without a thought to himself! We have a decent place to call home because of him! And you, you were never grateful. Only thinking about yourself, doing whatever the hell you wanted, your dad and I be damned!»

Evelyn staggered, almost fell. Becky moved to help her.

«No thanks, I'm perfectly fine. I've been fine for years without you.» Evelyn looked at her empty glass. «My glass is empty. I need a refill.»

She stumbled toward the door.

«You should really take it easy with the drink,» Becky said.

Evelyn pivoted, staring at her daughter fiercely. «You know, you move to the other side of the world where we don't see you for years. You don't care about me or your father or anyone. You didn't even think to call him on his—his last birthday. And now, poof! Too late. And then you just waltz into your lovely room, in the house he sacrificed so much to build for us, and you think you're in any position to question my judgment?»

Becky pressed back against the wall.

«You should consider yourself blessed to have been brought up by us in this luxury. And you should feel lucky to have been the one person your father adored more than anything or anyone while he was alive. So forgive me if I'm feeling upset with you, because you broke his heart! I'm feeling angry right now, and before I say anything else I shouldn't, I'm going to refill my glass and drink myself to sleep. I will see you tomorrow—if you're still here!»

Evelyn left, struggling to maintain her dignity.

Becky stood frozen for a moment, then grabbed the photo album and hurled it against the wall. Photos flew out, scattering across the floor.

Her breath came in short, sharp gasps. Panic attack. She knew the signs. She rummaged through her things, found her pill bottle, downed two tablets with the last of the wine from her glass.

Still trembling, she grabbed her mobile phone and scrolled frantically.

Sylvia Chang - Therapy.

She called. It went to voicemail.

«Oops, I can't connect with you right now, but please leave me a message or text me. I promise to reach out as soon as I can. Hope you have a wonderful day!»

Becky hung up, fell onto her bed, covered her face with a pillow, and screamed into it.

4

Bhutan, The Cavern, 8th Century

L ady Tsogyal and her disciples sat in deep meditation when the old man burst into the cave, spear in hand, moving with impossible agility for his age.

«The bad men are coming!» he shouted in Dzongkha. «We have to go right now!»

The disciples grabbed their belongings and ran toward the tunnel exit. Tashi reached for a wooden staff, ready to fight, but Lady Tsogyal smiled and shook her head.

She took the staff from the young girl's hands and gestured for her to join the others.

Tashi hesitated—loyalty warring with obedience—then ran.

Outside, blinding sunlight reflected off snow. They were at the top of the world, thousands of meters high, an inhospitable place at the edge of the sky.

Tashi stopped to adjust to the glare. The old man pointed toward their escape route—an extremely narrow trail that hugged the mountain's edge. One false step meant death.

The disciples moved single file, inches from the precipice, carefully navigating jagged rocks and scraggly branches. As Tashi waited her turn, she saw the old man jump onto a large rock and scan the distance.

Below them, a dozen thugs armed with spears, arrows, and swords trudged up the treacherous path.

The old man closed his eyes and moved his lips silently.

Thick fog suddenly materialized around the thugs. They looked at each other, afraid, but continued upward. The fog thickened.

A skinny thug, blinded by the curtain of mist, tripped and plummeted thousands of feet into the void, his scream echoing off the mountain walls.

The other thugs froze. Their leader—Tshering Chime, a tall, gaunt, aging man—scowled at them.

«Attack, you fools! Now!»

The thugs blindly fired a barrage of arrows toward the cave.

Lady Tsogyal emerged from the cave in her translucent tunic, walking on the snow with delicate bare feet, impervious to the cold, oblivious to the incoming arrows.

The old man leaped down with unnatural speed, spinning his spear like a propeller, making the arrows ricochet in all directions.

Tashi ran in front of Lady Tsogyal, shielding her. «My mistress, watch out!»

The old man looked back, distracted for a split second. «No! Run away!»

One arrow pierced Tashi in her lower belly. She fell to her knees, blood dripping and splattering on the snow.

She screamed.

Puerto Rico, Torres Residence, Present Day

Becky screamed, jolting awake in her bed.

The white bedsheet that covered her was stained with blood. She sat up like a bolt of lightning, lifting the sheet.

There was blood on her sleepwear near her lower belly.

«No, no, not today, dammit!»

She jumped out of bed, yanked the sheets off, and threw them onto the floor. In the bathroom, she cleaned herself up, changed, then gathered the bloodied sheets and clothes and rushed out of the room to deal with them before anyone saw.

Her period. Just her period. Nothing supernatural.

So why did her lower belly ache exactly where the arrow had struck in the dream?

The funeral chapel

The space was packed with dignitaries, politicians, lawyers—all the people who mattered in her father's world. Becky stood glued to the back wall, her face pale with dark circles under her eyes.

An elderly couple approached, offering condolences. She remained cordial but detached, her mind elsewhere.

At the front, Isabel stood next to their mother, trying to keep an eye on Becky while dealing with the endless stream of mourners.

Ana Ramos arrived and stretched her hand toward Isabel with professional courtesy. Isabel kissed Ana's cheek—friendly, but nothing more. Evelyn noticed, recoiled slightly, then turned her back.

Becky watched the dynamics with grim amusement.

A voice through the audio system announced the Mass. The crowd settled. A priest arrived at the altar.

In front of the altar, an elaborate, expensive casket overflowing with flower arrangements, and to the side of it, a large framed photo of Guillermo Torres taken at the peak of his age and power, elegant, stately, almost regal.

A young girl—maybe ten years old—walked in. She wore white linen with a large blue bow in the shape of a flower on her waist. She stood in front of Torres's framed photo and began to sing Schubert's *Ave María*.

Becky's smile vanished.

In the large framed photo, her father's eyes seemed to shift, turning to look at the little singer.

Becky fidgeted uncomfortably, broke out in a cold sweat.

The photo became blurry. She wiped her eyes.

Her father's expression changed subtly in the photo—lips slightly pursed into a grin, eyes fixed on the little girl.

Becky took a tremulous step back, cleared her eyes again.

Then the memory hit her like a physical blow.

Her father's fifty-year-old lips pursed into a grin, eyes fixed on seven-year-old Becky as she sat on her bed trying to contain her excitement.

He showed her a beautiful white linen dress with a blue flower-shaped bow on the waist. He placed it neatly on the bed, then helped little Becky take off her pajamas.

The pajamas fell to the floor.

He smiled, brushed little Becky's hair away, kissed her on the neck.

Little Becky shivered.

Adult Becky shivered. Her world collapsed.

Nauseated, dizzy, she backed up to the wall. The chapel seemed to be spinning. She scrambled toward the exit, shoving mourners out of her way.

Outside in the parking lot, blinded by sun and panic, she stumbled between a video camera operator and a news reporter.

«Cut, cut! Dammit, let's go again!»

Becky kept moving, diving into her purse for car keys. She pressed the beeper. A beep echoed in the distance. She moved toward the oound.

She reached Isabel's car, dropped into the driver's seat, turned on the ignition, slammed the door. She pointed the air conditioning ducts toward herself and pounded the steering wheel, clenching her teeth.

She rummaged for her pills and shoved one in her mouth, wincing.

Slowly, the anxiety began to subside.

She pulled out her mobile phone, scrolled to find Sylvia Chang's number, and pressed it.

The mobile phone's ringtone boomed through the car's speakers, startling her. The phone had connected to the car's system automatically.

To Becky's surprise, Sylvia Chang's smiling face appeared on the dashboard's LCD screen, her voice surrounded Becky,

«Hey, what's up, sweetie?»

«Am I interrupting you?» Becky felt the pull of New York city, of her newfound home, her friend and therapist. Becky suddenly felt terribly homesick and alone in her country of birth.

«I said you could call me anytime. I missed your call last night and then couldn't reach you when I called you back.»

«I had it muted, sorry. I'm at the funeral—well, I was until a minute ago.»

«Oh, is it over? How are you holding up?»

Becky's eyes welled up with tears.

«Becky, honey, what is it?»

«I'm seriously tripping, Syl. Right in the middle of the service. I started tripping, seeing things about me with my dad.»

«What did you see? What came up?»

«I was little. He showed me this pretty dress to try on, then he got me naked, and I felt bad, sick.»

Sylvia's expression changed. «Do you remember if he did anything to you? Touch you or something?»

Becky winced. «He... kissed me on the neck. Oh God, that made me so sick.»

«I'm so sorry, Becky. I don't want to jump to conclusions, but this could be something serious. I think you should call Roberto right away—the astrologer I told you about. I told him you might reach out.»

«I just want to leave, get back to the U.S. I can't stand it here with mom and now this shit.»

«I understand. But I really think you should calm down first, deal with the crisis at hand. If you try to book travel the way your mind is, who knows, you might end up in Timbuktu by mistake!»

Becky smiled despite herself. «You can be such a bitch.»

«Don't you know it? Please, do as I say. Call him.»

«I didn't plan on staying that long. What about my clients?»

«Your clients can wait. You're no good to them if you're a mess!»

«Wow, that was straight to the gut!»

«Gotta spank you in the butt once in a while, dear.»

«Okay, okay, whatever, I'll call him.»

«How are you doing with the meds?»

«Just took one now.»

«All right. Just don't abuse them.»

«Yes, mother. I mean, no, I won't.»

«Feeling better?»

«Yeah, thanks, Syl. Really.»

«I've got your back. Now hang up and call him!»

«Love you, thanks!»

Becky hung up and sat in the air-conditioned car, feeling the medication slowly smooth the sharp edges of her panic.

A ping from her mobile phone rang out from the car's speakers announcing a text message. Becky glanced absentmindedly at her phone's screen.

It was from Sylvia—Roberto Soto's contact information glowed on the screen. She'd text him later. Or tomorrow. Or never.

She looked at the chaos in front of the funeral home—press trucks, limos, throngs of onlookers, flags at half-mast.

Her father was dead. That was supposed to be the end of something.

Instead, it felt like the beginning.

She started the car and drove away from the funeral, away from her family, away from everything she'd been running from for years.

But she had a feeling that no matter how far she ran, some things would follow.

5

Torres Residence

Just like her bedroom, Becky's old bathroom had also been refurbished for guests who never stayed overnight. It was a study in excess—marble counters, rainfall shower, a bathtub almost deep enough to swim in. Becky ran the water as hot as she could stand it, then poured herself a generous glass of red wine from her father's wine cellar.

She caught her reflection in the steam-fogged mirror and paused. Dark circles under her eyes. Hair a mess. The face of someone coming apart at the seams.

She gulped down two of her pills with a swig of wine, knowing Sylvia would disapprove but not particularly caring. Then she slid into the tub, letting the heat seep into her bones.

The wine went down smooth. Too smooth. She poured another glass.

The pills and wine were doing their job, making everything soft and blurry. Becky leaned back, closed her eyes, and let herself drift.

Colorado River, 1876

The sun was being swallowed up by the mountains over the amber and red painted desert. All kinds of creatures on the ground and in the sky began filling the air with their night songs as twilight descended.

Wa'a-Mama-ci of the Ute people moved silently to the riverbank, checking in all directions to ensure she was alone. At twenty-seven, she had learned the cost of carelessness. Her people considered her a powerful shaman. White men called her a witch, or worse.

She lit a small fire with practiced efficiency, spread a blanket on the ground, and disrobed. The night air raised goosebumps on her copper skin, but she ignored the cold. She grabbed one of the flaming embers like a torch and waded into the river.

When the water reached her waist, she stopped and closed her eyes.

«Om Ah Hung, Benzra Guru Jnanasagara bam ha ri ni sa siddhi Hum.»

The words were old, completely alien to her tribe or her ancestors. But somehow she knew them, had always known them. They had been etched into her soul for centuries before she was born.

Blue flowers appeared in the water around her, floating on the current. Impossible flowers that didn't belong at all in that area or anywhere in her country. They glowed with their own light.

Beneath the surface, a translucent figure materialized—a woman, beautiful and ancient, smiling up at her through the water.

Lady Tsogyal.

Wa'a-Mama-ci took a deep breath and dove, flaming torch and all, staying under the surface for what seemed like an eternity. When she burst back to the surface, the torch was still burning—impossibly, miraculously burning despite being submerged.

In her free hand, she held a small wooden chest.

The blue flowers cascaded down her naked body, some clinging to her long black hair. She waded back to shore, placed the burning ember back in the fire, and set the chest on the grass.

She dried herself and donned her garments, then opened the chest carefully. Inside were golden scrolls covered in strange writing, perfectly preserved, as being hidden in the water for centuries had no effect.

Then she heard it: the thunder of hooves.

Four U.S. Army cavalry soldiers on horseback emerged from the darkness, their blue uniforms worn and tattered, their faces hard. Wa'a-Mama-ci grabbed the chest, covered it with her blanket, and stood, facing them.

A fifth rider appeared behind the others.

He was an officer, his uniform crisp despite the desert dust. But his face—South Asian features, a neatly trimmed goatee—didn't match the uniform. And when he looked at her, his eyes glowed red.

Druk Dorji.

He spoke in perfect Shoshonean, the language of her people: «There's nowhere to run.»

Wa'a-Mama-ci straightened her back, self-assured. «I feel your spirit. It is very old and consumed by rage. My brother, leave that hatred with your ancestors. It is not for you to carry.»

Dorji's mouth twisted into a cruel smile. He switched to English:

«Find what the squaw is hiding, then do whatever you want with her.»

The soldiers spurred their horses forward. Wa'a-Mama-ci spun and ran into the river, stumbling in the current.

A red-bearded soldier overtook her easily, running his horse into the water, he jumped off, and grabbed her by the hair, making her yell in pain.

She pulled a knife out of nowhere and slashed at him. He yelled angrily, punched her viciously in the jaw, sending her tumbling into the water as the other two soldiers laughed at his injuries.

Red beard pulled her up by her hair, unsheathed his bayonet, touched its gleaming steel point against her neck.

«Wait!» Dorji called out. «I need the object she's hiding before you kill her.»

Dorji rode closer, his horse's hooves somehow finding purchase on the riverbed. He switched back to Shoshonean, «Where is it? I know you have it.»

Wa'a-Mama-ci shook her head, defiant despite the blade at her throat.

Another soldier dismounted, found the chest under the blanket, and brought it to Dorji. The officer opened it, examined the scrolls with satisfaction, then carefully packed it in his saddle bags.

«The whore's all yours.»

The red-bearded soldier grinned, revealing rotten teeth. He used his blade to tear Wa'a-Mama-ci's clothing, her eyes wide open with horror.

An arrow hit her attacker square in the back.

More arrows followed—a group of Ute warriors on horseback burst from the opposite bank, firing as they charged across the river.

Wa'a-Mama-ci ran, ducked low. Arrows flew. Soldiers screamed. One took an arrow to the throat. Another fell with a tomahawk buried in his skull.

Dorji remained calm. He unholstered his rifle and, with unnatural precision, shot every single warrior before they could reach the shore. One by one, they fell from their horses into the water, dead before they understood what had killed them.

Wa'a-Mama-ci stopped running. She turned to face Dorji, standing in the shallows, water lapping at her feet.

He raised his rifle.

She smiled at him—not with fear, but with compassion. Like a mother looking at an errant child.

«All life is precious,» she said in perfect English.

The rifle's blast echoed through the canyon.

Wa'a-Mama-ci's body fell back into the water, bleeding, swallowing water.

Dorji fired again, just to be sure.

***Torres Residence,
Present Day***

BANG!

Becky's head burst out of the bathwater, coughing, water shooting from her lungs, arms flailing wildly. She'd fallen asleep. Nearly drowned.

BANG! BANG!

The sound was coming from the door.

«Becky? Becky! Open up! Are you okay?»

Isabel's voice, frantic.

Becky tried to stand, slipped, and slammed onto the bathroom floor in a wet heap.

«Ow! Fuck!»

«Becky!»

She got up, threw on a robe, and opened the door. Isabel's face was pale with fright. She rushed in and hugged her sister tightly.

«Oh, thank God! I saw you run out of the funeral, and the car was gone, and I thought—I thought you'd—Jesus!»

«What? You thought I'd come here and end it all? Really?»

Isabel pulled back, mascara and tears streaming down her cheeks. «I didn't know what to think! Everything's been so horrible. I'm so sorry.»

«Always looking out for me.»

«You're the one that looks out for me, little sis. Always! I love you!»

«I'm still here so you're gonna have to put up with me, I hate to say.» Isabel hugged her again, Becky winced. «Ouch!»

«What? What is it?»

«I just fell on my ass getting out of the bathtub. I was asleep.»

«Did you have any nightmares?»

«Yeah. They just keep coming, and getting worse.»

«I'm so sorry. I can't even imagine.»

«There's one more thing I'm gonna try. A person my friend, Sylvia, the therapist I work for, recommended. I texted him earlier. I'm just waiting for him to give me an appointment.»

«I hope this one works. I really do.»

«Where's mother? Is she really pissed with me?»

Isabel shrugged. «Yeah, well, she drank herself to sleep as usual. So, do you want to come over to my place? We could get drunk too.»

Becky laughed. «What about your attorney-client privileges? Won't she object, your honor?»

«Hello, you're my sister! Besides, she's working late on setting up the inheritance papers, and the appointment at the bank, all that stuff. So it's just you and me, kid.»

«Okay, let me get dressed.»

6

Bhutan, The Eternity-Field Foundation

The laboratory was a study in contradictions—ancient and modern, spiritual and scientific, beautiful, and deeply wrong.

Shelves lined the walls, filled with disturbing specimens: fetuses floating in formaldehyde, preserved organs, body parts that shouldn't exist. Ancient oak tables held an eclectic mix of modern chemistry equipment and apparatus that looked like it belonged in an alchemist's workshop from the Middle Ages or even more ancient.

Druk Dorji, looking decrepit and withered, carefully handled large tongs, pouring molten mercury from a cast iron crucible into a complex distilling contraption. His hands shook with age. His hair was gray and thinning. His face was a mass of wrinkles.

He adjusted valves, checked readings on a computer screen, then shuffled to the other end of the still. He placed a beaker under a spigot and opened a valve. Out poured a pale, shimmering fluid, steaming slightly.

He closed the valve, lifted the beaker, and drank.

The transformation was immediate and horrifying.

His gray hair darkened to black. The wrinkles disappeared. His muscles filled out his clothes. His back straightened. Within seconds, he looked like a man in his mid-forties—vital, powerful, dangerous.

A chime rang. Dorji glanced at a video monitor showing multiple angles of the Foundation's property.

On screen: Bhatua and Mohammed entered through a doorway, Bhatua carrying a backpack.

The library was vast, endless bookshelves reaching toward a ceiling two stories high. At one end, a massive stained-glass window depicted the Kalachakra Mandala, the sun filtering through it created dazzling patterns of colored light in the dusty air and across the floor.

Bhatua placed his backpack on one of the reading tables. Mohammed stood guard at a distance. Druk Dorji entered, moving with the fluid grace of a much younger man.

They spoke in Dzongkha.

«You did well,» Dorji said.

«My pledge is to serve you, Guruji.»

Dorji opened the backpack and pulled out the stone Bhatua had stolen from Jiménez.

Every light in the library shut off.

Mohammed jumped back, startled. Druk Dorji's laughter echoed through the darkness—deep, amused, terrible.

«As the oracles predicted,» he said, «the Dakinis are debilitated.

Otherwise, the three of us would be dead right now. Everything favors us. My moment of glory approaches.»

He ran his fingers over the stone lovingly. «This proves the last of the eleven disciples of that wicked bitch is on that island, soon to be awakened.»

«How soon, Guruji?» Bhatua asked.

Dorji's gaze became distant, remembering. «I have learned to have much patience. Enough to withstand over a thousand years of this hunt... But to savor the destruction of each one of them one by one...» his eyes wandered, smiling...«that has made it all worthwhile.»

His focused intensity returned. «As soon as I find the last one and seize their treasure, my power will become beyond measure.»

«Forgive me, master, but have you seen who it is in your visions yet?»

«Not yet. But this would not be the first time. I cannot see them clearly until they are awakened.»

«Awakened?»

Dorji looked irritated at his servant's ignorance. «Yes, yes! The disciples cannot uncover their treasure until they are initiated—awakened to their true nature. I have been fortunate to find signs like this before, omens that presage their awakening. But until they are initiated, they are worthless to me. So we wait.»

Dorji placed the stone back in the backpack.

The lights immediately came back on.

Mohammed jumped again. Dorji glanced at him with contempt.

Dorji carried the backpack to one of the bookshelves and stood before a book titled *The Golden Eye of Buddha* with a gold-embossed image of an eye on its spine.

He stared straight at it.

A beam of light shot from the book's gilded eye, scanning Dorji's pupil. The bookcase slid open with an almost imperceptible mechanical whir.

Behind the false bookshelf was a temperature-controlled vault. Thick glass doors with humidity indicators protected the contents.

Inside the doors, on illuminated shelves, sat familiar objects: The bronze statuette taken from Juliane in Germany, the wooden chest stolen from Wa'a-Mama-ci in America, and other objects—talismans, scrolls, precious stones—that Lady Tsogyal had presented to her disciples more than a thousand years ago.

Dorji opened one of the airtight doors with a hiss. He placed the backpack carefully on a shelf and closed the door.

Ten treasures recovered. One remained.

After a thousand years of hunting, killing, and stealing, his quest was almost complete.

Back in the library, the vault door slid shut behind him.

Dorji stood before the Kalachakra mandala window, closing his eyes, allowing the colored light to bathe his rejuvenated face.

7

Puerto Rico, Roberto Soto's Office

 poster of the Kalachakra mandala, worn and faded adorned one wall—images of Vedic and Buddhist deities, most of which had seen better days, decorated the rest.

The space was small. Modest but clean, tucked into a nondescript building in a middle-class neighborhood.

Roberto Soto sat behind a small desk, going over information in books and on his laptop. He was forty-five, with kind eyes, an easy smile, and the bearing of someone who'd spent years gladly attending to other people's problems.

Across from him sat Manuel Meléndez—sixty-three, bald, overweight, with a peppered goatee.

«Mars is staring at Mercury from Gemini,» Soto explained, «and that's why you have to be careful with your oral and written communications until the fifteenth. I know you love to shoot from the hip at work, but you have to be careful with contracts, emails, even board meetings or employees during this period.»

Soto lifted his eyes from behind his laptop for a second and looked at Meléndez straight in the eyes, «Also, the strength of Mars is heightened from its retrograde movement creating an aspect with Ketu, the Southern Node, which is at Virgo right now.

Meléndez's shoulders dropped. «You lost me. Cut to the chase, please. You sound like my mechanic with all this technical stuff. Just tell me what it all means, give me the bottom line.»

Soto smiled patiently. «It means, take care of your digestive system. Watch for inflammations, viruses, infections.»

«Jesus, anything else?»

«Yeah, well, with Mars in Gemini there's also a chance of respiratory problems.»

«So I can't eat or breathe?»

«You can. Just be careful where and what you eat. On the other hand, it's a great time for physical and emotional healing. If you ever considered exercising, this would be a good time. I just can't underline enough the importance of taking care of your sensitive documents and communications, which might get lost or data corrupted. But most importantly, this is a time to start taking care of your body.»

«Any good news?»

Soto checked his laptop. «In about a week, on the first day of the crescent moon, you have a very good moment to start new projects. That's when you should start planning for new enterprises.»

«A week. Okay, that isn't too bad.»

«Just remember, my recommendation is that until then, you should listen before you speak. Don't make judgments or reach conclusions until you have all the information at hand, so you don't get into trouble.»

Meléndez nodded silently.

«I'll send you a list of important dates so you can put them in your calendar. How's that?»

«Yeah, great! Thank you very much! I appreciate it!»

They shook hands. Meléndez left, and Soto returned the books to his bookshelf.

He glanced at his watch, then at a framed photo on a low console table—Dr. Krishnaa Bhat, an Indian woman in her late seventies. He opened a drawer, lit candles on each side of her picture, turned off the office lights, kicked off his shoes, and sat on the floor facing the table in the lotus position.

He began to control his breathing, slowing it down, relaxing. His eyes were half-open, looking at the floor.

The flickering candles made the posters appear alive, dancing.

A wavy, translucent presence slowly materialized beside him—Dr. Bhat's astral body, separated from her physical form thousands of miles away in India.

Her lips didn't move, but he heard her whispered, ethereal voice in his mind. «You are late again, shishya. You kept me waiting in the never-after.»

A faint glow appeared around Soto's body. It slowly separated from him, became more dense, until it resembled a hazy human silhouette —his own astral form.

His lips didn't move either as his ethereal whisper responded. «I apologize. I was with a client—»

«That is not important right now. What is important is that you need to learn to take your time, and relax more. Always being in such a hurry makes it harder.»

«I feel relaxed.»

«If you were truly relaxed, our bodies would appear completely solid. There would be no distinguishing them from real blood and bone. I can barely recognize you, or myself! You are getting much better, yes, but you must practice more.»

The real Soto took slow, deliberate breaths, his body slumping slightly, more relaxed. Soto's astral silhouette became more defined.

Dr. Bhat's astral projection smiled. «See? Much better. People think the solution is to concentrate until their brains burst. All this mindfulness business makes me crazy. It is mindlessness that you must master in order to transcend.»

Their whispered, ethereal voices continued the dialog.

«I understand.»

«So relax even more, my dear shishya. We will need to perfect this practice in the coming months.»

«Why?»

«I see there are challenges ahead. Have you not studied your own chart?»

«I have. But I didn't see anything out of the ordinary.»

«Go over it again, carefully. I still cannot determine what the true nature of the issue is exactly. But whatever it is, it may be extremely dangerous—for both of us.»

Wisps of smoke began to waft from Dr. Bhat's astral body.

«What... What is that?»

«That is not important. Just continue to relax.»

«I'm trying to, but I see smoke. Are you all right?»

«Relax. I'm just rescuing another of my students from a fire right now. No need for concern.»

Soto jolted out of his trance, shaking his head. The astral figures vanished instantly.

«What? A fire?»

He scrambled to his desk, grabbed his mobile phone, and dialed. Dr. Bhat's recorded voice came over the speaker:

«I apologize, but I cannot answer your phone at this moment. Please feel free to leave a message—»

He tried again. Same recording.

Soto hung up, blew out the candles, turned on the lights, and sat down heavily to put his shoes back on. He looked at Dr. Bhat's photo, with worry creasing his face.

«Please be safe, Guruji,» he whispered.

8

The Bank

Becky found herself in a conference room that smelled of coffee and anxiety.

The bank management had brought in a spread—pastries, fruit, coffee service—as if this were a business meeting rather than the dissection of a dead man's assets. Isabel fidgeted with her makeup compact, seriously concerned about her appearance.

Becky slumped in jean shorts and a tank top, feet up on the conference table, stirring a cup of coffee with the enthusiasm of someone at a dental appointment.

«You threw your photo album against the wall?» Isabel asked quietly. «What was that all about?»

Becky didn't look at her. «My God, mother is such a drama queen! I found the damn thing in my panty drawer, so I threw it in the trash to get it out of the way. She saw it, got pissed, and started shoving it in my face!»

Isabel opened her mouth to respond, but Evelyn entered with Ana. They sat down. Ana inadvertently brushed against Isabel as she adjusted her chair. Isabel moved away too abruptly, colliding with Evelyn. Evelyn scowled. Becky smiled faintly, amused.

Ana cleared her throat. «The tax inspector just arrived. This shouldn't take much time.»

Miriam García, the bank's manager—pleasant, professional, entered. She escorted Juan Ramírez—a thin, officious man who looked like he'd been born wearing an ill-fitting, government issue suit.

Ana made introductions. «This is Mr. Ramírez from the Treasury Department.»

Ramírez nodded curtly.

García's gaze went from Evelyn to Ramírez and back again. «One of the boxes is registered jointly with your husband, and the other one is under his name.»

Evelyn's back stiffened. «What other one? Under his name?»

«I thought you knew, Mrs. Torres.» García replied, taken off guard.

«Maybe it slipped your mind, ma'am?» Ana offered carefully.

Evelyn's stare could have frozen magma. «I don't think so. Things like that don't slip my mind.»

Isabel shot Ana a look—*back off*.

Ana got the message immediately. «My apologies, of course not.»

Becky continued smiling, enjoying the show.

«Excuse me, ladies,» Ramírez interrupted. «I have a long day, and I changed my regular appointments to attend this one.»

«Yes, of course. Right away.» Ana stood, gathering her materials.

The group filed out, Becky trailing behind like a reluctant prisoner.

The vault room was claustrophobic—designed for privacy, not comfort. Four people crammed into a space meant for two. The walls seemed to press in, the air recycled and stale.

García brought in the first safety deposit box. «This is the jointly-held box. I'll bring the other one as soon as you're done.»

«Thank you, Miriam. You're very kind,» Evelyn said with forced warmth.

Ramírez was meticulous, formal, dry as desert sand. He removed each item and cataloged it with bureaucratic precision: men's and women's jewelry, watches, cash, gold bars, stacks of foreign currency, commemorative coins.

«Just so you know, madam,» he said without looking up, «you need to provide evidence of where and how these items were obtained.»

«I'm sure my lawyers will handle it.» Evelyn's voice was ice.

Becky slurped the last of her coffee. The sound echoed in the small space. Evelyn's glare intensified.

Ramírez finished his inventory, placed the items back in the box, closed it, stood awkwardly—there was barely room to stand—and signaled García by tapping on the door.

She came in and took the box away.

There was an awkward silence, everyone avoiding each other's eyes.

«Watch the other box have fake passports, a walkie-talkie, and a gun,» Becky muttered. «Straight out of James Bond.»

Isabel covered her face, struggling to hold back her laughter. Evelyn struggled to hold back her anger.

García opened the door just in time to avoid an incident, placing the second box on the table.

Ramírez opened it and pulled out a thick stack of printed papers.

«What are those?» Evelyn leaned forward.

«Federal Treasury bonds, ma'am. I'll report the amounts in my inventory, but your lawyers will need to file a formal report of their values.»

«Did you know about this, mom?» Isabel's voice had an edge.

«No.»

«My, my. Surprise, surprise.» Becky's tone was all mockery.

Evelyn shifted uncomfortably. Isabel busied herself fidgeting with her mobile phone. Ramírez continued his work, unfazed by the family drama unfolding around him.

Then he reached into the box again and pulled out small velvet bags. When he opened them, loose diamonds tumbled onto the table, stunning Evelyn and Isabel. Becky seemed disconnected.

Ramírez kept his dry manner. «Same thing with these. I'll need them appraised by a third party, and you'll need to establish evidence of their origin.»

«Mom, did you know about these?» Isabel's pitch had gone up.

Evelyn shook her head, visibly rattled. «I don't know of any evidence of their origin. This is clearly new to me, but as I've stated before, my lawyers will take care of it.»

«Ooh! More surprises by the minute.» Becky was enjoying this far too much.

Evelyn gritted her teeth, her fists clenched, her knuckles white.

Ramírez, immune to emotional displays, continued methodically. He found some badly worn manila envelopes at the bottom of the box. He opened them carefully and pulled out a set of photographs.

Photos of seven-year-old Becky.

«May I?» Evelyn reached for them.

Ramírez handed them over. Evelyn examined them, then passed them to Isabel, who looked confused.

«Why on Earth would he keep those in there?» Isabel asked.

Evelyn's voice dripped sarcasm. «Maybe so your sister wouldn't throw them in the trash.»

Becky suddenly became tense, she didn't feel amused at her mother and sister rambling on about some old photos of her. She was puzzled that it was only her, no Evelyn, no Isabel, no group shots of the family together.

Ramírez opened the next envelope.

More photos of young Becky. But these were different. The child wore women's makeup. Provocative lingerie. Poses that no child should know how to make.

«What the fuck!?» Becky sat bolt upright, the coffee cup clattering to the floor.

«Mom! What is this?» Isabel's hand flew to her mouth.

Evelyn stared in disbelief, then lunged forward to cover the photos. «Don't you dare open any more!»

«Madam, it's my job.» Ramírez's voice remained flat, bureaucratic. «I'm sorry, but I don't have a choice.»

His hand reached for the third envelope. Evelyn grabbed it. The old manila tore open, and dozens of photographs flew across the table and onto the floor—nude images of young Becky, posed, provocative, obscene.

«Oh my God!» Becky's voice was barely a whisper, suffocated, breathless.

«Mom? What?» Isabel looked like she might vomit.

«You better keep your mouth shut about this, sir,» Evelyn hissed at Ramírez, «or you will hear from my lawyers!»

«Madam, this has nothing to do with my business here today. I'm done.» Ramírez gathered his materials with shaking hands and fled the room like it was on fire.

«You just keep this to yourself!» Evelyn called after him. «If word gets out, I'll know it was you, and I swear I will sue you!»

The door closed. The room felt even more claustrophobic with his absence. The three women stood frozen inside, almost suffocating, red-faced, dozens of photographs scattered at their feet like evidence at a crime scene.

Becky lost it. She snatched up a handful of the photos and shoved them at her mother's face.

«Mom, what the fuck is this? Who took these? Was it my father?»

«Don't you dare disrespect your father like that!» Evelyn's voice shook. «You were always so depraved, flirting with him all the time to get your way!»

The walls seemed to close further in. The space became even more oppressive. The three women stood up, legs and knees banging the desk, chairs toppling backward.

«What are you saying?» Becky's voice rose to a shout. «Are you fucking crazy? I was just a baby! How much did you know about this? You said it was his goddamn hobby! Was that all bullshit? Did you know?»

Evelyn frantically tried to gather the scattered photos. «That is disgusting! How could you even think that way about me? Or about him? You were always the little whore in the family! You still are— look at you!»

Becky shook uncontrollably, her entire body trembling with rage. «Well, maybe if you hadn't been drunk all the time, he wouldn't have had to jerk off to me!»

The slap came fast and hard.

Evelyn's palm connected with Becky's cheek with a crack that seemed to echo forever in that tiny room.

Becky stood frozen, touching her face, her eyes wide with shock. Isabel pressed herself against the wall, paralyzed.

«I want you out of my house.» Evelyn's voice was low, venomous. «Out of my life! You will never disrespect me or this family again!»

«Your whole life's one big fucking lack of respect!»

Becky threw the photographs at her mother's face. They fluttered down like poisoned snow. She squeezed past Isabel, nearly knocked her mother down, and burst out of the vault room.

In the corridor, she collided with Ana.

«Becky, what happened? What's the problem?»

«Ask your fucking girlfriend!»

जल

Water

9

Bhutan, Cremation Grounds,
Present Day

The sun seemed to hide behind the mountains earlier than in most other parts of the world because of the sheer height of the Himalayas.

Between a natural barrier of trees and shrubs, in a clearing near the riverbank, funeral pyres stood like ancient altars—mounds of brick and charcoal scattered at deliberate intervals. The air was thick with smoke and the sweet-rot smell of burning flesh.

A small group of mourners walked away from one smoldering pyre, their chanting and crying fading into the gathering darkness.

Bhatua crouched behind a large rock, watching them go. When the last mourner disappeared down the path, he signaled. Mohammed's massive form emerged from the shadows, dragging a large, tightly wrapped bundle. The bundle lurched and swayed. A muted scream came from inside.

«Shhh! Quiet!» Mohammed hissed in Dzongkha.

They navigated between scraggly bushes and trees, pulling the bundle toward a secluded pyre with a pile of fresh wood. Druk Dorji sat naked atop the rotting corpse of an old woman, his body painted with a mixture of white ash and red markings that looked like Sanskrit but weren't quite. His eyes were closed, his face a mask of concentration.

Mohammed gave the bundle a final shove. It fell to the ground with muffled cries. Bhatua drew his commando knife, sliced the ropes and unwrapped the bundle.

A young girl tumbled out—Ayla, barely sixteen, beautiful and terrified, head covered by a burlap bag. Bhatua uncovered her head. Her mouth was gagged, her eyes wide with animal panic.

She tried to scream through the gag.

«Thank you, my dear servants,» Dorji said without opening his eyes. «You have outdone yourselves.»

Bhatua and Mohammed bowed.

«Serving you is our life, Master,» Bhatua said.

Dorji's lips moved, reciting something in a language older than Dzongkha, older than Sanskrit. An incantation that made the air feel heavy, wrong.

Bhatua cut Ayla's hands loose, tore off her clothes, yanked the gag from her mouth and kept his knife pressed to her naked back.

Dorji opened his eyes.

They were blood red, glowing with infernal fire.

He fixed his gaze on Ayla's terrified face. Her body went still. Her will evaporated. She became a puppet with cut strings, conscious but powerless.

Dorji nodded. Bhatua sheathed his knife and melted into the darkness, taking Mohammed with him.

Ayla walked toward Dorji without resistance, transfixed, obedient. She squatted and sat on his lap, her arms wrapping around his shoulders as if embracing a lover. Nearby, Bhatua set the pyre on fire. The flames danced, creating twisted shadows across the clearing.

Dorji grabbed Ayla's bare flesh, his fingers searching for specific points. He pressed both index fingers into pressure points on her buttocks.

Ayla moaned—not with pain, but with pleasure. Her eyes rolled back. She kissed him furiously, squeezing him against her body. Dorji remained completely detached, emotionless and clinical.

Ayla's hands moved down to caress the corpse beneath them—a grotesque *ménage à trois*. She growled, possessed, gyrating obscenely. The dead woman's body swayed beneath them.

Dorji shifted his pelvis forcefully, penetrating her.

«I take your bodily fluids,» he said, his voice flat. «Your energy. Your essence. Your soul.»

The rhythm became wilder. Ayla screamed with pain and pleasure. Her body began to change—shriveling, losing color, her cheeks sinking in. She was being consumed from the inside.

Dorji showed no emotion. No pleasure, no satisfaction. Only cold focus.

«Your essence is mine. You belong to me. You are in me. You are no more.»

Ayla gasped. Her body had become skin stretched over bones, barely alive.

Bhatua appeared from nowhere, grabbed her by the hair, and drew his dagger across her throat. Blood splashed onto Dorji's face. He didn't flinch.

Bhatua dragged Ayla's skeletal body to the pyre and, with Mohammed's help, threw her into the flames. She was still alive—barely—when the fire took her.

The wind picked up suddenly, violently, sending flames and sparks flying in all directions. The fire reflected in Dorji's dark red eyes—unmoving, shark-like, inhuman.

Ayla screamed. The fire burst with a loud boom.

Puerto Rico, Torres Residence

BOOM!

The explosion reverberated in Becky's dream.

She screamed, bolting upright in bed, blinking in the darkness. Her body was drenched in sweat despite the air conditioning. The dream had been so vivid—fire, death, violation, evil so pure it felt like drowning in sewage.

She fumbled for the lamp and knocked over a water glass. It shattered on the floor.

KNOCK, KNOCK, KNOCK!

Becky was disoriented, finding her bearings as she got up, trying to avoid stepping on the glass fragments. «Stop that! Leave me alone! I'll be out of your goddamn life in a fucking minute!»

«It's me!» Isabel's voice sounded muffled by the door, her tone urgent.

Becky paused, recognizing her sister's voice. «I don't give a shit! Go away!»

But Isabel kept knocking. «Please, I need to talk to you.»

«I don't give a fuck! Just go away!»

Isabel banged harder. «Please, I beg you, let me in!»

Then, louder: «Mom's not here, I swear! We really need to talk!»

Isabel banged her head against the door. Becky could hear her crying.

«Goddammit! Stop it already!» Becky opened the door.

Isabel rushed in to hug her, but Becky stopped her cold, spun around, and grabbed her backpack. She started packing frantically. «Whatever it is, make it quick. I'll be outta here in a second.»

«Becky, I swear to you, I didn't know.» Isabel's words tumbled out. «I was away, in the States, at school, remember? I never saw anything when I came back here! I don't think that mom knew either.»

«Really? I think she knew. She just looked the other way. Or she was too drunk to notice—same thing! Just like she didn't notice you getting beat up by that asshole!»

«Wait, that's not fair! There's no way she could've known what he did to me. So maybe it was the same with you. I—»

«Really? Come on! Mothers always know! She just kept her mouth shut while your motherfucking husband beat the shit out of you! Can't stain the name of the great Torres legal empire, with a scandal, no? All she ever cared about was her own ass!»

Isabel backed up against the wall, shaking.

«Come on, Becky, mom wasn't like that. She took care of us. She—»

«That shit never happens in good homes, right? It only happens to other people! Well, guess what? It fucking does—to you and to me!

We just found out our father was a fucking pervert, jacking off to pictures of me! Try and wrap your head around that! And where was our dear old mother, huh?»

Becky started panting—a panic attack building. She scrambled for her pill bottle. Half of them spilled across the floor. She dropped to all fours, frantically collecting them, bumping into furniture, cursing, trembling. She managed to gulp one down dry, wincing.

«Imagine the headlines,» she said, her voice breaking. «The country's most respected attorney peddles kiddie porn. Wife claims it was her baby girl who made him do it, swears she was a little whore!' What about your other daughter, Mrs. Torres? Was she to blame for getting beaten up? What was she, a punching bag?»

Isabel slid down the wall, shaking uncontrollably. Her eyes went glassy, staring at the ceiling, sobbing.

Becky propped herself against the bed, heaving. She punched her own temples with her fists, bit her lips and slowly calmed down. Her breathing became more controlled.

«I'm sorry! I shouldn't have said any of that. I wasn't thinking! Please, Isa, I didn't mean it!»

Isabel looked catatonic.

«Listen, everything will be fine. I promise. It's all gonna be okay. I just need to get outta here. Outta this house, outta the fucking country, outta everyone's way! And everything will be back to normal. Just forget what I said. I'll just go to the airport and get out of everyone's hair, okay?»

Isabel blinked. A tear streamed down her cheek.

«Becky. Don't. Please.»

«I can't stay, Isa. I just can't.»

«With all that's happened, you shouldn't be in that shitty, cold place all alone. It's not good.»

«I wouldn't be alone. I've got Sylvia. I'll be alright.»

Isabel closed her eyes, shivering, holding back tears. «I can't be in this shitty place all alone. I need you. I really need you. I can't handle all this alone. Please! Don't leave me. Not like this!»

«Come on, Isa, I really need some space. You'll be fine with your—with Ana.»

«It's not the same thing. You're my sister. I need you. We need each other right now. I'm begging you!»

Becky closed her eyes, then crawled on all fours to Isabel and lay down, resting her head on her sister's lap. Isabel caressed Becky's hair gently.

«Just come stay with me for a while.»

Becky nodded, eyes closed, a faint smile on her face. They sat in silence, enveloped in their sisterhood.

«Okay,» Becky whispered. «But just for a couple of days.»

10

Roberto Soto's Office

S oto worked on his laptop, checking his calendar, making notes. A knock at the door. He checked his watch, sprinted up and opened it.

Becky stood there, looking like she'd been sent to the principal's office in high school.

«Oh my, I'm so sorry,» Soto said. «Time flew by. I didn't realize it was this late. You're Becky, right? Sylvia's friend? Come on in, please.»

Becky walked in slowly, surveying the small office. Her eyes lingered on a faded poster of the Kalachakra mandala—its intricate circular design of interlocking geometric patterns and symbols intriguing to her. Then she moved to the photo of Dr. Bhat.

«Is that a relative?»

Soto smiled warmly. «That's one of my teachers. My most important one, in fact. Please, have a seat.»

Becky's attention was drawn to another poster—a blue-skinned, four-armed, princely figure riding a wave on top of a large sea turtle.

«What's the story with this guy? He's hitching a ride on a turtle?»

Soto laughed. «That's Kurma, the second incarnation of Lord Vishnu, the protector of Earth, of life itself. The ancient writings say he took the form of a huge turtle to carry the world on his back, and help good triumph over evil.»

«The weight of the world on his back, literally? I can relate.»

«Well, some would say metaphorically. Can I get you anything?»

«I'm fine, thanks. Well, not so fine if I'm here, I guess.»

«How can I help you?»

«Didn't Sylvia tell you?»

«No. She said you might call and asked me to help you any way I could. But she didn't mention any specifics. She wouldn't without your permission. Neither would I.»

Becky eyed Soto carefully before continuing. «I've been seeing her for some time because of these horrible nightmares. I don't sleep 'cause I'm scared to dream, so I basically walk around all day in a daze. When I do zonk out, boom! I wake up screaming 'cause someone in my dreams either dies or gets tortured or some other horrible shit.»

She took a deep breath. «And now, my mother just threw me out of the house, so I'm staying at my sister's for a couple of days until I fly the fuck outta here back to my apartment in the States.»

«How long have you suffered these nightmares?»

«Shit, most of my life, I think. But they've been getting worse. And now, recently, I'll just zonk out unexpectedly, so the dreams happen anywhere, anytime. Yeah, the pills Sylvia gave me calm me down sometimes, but not always.»

«What does she give you?»

Becky pulled out the bottle, read the label. «Kava extract.»

«Strong stuff.»

«She'd rather I didn't take 'em, but I guess it's better than never sleeping. And yesterday—like, things took a really nasty turn when my mother kicked me out. I took more than usual and kinda passed out in the middle of the day. And I had another fucking nightmare anyway!»

Becky slumped in her chair, biting her fingernails.

«Tell me about these nightmares.»

«Well, they always happen in weird, exotic places I've never been to. Like in ancient times and stuff. And there's always this evil motherfucker—pardon my French.»

Soto smiled. «No worries. Go on.»

«This guy, no matter when and where the dream happens, he's always the same, but dressed according to the time and place. And he's always chasing somebody different, but I feel I know them somehow. Then the evil dude steals some shit from that person and kills them. That's when I wake up. I mean, I know all this sounds crazy, but you asked!»

«And that man, the recurring character—how would you describe him?»

«He's like, around your age, a little taller than you, I guess. Oriental, straight black hair, sometimes long, sometimes shorter, depending. And his eyes are dark, but they can become dark red. Not like irritated red—I mean creepy, glowing red.»

«Wow. That's a pretty amazing amount of detail.»

«Well, he's been there almost every night for years, so yeah, you could say I kinda know him pretty well. But I just wish I could forget the damn thing. Him, the places, the people—I hate it. It's horrifying!»

«Why don't we start with your natal chart and see where that takes us?»

«Sure, whatever.»

Soto looked at his laptop. «You were born on August 10, 1991, at one forty-five AM, city of Dorado, right here in Puerto Rico, correct?»

«So I've been told.»

«I know your father passed away recently. How do you feel about that?»

Becky clenched her teeth. Her entire body tensed. «You want the truth?»

«Of course.»

«I wish he would rot in hell!»

«That anger toward your father—it's been there for a long time?»

«More now than ever. I really don't wanna get into that right now.»

Soto looked up from the screen. «What about your mother? How is your relationship with her?»

Becky frowned. «Seriously? I just told you she kicked me out of the fucking house!»

«None of this is recent, is it?»

«Well, this was a bit over the top, even for her. But yeah, dad was horrible, but maybe she was worse.»

«How so?»

«She was never there for me. For neither of us.»

«Neither of us? Meaning your father or your sister?»

«Wait—how'd you know I have a sister? Did Sylvia tell you?»

«No, she didn't. I can see it in your chart.»

Becky's eyebrows rose. She eyed Soto suspiciously. «Okay, that's weird.»

«So you felt she wasn't there for you and your sister, is that correct?»

«When she was there, she was on another planet.» Becky mimed drinking.

«I see.»

«When I grew older, all she wanted was to get me hitched with some rich asshole, like she did with my sister. But I never buckled, and that would really piss her off. So as soon as I was able, I moved out as far away as I could.»

«So would it be fair to say you were angry with both of them because you didn't get much support from them? Only from your sister.»

«Yeah, I've always loved her. When I was little, they sent her away to boarding school, so I grew up mostly alone. But whenever we got together, we were great with each other. Even to this day.»

«How about your relationships with other men? Have you had a hard time trusting them or being intimate with them?»

«How do you mean?»

«Well, in your relationships with men, have you ever felt uncomfortable when they touch you in certain ways or in certain parts of your body? Does it make you feel uncomfortable or make it difficult to have sexual intimacy?»

Becky straightened up. «Hey! I'd say you're getting too damn intimate right now! What the fuck are you talking about?»

Soto turned his laptop around so Becky could see the screen—her natal chart, a complex grid of symbols and lines.

«I'm talking about what I see in your childhood. The cause of your fear of intimacy, your lack of trust toward men. More than justified from what I can see here.»

Becky sprang up, angry, shaking her head. «Enough of this bullshit. I didn't come here for this. I'm outta here!»

«With all you've been through, it's no surprise you suffer from these nightmares, Becky. That's my point. That's why you're here. Let me help you.»

«What the fuck do you know? Yeah, my father was a creep, so he took some photos of me. But so what?»

«You don't remember anything else?»

«No! What do you mean? Fuck you! This shit's over. I'm done!»

Becky turned toward the door but started to shake, her breathing labored.

«Breathe, Becky. Just breathe. Can you tell me what was in those photos?»

Becky froze, trembling more intensely.

«No. Stop! I don't want to do this!»

«I know this is extremely difficult for you. There's probably a lot of pain boiling inside you. If you don't let it out, it will just continue to grow and hurt you in other ways. Can't you see that? Why not let it all out? Let it explode. You're safe here. Let it all out.»

«I didn't come here for this shit!»

«Locking all that pain inside takes a toll on your body, on your mind. It's got to be eating you alive.»

Becky struggled to move, paralyzed.

«How would you know? You asshole! Why're you doing this to me?»

«Okay, okay. Just breathe, Becky. Take deep breaths, slowly.»

Becky managed to turn to face him, eyes wide, struggling to breathe, face pale with shock.

«What is it you think you know, you son of a bitch? What'd you see in my fucking natal chart?»

Soto nodded softly, reassuringly, with a knowing expression.

«Why did you ask me all those questions if you already knew? What kind of sadistic son of a bitch are you?»

Becky cried inconsolably, her body shaking. Soto stood up slowly, trying not to appear threatening.

«Let it out, Becky.»

Becky let out a howling yell. Soto moved closer.

«They're just pictures of me naked! Okay? Dirty pictures of when I was a little girl! That's all! There! You satisfied? Are you getting off too?»

Becky shook so hard she could barely stand. She clutched the back of the chair. Soto inched closer.

«Just keep breathing. Do you remember what else happened?»

Becky slid to the floor, eyes darting wildly, blinded by tears.

«What else? What're you saying?»

«What happened with your dad, Becky?»

«Nothing! What do you mean?»

Becky let go of the chair, clenched her fists, her jaw locked. She crouched, about to punch the floor. Soto grabbed a cushion, placed it on the floor under her hands. Becky pounded on it with all her strength. Soto moved behind her, made a series of movements with his hands along her back without touching her.

«That's it, come on, let it out! What did he do to you? Do you remember now? Scream if you have to!»

Becky uttered a primal scream.

She grabbed the cushion with both hands, brought it to her face, bit it hard. Her eyes rolled back. She continued to scream into the pillow, bit it like a rabid animal, came up for air, and screamed again, her body convulsing slightly. «Stay away! Don't touch me!»

«Is he touching you?»

Becky's whole body rocked back and forth. Her eyes went white. The pitch of her voice went up, like a little girl's.

«No! Stop it! Go away! Please, stop—it hurts! Mommy? Where are you?»

Her cry was agonizing, her face contorted. She began to gag.

Soto reached for a small wastebasket. Becky vomited into it. Soto tapped Becky repeatedly on her forehead with two fingers.

«Becky, listen to me. What happened is in the past. Gone. It's over. You're going to look at whatever it was from up above, like you're watching a movie. What do you see?»

«Daddy. Father, he caresses me. Then he kisses me in the mouth. His tongue—ugh—he puts it in me. Then his fingers in my—oh God, no!»

Becky gagged again, vomited again.

«What happened is in the past. You've seen it now. You know what happened. You don't have to stay there. You can come back here, to my office. You are safe. Come back to here and now.»

Becky cried intensely, clutching the cushion, curled into a fetal position. Soto placed another cushion under her head, got some tissues and placed them near her.

«You're safe. Take a deep breath. Feel your body. Feel the floor. What's past is past. You're okay. You're here now, with me. Just exhale deeply, saying 'aaaah'.»

Becky exhaled, shuddering. «Aaaah.»

«That's it. Just keep breathing. Slow it down if you can.»

Becky slowed her breathing, opened her eyes slowly, still rocking back and forth.

«I was so little. Six, seven maybe. How could he? Oh Jesus!»

«Keep breathing.»

«What just happened to me? I lived it, felt it in my stomach. Oh God, did I feel it! No images, no memories really. More like a horrible sensation.»

«I'm guessing you might have had a spontaneous regression.»

«How come I couldn't remember any of this before? I mean, did I imagine it? Am I making it up?»

«I've worked on natal charts just like yours for years, verified them with my teachers and many other experts. When Mars is in the fourth house of someone's horoscope, like yours, it is almost absolutely certain that the person was sexually abused at an early age. And that the incident has probably been kept secret from everyone. That's an extremely painful burden to carry. And in your case, with no support from your mother, it's probably much worse. And I can see it likely happened to you later with other men, correct?»

Becky nodded slowly, staring at Soto with equal parts amazement and skepticism. She pondered whether to open herself to sharing the truth, possibly the darkest truth she had ever hidden inside.

«I was in high school. Got taken to the hospital because, well, cause I tried to kill myself with a shitload of pills and alcohol. Didn't do a very good job, obviously. I'm still here.

«I'm very glad you didn't,» Soto replied calmly.

Becky smiled weakly then turned serious.

«So, I'm lying there in this hospital bed, alone, all by myself, completely out of it. My father was off somewhere traveling for work and he never found out. Mother was completely devastated, which, come to think of it, was probably why I did it in the first place. So she went home that night. I mean, what would be the point of staying overnight with her unconscious daughter, right?

Becky shook her head, closed her eyes, remembering. Tears streamed out.

«Yeah, well, I remember this guy wearing scrubs, an orderly, a nurse or whatever. He came in, and took advantage of me. I barely felt anything, you know. I was almost in a coma.»

Becky shook her head, took a deep breath.

«That's such a bullshit, white-wash expression: 'Took advantage of me.' It kind' a keeps me from calling it what it really was. Like with my father. I just swept the whole thing under the rug. I just grew to hate him and my mother without really knowing why. Better to forget, right?

«Denial never helps. When you do that, it usually manifests itself in other ways, none of them healthy.»

«You're the first person I've ever told any of this to. Not even Isabel or Sylvia.» Becky smiled, this time sincerely took a deep breath. «So, given that I'm totally fucked up. Is there any cure for me, doc?»

«There can be. If you look at it as something you had to go through because of your karma, then we can move on from there.»

«Oh, so I'm being punished for something I did many lives ago?»

«It's not about punishment. It's just the law of cause and effect. One action generating a reaction. There's no judgment in it. You simply accumulate karmic seeds with every action you take. Whether or not those seeds grow and manifest themselves depends on many things.»

«How can there be no judgment? No right or wrong? Are you kidding me? What about what my father did or that guy? It sure as hell wasn't right—it was evil, fucked-up shit!»

«Actions we take that create pain and suffering for others in one life eventually catch up to us in another. And we've been alive endless times. So imagine all the seeds we've planted for millions of years. Same thing with actions that create joy, happiness, and pleasure in others. They will also, at some point, generate joy and happiness for us. But here's the kicker: all those emotions—pleasure, pain, joy, suffering—all of them are in our mind, in our ego. If we can control our mind and get rid of our ego, of our sense of self, which is just an illusion, then there will be no more pain and suffering.»

Becky stared, puzzled.

«And no joy or pleasure either. Who the hell wants that? I wanna be happy!»

«And what does that happiness depend on? Something outside yourself? So if you lack that which makes you joyful or happy, you're right back to pain and suffering in an endless cycle. You see?»

Becky tried to sit up with Soto's help.

«So what's the solution? How do we stop that cycle?»

«The question you should be asking is: Who is experiencing the pain or the joy? If these actions and reactions carry over from one lifetime to another, then who or what is it that's coming back over and over in a different time and place to go through all this?»

«You lost me. Our soul, our spirit? What? You're even crazier than Sylvia is, and that's saying a lot!»

Soto smiled. «It does seem crazy, I know.» «Yeah, well, what does all this hocus-pocus do for me now, with my nightmares and the shit I went through? I'm still freaking out with this news of what my father did to me. It's stirring up all sorts of horrible shit. I can still feel it in my stomach.»

«Healing is a process. One that requires hard work and practice. It's not linear, so progress might seem slow. But hiding from it simply doesn't work. The best way to heal is facing it head-on, and that may mean stirring up painful memories and feelings. But I promise you, you always come out stronger at the end, and more aware. I'll be happy to guide you through it, if you wish.»

«I'm not sure how much longer I'll be here on the island.»

«We can set a date and, if you have to go, we can connect remotely. How's that?»

Soto looked at Becky with a soothing, comforting expression. «Let's work on the pressing issue of your childhood trauma first, but that doesn't mean we're not going to work on your nightmares. We just need to take care of one thing at a time. Is that okay with you?»

«I guess. I don't know. Both things are horrible to deal with.»

«Okay, let's do this. Try to keep a notebook with you and write down all the details you can remember from your dreams when you wake up. Let me look at my calendar and I'll text you some dates, and we'll work on both these things as best as we can. Just know that if you need to, if you become activated or get into a crisis, you can call me anytime.»

«Yeah, sure. Thanks.»

Soto pointed at Dr. Bhat's photo.

«I wanted to ask your permission to consult with my teacher about your case. She's an extraordinary human being and a far better astrologer.»

«I'm so fucked up that you need to bring in the heavy guns?»

Soto winked. «As heavy as they can be! I want to validate some aspects of your chart with her, if you don't mind.»

«Sure, what the hell? At this point I could use all the help I can get.»

Becky's eyes locked onto Soto's for a moment, smiling. It became awkward. She shifted her gaze toward the Kurma poster.

«You can even bring in the turtle man if it'll help me!»

They both smiled warmly.

11

India - Institute for Human Consciousness

A medium-sized turtle dipped into an artificial pond, its shell breaking the surface among beautiful blue lotus flowers. The pond was surrounded by lush, exotic plants and trees divided by winding footpaths—a carefully cultivated paradise of learning.

Dr. Krishnaa Bhat walked along one of the paths, followed eagerly by a group of college-age students. Despite being in her seventies, she moved with the energy of someone half her age. She stopped at a leafy bush dotted with small red berries.

«*Ashwagandha*,» she announced, her voice carrying authority and warmth in equal measure. «Also known as Winter Cherry or Indian Ginseng. It's a good stress reliever, reduces blood sugar levels, and can help you sleep. Some even say it may have anti-aging properties, which explains why I don't look a day over eighty.»

The students laughed.

«However, who can tell me what happens if taken excessively?»

A young woman named Swathi raised her hand. Dr. Bhat pointed to her.

«It may upset the stomach, cause vomiting, or even lower your blood pressure dangerously. There is also a risk of liver disease.»

«Very good! So, ladies, consider that before you use it to maintain your youthful beauty.»

More laughter. Dr. Bhat smiled—she enjoyed teaching, always had.

«And are these beautiful berries the source of all those properties?»

A nineteen-year-old boy named Amir timidly raised his hand from the back of the group.

«Go on, Amir. The plant does not bite, and neither do I.»

The students giggled.

«It is not the berries, Doctor Bhat. It is the root that hides the active ingredients.»

«Very well, Amir. See? No need to deprive us of your knowledge!»

Amir's face turned red, but the exchange brought out a bright smile on his face.

An Indian man strode quickly toward them, holding Dr. Bhat's mobile phone.

«Forgive me, Madam Doctor, but you left your mobile phone in your office.»

Dr. Bhat looked miffed. «Precisely. I left it there on purpose.»

«I apologize, Madam Doctor, but you asked us to inform you if the call was long distance.»

Dr. Bhat examined her phone, checking her messages. «Oh, I see. My most sincere apologies. Thank you.»

She turned to her students. «Excuse me for a moment. Please be careful not to touch any leaves in here. I wouldn't want your fingers to fall off!»

Her students giggled as she moved to a secluded corner and made the call.

«My dearest Roberto, what a pleasant if ill-timed surprise. I'm in the middle of a lecture.»

She listened, then her expression changed. She moved deeper into the gardens for privacy.

«Does she know? Is she aware?»

Many hours and thousands of miles away, Soto cradled his mobile phone awkwardly between his shoulder and neck—an impossible task. He gave up, put it on speaker, and stared excitedly at his laptop screen.

«She doesn't seem to have a clue,» he said.

«Did you mention anything to her?»

«No, not at all. Not before I am completely sure. Besides, I don't think she'd be ready to handle something like this right now. That's why I'm reaching out to you. Could you please verify my reading?»

«Of course. It would be my honor.»

«Do you think it's possible? Could she be one of the disciples?»

Back in the botanical garden, Dr. Bhat's voice was careful, measured. «Anything is possible, but let us not get ahead of ourselves. Where is she from?»

«She was born here in Puerto Rico, but she's been living in the States for a while. She's visiting for a few days and came to consult with me.»

«Are you going to see her again?»

«I hope so. She's going through a serious crisis. I offered to help her through it, but since she's here only in passing, she's not sure if she can meet with me again.»

«I agree with your decision not to say anything to her for now. We have to be completely sure, and even then, this is extremely delicate. So please, keep it between us.»

«Of course, I understand!»

«Very auspicious, your call. Just this morning I received an invitation for a lecture on the subject of Yeshe Tsogyal's disciples and the *terma* tradition.»

Soto's excitement was palpable through the phone. «Really? Incredible timing!»

Dr. Bhat pulled out a brochure from her pocket, glanced at it. «The lecture is being given by a scholar who claims he is one of Yeshe Tsogyal's reincarnated disciples. If that is true, that would make him uniquely qualified to help us determine if your client is indeed another one of them.»

«That would be amazing!»

Dr. Bhat studied the brochure. The title on the facing page read: «HIDDEN TREASURES OF BUDDHISM.»

«I believe it is now imperative that I attend this event. Do you give me permission to share her information with him if I find it pertinent?»

«Of course! It would be wonderful to bring in his expertise!»

«The lecture will be at this scholar's foundation in Bhutan. Now, remember to keep up with your astral travel practice! It will save us both a lot of money in long distance calls!»

Dr. Bhat's laughter was infectious. «Namasté! Talk to you soon!»

She turned over the brochure. The back page showed a photo of the event's host: Druk Dorji.

12

Bhutan, King Sindhu Raja's Palace
8th Century

Thin beams of sunlight crisscrossed the smoke of incense floating in the air along the shadowy hallways. The entrance to the king's bedroom was ornate, colorful, adorned with elaborate cornices of snow lions and dragons. The walls and columns were so dense with colorful, intricate designs that they were almost overwhelming to the eyes.

But now all the astounding artistry seemed dark, dust filled, decaying, dead.

Two guards opened the doors for three visitors to enter the king's bedroom—Tobgay, one of the king's closest advisors, an old man in his early eighties, incredibly agile for his age, followed by Guru Padmasambhava, the ageless sage from the kingdom of Oddiyana, around one thousand miles to the West of Bhutan.

Padmasambhava was light skinned, his face adorned by a thin goatee and twirly mustache, and an intense gaze that could see right through your very essence.

The third visitor, standing close to him, was the always radiant, delicate, and beautiful Yeshe Tsogyal.

The king's chamber was even darker than the hallways if that could be possible. Tobgay, Padmasambhava, and Lady Tsogyal bowed from a distance at the pale and consumed King Sindhu Raja, his once-powerful frame now reduced to trembling hands and labored breathing. His body was almost hard to discern, buried inside his immense bed, wrapped in silken sheets.

In the corner sat a young maiden, face hidden behind a veil, body covered in royal vestments. She rose and bowed as the visitors entered.

Tshering Chime, the same man that had led the attack against Lady Tsogyal and her disciples in Becky's dreams, seemed to materialize from the shadows. He approached the head of the bed, leaned over, and whispered to the king, his voice dripping with poison, «My Lord, why would you allow a man such as this into your chambers.»

The king dismissed him with a scowl and a trembling, faint, hand gesture.

Tobgay took half a step toward the foot of the king's bed, «My lord, these are the great sages that you summoned to examine your health: Guru Padmasambhava and his consort, Lady Yeshe Tsogyal.»

Guru Padmasambhava and Yeshe Tsogyal bowed reverently again. The King eyed them up and down. His voice cracking and wheezing, he pointed his bony finger at Tshering Chime with derision, trying to control his anger.

«When I sent my son into battle I asked this one, my most trusted wizard, to summon our most powerful deities in order to protect him.»

Tshering Chime avoided looking at the visitors and instead leaned over to the king eying him with a cold, acid stare, «My Lord, I invoked their spirits as you commanded, but once unleashed, no one can really control them.»

«Silence!» The king's voice cracked with sudden force. «My son is dead! My army was defeated! And when I renounced those devilish deities and had their temples destroyed, I became ill with this sickness no doctors can understand—not even you, you cursed witch!»

«My Lord, the spirits are angry. They feel betrayed. We must appease them!»

«One more word from you, witch, and I swear it will be your last!»

Chime retreated into shadows like smoke.

The king turned to Padmasambhava. «They call you Precious Guru. Are you as powerful as people say? Can you rid me of this disease and bring prosperity to my lands?»

Padmasambhava replied with a measured, mellifluous voice, «I cannot speak for what people say about me, my Lord. I can only speak of what I see: your palace, your realm, and your highness have been overtaken by deadly, wrathful spirits that must be subdued. If you will allow me, I will bring these dark forces into the light.»

«Will you vanquish them? Destroy them? They have almost destroyed me and my kingdom!»

«No, your highness. Such is not the way of sadhana, our spiritual practice. We seek not to destroy but to heal. We do not cut the poisonous tree—we transform it so it bears healing fruit. Such are the ways of Buddha Dharma.»

The king contemplated this, nodded softly to Tobgay, his trusted advisor, before closing his eyes.

Tobgay bowed before his king, then turned to face Padmasambhava.

«You have the King's permission, with all of his authority, to do what is needed, great Guru.»

Padmasambhava moved to the windows, opening them wide. Sunlight and fresh air flooded the room. Everyone squinted at the brightness.

Tshering Chime slithered deeper into the shadows.

«Breathe deeply, my Lord,» Padmasambhava uttered, «breathe in the light, the sun, and the fresh air. I will help you with these deities. I will bring the light of wisdom and compassion into their hearts. For it is from darkness and ignorance that they derive their unholy power.»

The king opened his eyes, squinting from the sunlight, breathed deeply, tried to sit up to bask in the sudden warmth and fresh air.

Tshering Chime moved to help him. The king brushed him off.

«Bring the light back to my kingdom and my health back to me,» the king said, «If you succeed, you can have anything you wish from my kingdom—lands, gold, jewels, women, men, anything.»

He pointed to the young maiden. «And as a token of my trust, I offer you my only daughter along with the most generous dowry.»

The maiden's body stiffened and took a step back in fear.

Tshering Chime approached once more, whispering urgently. «Forgive me, my Lord! Your illness must be affecting your memory. Your daughter was promised by your highness to marry my son. I took your word as a solemn oath!»

The king sat upright, his voice growing stronger. «A promise I surely made under one of your feverish spells after my son's death. My mind was not well then, but it is becoming clear now. My throne is in peril, my country suffers, and we must all do what is necessary. My daughter understands her duty is to her king and her realm!»

«Forgive me, my Lord. My son is very much in love with your daughter, he is completely devoted to her, to you, and to these lands. Together they could do wonders to protect our kingdom and dispel these evil spirits!»

«What insolence! I will hear no more! This is my kingdom! You will immediately renounce your position as Chief Wizard and are hereby banished from these lands! Neither you nor your son are allowed in the kingdom under penalty of imprisonment or worse! You have two days to leave!»

Tshering Chime tried to control his rage, bowed, and retreated. For a moment his icy, hate-filled eyes fixed on Padmasambhava and Yeshe Tsogyal with seething contempt as he exited.

King Sindhu Raja waited for the wizard to leave before addressing the sages from the West.

«Forgive me, great Guru, for allowing such a scourge into a place of trust beside me. Once again, I beseech you, heal me, heal my land, and my daughter is yours!»

Padmasambhava nodded softly. «I humbly thank you, my Lord, but I have no interest in material possessions or offerings of the flesh. They are but illusions, fleeting, impermanent, that generate attachments within us that eventually turn into pain and suffering.»

«You refuse the offering of a king of his most precious jewel, his very flesh and blood?»

Yeshe Tsogyal whispered in Padmasambhava's ear. The Guru nodded.

«My lord, great king,» Yeshe spoke, «your daughter is indeed a precious jewel. I sense within her the auspicious signs of an enlightened being, a Tulku, reborn, that should be nourished with the tree of knowledge. I humbly request your blessing to take her under my wing as one of my precious disciples. No need for dowries—the greatest gift will be to help her fulfill her destiny as a guru in her own right.»

The maiden trembled.

«And if I may be so bold, your highness,» Padmasambhava added, «when we succeed in subduing these evil spirits, I beg that you open your heart and allow us to share the teachings that Lord Buddha bestowed upon us with you and your people, so you may all reach enlightenment.»

The king closed his eyes, breathed deeply, feeling fresh air entering his lungs along with the hope of healing his mysterious ailments and restoring peace and abundance to his kingdom.

«On the soul of my dead son, it is done! My dear child, go to them. It is a rare honor to be recognized by a great Guru!»

The maiden bowed, moved shyly toward Yeshe Tsogyal.

«May I see your face, child?» Lady Tsogyal asked.

The maiden looked to her father, hesitating.

«Do as she asks. She is your Guru now!» Her father, the king, commanded.

The maiden removed her veil. It was Tashi Chidren—the young disciple from Becky's dreams.

Lady Tsogyal's voice flowed as warmly and smoothly as Centauri honey. «You are beautiful, my child. You will be my greatest disciple, and you will bring great blessings to your father, your kingdom, and to all sentient beings now and forever.»

Tashi bowed, keeping her head down.

Padmasambhava bowed before the king once more. «We thank you, your highness. Now, if you will allow us, we must bid farewell. We have a great task ahead.»

«Come along, child,» Yeshe said to Tashi. «Your teachings begin right now. Although I suspect you have foreseen our arrival in your dreams many times before.»

Tashi's eyes opened wide, mouth slightly ajar in awe, shocked that anyone would know about the many strange dreams that had haunted her since she could remember.

No one knew, she had never told a soul.

Yet this strange but enchanting woman seemed to know her secret. Tashi nodded in slight reverence, took one last look at her father and left with the two gurus.

Outside The Cavern

This was the same entrance to the cavern that had appeared in Becky's dreams so many times before—nearly buried by snow, dotted with scraggly bushes and jutting rocks, with the treacherous path that led to it, winding along the precipice.

Guru Padmasambhava and Yeshe Tsogyal danced together in front of its entry in bright, flowing ceremonial attire. They floated and swayed, unaffected by the cold. Their movements were beautiful, enthralling, perfectly synchronized.

Tashi Chidren knelt nearby, wrapped in thick furs, dazed.

As Padmasambhava and Yeshe jumped and spun, translucent figures materialized around them—frightening, demon-like. The spirits' gazes were transfixed, swaying slowly in unison with the two gurus.

Tashi sprang up and cowered back, terrified.

Yeshe Tsogyal spun her head toward the young maiden. Her eyes glowed beneath her mask. She smiled.

Tashi immediately calmed down.

The dance stopped. Guru Padmasambhava removed his mask and addressed the ghostly, demonic spirits surrounding them.

«You accept the teachings of Buddha,» he said. «You vow to stop hurting the people of these lands, and indeed swear to become their protectors. You will from this moment forward be defenders of the Lord Buddha's teachings on all the kingdom.»

The ghostly deities bowed down with respect.

«One of you still remains inside this cave, resisting me. A very obstinate demon!» Padmasambhava pointed to a shiny copper vase next to Tashi. «Tashi, if you please, run and fetch me some water. Use that vase!»

Tashi glanced at Yeshe Tsogyal. Yeshe nodded reassuringly.

Tashi grabbed the vase and ran up the path, trudging through the snow. The path was treacherous. One misstep meant falling thousands of meters to the abyss below.

She maneuvered carefully up the snowy terrain. She found a small stream cascading down the mountain wall, filled the vase with icy water, and retraced her steps.

Tashi moved slowly back toward the cavern entrance, terrified at the eerie sight of Padmasambhava and Yeshe Tsogyal surrounded by ghastly demons. She handed the vase to Padmasambhava and knelt nearby.

Padmasambhava moved to catch the sunlight at just the right angle, reflecting it in a wavy pattern toward the cave.

A terrifying roar thundered from inside.

Tashi recoiled in terror. Yeshe ran to her, embraced her.

A humongous, unworldly thing leaped out from the cave—half snow tiger, half dragon, engulfed in bluish flames. The other deities flew to the front of Padmasambhava to shield him.

Tashi fainted. Yeshe held on to her.

Padmasambhava remained unfazed.

The Dragon-Tiger moved closer, snarling. Its powerful claws slashed right through the other deities' defenses. Its enormous canine teeth drooled, inches from Padmasambhava's face. Eerie vapor oozed from its nostrils.

The Guru remained still, eyes locked onto the demon's face.

The fiery beast got up on its powerful hind quarters, ready to pounce. The deities regrouped to stand up to the attacker.

The Dragon-Tiger roared. The echo boomed throughout the valley.

Padmasambhava dropped to his knees, arms open at his sides.

«If it is my body you need, take it, it is yours, I do not need it,» he said. «If it is my soul you seek, I am but an emanation of *Avalokiteśvara*, and the Buddhas, eternal, formless, and compassionate beyond measure. I am you, you are I, we are one. Take me for I am willing to give this body to you to advance your enlightenment, and that of all living things.»

The Dragon-Tiger closed its jowls. Tears welled in its eyes. It fell to the ground, calm, docile, bowing until its huge forehead touched the snow in front of Padmasambhava.

The Guru caressed the fiery beast's head gently.

The creature looked up with love in its eyes, its bluish flame not as intense. Nearby, Yeshe Tsogyal smiled and shook Tashi gently.

A groggy Tashi came to, holding on to Yeshe tightly. But slowly she began to understand—her gurus had powers beyond compare.

The deities began to spin and jump around in joy, performing the same dance Padmasambhava and Yeshe had done before. An unreal, ghostly celebration.

The Dragon-Tiger purred softly and retreated into the dark recesses of the cave. The demonic spirits slowly faded away.

«I need time to meditate inside this cave,» Padmasambhava said. «I must honor these proud and powerful spirits and their birthplace. They have been unwitting slaves to evil wizards for years, serving their unholy pursuits. They deserve my respect, my admiration, and my gratitude for opening their hearts to me, and to the buddha dharma. In a few days' time, I will meet you at the palace.»

Yeshe nodded, rose, helped a still shaken Tashi to her feet and carefully treaded with her down the treacherous mountain path.

Inside the Cavern

This was the same magical cave from Becky's dreams where Yeshe Tsogyal had distributed the treasured objects to her disciples.

Sunlight barely made it inside. The iridescent blue glow of the Dragon-Tiger bounced off the walls and ceiling like a pale lantern. The beast lay peacefully on the floor.

Padmasambhava sat in the lotus position, his hands forming a mudra, fingers locked in a mystical gesture. He breathed calmly, staring at nothing, at everything.

Outside, across the imposing Himalayan mountain range, the sun rose behind the imposing snow-covered peaks and night became enveloped in a blanket of stars—over and over again, in quick succession. At least three days and nights went by.

Inside the cavern, Guru Padmasambhava floated in mid-air, eyes slightly open, smiling softly, in absolute peace. A fiery, dazzling rainbow surrounded his body, bathing the cave in colorful rays of light.

He took a deep breath, slowly descended, unfolded his legs and landed softly. The rainbow-glow faded.

The solid granite wall behind where he'd been floating was now indented with the imprint of his body—exactly as it had appeared in Becky's dreams.

«I call upon you, great spirit!»

The Dragon-Tiger's growl reverberated all around. The gigantic beast slowly got up, shook its body from its sleep-like trance, lighting the cave with its bluish glow. It approached the Guru with its head down.

Guru Padmasambhava grabbed onto the Dragon-Tiger's back and with a swift, gracious movement climbed on top of it. He rode the beast out through the tunnel that led outside.

Guru Padmasambhava rode out of the cavern atop the Dragon-Tiger at full trot, straight toward the edge of the precipice.

The beast leaped into the abyss, took flight, gracefully gliding in the air thousands of feet above the valley, into the clouds like a blazing blue comet.

Isabel's Apartment, Guest Bedroom
Present Day

Becky woke up, her eyes open wide with excitement and awe. She smiled, stretched, looked around to find her bearings.

She reached for a notebook and scribbled in it, pausing only to recall details of her dream.

The screech of Isabel's espresso machine interrupted her reverie.

Becky jumped out of bed, threw on a robe, and ran out into the hallway. Isabel sat on the sofa with a fresh mug of coffee in hand.

Becky ran in and hugged her. Isabel almost dropped the mug.

«Whoa! What's up with you?»

«I had a good night's sleep, thank you, for the first time in a long, long time!»

«I'm happy to hear that but, next time, try not to get us both burned.» Isabel looked toward the kitchen. «I didn't think you'd be up so early.»

Becky eyed her quizzically, then smiled mischievously. «What's going on?»

The espresso machine screeched again.

«Oh. So we're not alone.»

«Here, take mine, I'll make another one for me.» Isabel darted up, gave Becky her mug.

«A full house! I might have to go out and do a coffee run!» Becky said, winking mischiveously.

«Shut up and behave!»

«Hey, I ain't the one misbehaving!» Then, loudly: «Good morning, Ana!»

Isabel gave Becky the eye and ran into the kitchen, almost bumping into Ana Ramos as she walked into the living room in nightwear, fresh coffee mug in hand.

«Good morning, Becky. Did I hear correctly? You slept well? No nightmares? That sounds great!»

«Mmmm, thank you, thank you! I mean, it was still a fucking weird dream, but it was different, it had a happy ending for a change, nothing horrible, nobody dying or anything.»

Ana sat quietly in one of the chairs, sipping her coffee. «What are your dreams about?»

«There's always this evil creep killing people all over the world at different times in history, always the same guy, over and over. Then there's this beautiful woman, like a princess or a goddess or something, who shows up like a mirage or a spirit kinda' thing. And she's always leaving these weird objects for different people to find, you know? Like a scavenger hunt but all over the world, and through centuries. But then the evil creep shows up and kills these people to steal these objects. That's usually when I wake up because, well, it's like I can literally feel it when they get killed.»

Ana stared at Becky intently, eyes wide open. «Oh, my God, that sounds horrible! No wonder you're scared to sleep. And this has been recurring for how long?»

«Most of my life, really.»

«Jesus, Becky, that's really awful! I can't begin to imagine what that must be like!»

«Yeah, well, this last one was different, thank God! The beautiful woman, you know, the goddess, she showed up in my dream but this time in the flesh, not like a ghost, and there was another guy with her, like a very powerful, spiritual being. They seem to be like a couple, you know? They kinda' work together..»

Becky paused for a second to recollect. Tears welled up in her eyes. She shivered, in a daze.

«Are you okay?»

«Yeah, it's the weirdest feeling. Like I really know them, and I miss them.»

«Well, if this has gone on your whole life, I guess they're almost like a family to you.»

«Yeah, better than my real family for sure. Except for Isa, of course!»

Ana smiled. «Of course.»

Becky shook her head, got out of her reverie. «And then I remember: There was this young girl, barely in her teens, a little princess, and her dad's the king, of course. It sounds kinda' like a fairy tale. I mean, I know I'm rambling like an idiot.»

Isabel walked in with her coffee, sat next to her. «A powerful man? A little princess? You do see the parallel, don't you?»

Becky frowned. «Oh, please, don't even go there! I don't think it's got anything to do with me!»

«Just saying.»

«Don't be an asshole! What kind of dreams have you been having lately?»

«I honestly can't remember.»

«Well, then, spare me your expert opinion.»

Isabel's eyes rolled up. «Okay, forget it. So, your dreams are getting better. That's good. Maybe seeing that astrologer is helping.»

«He asked me to keep a diary of my dreams so I can work on this.»

Isabel winked. «Did he show up in your dream?»

«No, you idiot.»

«Just checking.»

«Come on, this shit is serious.»

«I know. I'm just teasing.»

«And, before you go off on another tangent, I need to ask you a favor.»

«Oh, oh.»

Becky looked sideways at Ana. Ana took the hint, got up and went back into the kitchen.

«I have to get ready for work, ladies, if you'll excuse me. You have a great rest of the day, Becky.»

Becky waited for Ana to be out of earshot. «I mean, I don't wanna ruin your love life, you know, but, do you think I could stay with you for a little longer? I really want to work with this astrologer in person if I can, you know?»

Isabel put on a funny, tragic pose. «Oh, God, no! My peace, my freedom, my privacy, my love life, ruined!»

«You're such an asshole!»

They both laughed.

Becky sprang up, hugged her sister tightly. Isabel's coffee mug almost spilled over again.

«Now I know you're trying to get us both burned! Stay for as long as you need. Well, at least until I get sick of you and kick you out.»

They both smiled.

13

Torres Residence, Becky's old bedroom

Isabel scurried about, trying her best to choose which of Becky's belongings she needed to pack quickly.

«Hello? Who's there?» Evelyn walked in, drink in hand. «Isabel? What are you doing here? You scared me out of my wits!»

«I'm just packing some stuff.»

«Some stuff? Like what?»

«Just clothes for Becky.»

«Oh, so she's still around? What, she's slumming at your place now?»

Isabel raised her eyebrows, shook her head and continued packing.

«Are you taking her side now?»

«This isn't about sides, mother! How can you even think that way? We all saw what father did and you still—»

«We don't really know what happened! I just can't believe that he could've done something like that. Maybe somebody else took the pictures and, and he hid them so they wouldn't be found, we just don't know!»

Isabel stopped packing, her face red, holding back anger.

«Really? Somebody else? Who? And why wouldn't he just destroy them?»

«What if it was proof against someone, have you thought of that?»

«Proof that someone else did that to Becky years ago?and he just held on to that proof for twenty years? Is that seriously what you're thinking? Christ, mom!»

«I just know there is no way Guillermo would have done such a thing! And, and, if he had done that, and I'm not saying he did, she should have said something to me, unless she was in on it!»

«How dare you blame her! My God, mother! She was just a baby! It was her own father! Your husband! She didn't know any better, she just obeyed him! And you turned your back to her. Worse, you spat on her face! I don't know what the hell is wrong with you! Evelyn opened her eyes wide, her face a mixture of guilt and anger. Her glass slipped from her hands onto the carpet.

«No! Stop it! There is no way he would do anything to her, or to you, no, no way! Guillermo was always there for me, for all of us, he loved Becky more than his life!»

«Yeah, well, it seems he had more love for her than you and I knew about. You better think all of this through, mother, before you lose Becky and I forever and you end up alone!»

«I've always been alone! She always hated me, and I know Guillermo would never touch her unless she wanted him to! It makes no difference to me! So go on, go away, see if I care!»

Evelyn broke down, sobbing, and plopped down on the bed.

Isabel turned away from her, face red with rage. She finished packing.

«I thought I would never say this, ever, but today I am ashamed to call you my mother!»

Isabel left, slamming the door.

Bhutan, Woods Near Raja's Palace
8th Century

Night had fallen.

Padmasambhava walked along a tree-lined path toward the imposing walls of Raja's palace. Four royal guards, armed with spears, pounced out of the woods—two in front, two behind him.

Padmasambhava stopped and bowed. «May I assist you?»

A frightening, booming voice came from within the woods. It was Tshering Chime's, but he was nowhere in sight.

«We no longer desire your assistance. You are not welcome here. You will join your unholy consort and the king's whore daughter in hell. Guards, bring him to me!»

The royal guards hesitated, frightened, tightening their grip on their spears, bringing their gleaming, sharp points menacingly closer to Padmasambhava.

The Guru shrugged and followed them into the woods.

They reached a clearing at the edge of a river, beyond the natural barrier of trees and shrubs. The clearing was charnel ground, a cremation site. Mounds of burnt wood and charcoal were dispersed some distance from one another, surrounded by a thin layer of fog.

The royal guards and Padmasambhava reached a pile of firewood. Yeshe Tsogyal and Tashi stood on top of it, bound and gagged.

Tashi's eyes opened wide when she spotted the Guru. She let out a muffled scream, trembling uncontrollably.

Yeshe looked at the Guru lovingly, without a hint of fear in her eyes.

Two royal guards tied Padmasambhava and tried to gag him.

«No need. I will not scream.»

The royal guards shrugged, threw away the piece of fabric and tied the Guru on top of the pile of wood between the women.

Tshering Chime emerged from the shadows followed by his son, Druk Dorji. At fifteen-years-old, he was a scrawny, wiry boy. Young Dorji struggled to catch up to his father while carrying a lit torch.

«I hoped you would have joined your king in the practice of Buddha Dharma, but I always knew that was not your destiny. You were predestined to be an enemy of the Dharma in this lifetime, and your son, unfortunately, even worse—»

«Silence! What do you know of my destiny? You have no power over me, you fool!»

Tshering Chime glowered like a slimy lizard under the glow of the flaming torch.

«I was in control of those spirits until you appeared! My son's destiny was to marry her, the king's daughter, and you stole her from him even as you're trying to steal the throne! You said you wanted to bring light into these lands, but all you have done is bring darkness into our lives! I will now bring the burning light of hell upon thee!»

Tshering Chime made a gesture, signaling his son.

The young Druk Dorji looked puzzled.

«Do it, my son, burn these heathens!»

«What? Please father, let Tashi go, she has nothing to do with this! She was forced to join them!»

Tashi's eyes bulged with fear, looking back and forth between Chime and Dorji, pleading for her life.

«Fool! She is the consort of this devil now! She is nothing to you!»

«How can you say that? I love her! Please father, I cannot do this!»

Dorji threw the torch on the ground and prostrated himself before his father, face buried on the ground, pleading.

«I would never disobey you, father, but not this, please, no!»

Tshering Chime scowled, grabbed the torch, scrambled to the pyre, and pressed it to the wood pile until it burst into flames.

Tashi shook hysterically, with muted screams. A royal guard grazed her belly with the tip of his spear until she stopped, her eyes bulging in terror as the flames rose.

Dorji raised his head, looked in horror and punched the ground. The hellish glow of the flames reflected in his eyes.

«No, father, please, stop this!»

Tshering Chime and the four royal guards stood by, watching. The dancing glow of the fire on their faces made them look even more menacing.

Young Druk Dorji got up. He wiped tears off his face, distraught, helpless and ran toward his father.

«Father, please, there's still time to stop! Save her, I beg you!»

Tshering Chime glowered at Dorji, signaling for the guards. They restrained him.

Dorji squirmed and heaved, but he was overpowered.

«In time you will thank me for saving you from that devil's whore!»

Dorji collapsed in the arms of the guards, completely defeated, eyes blinded by tears. He slid to his knees.

Guru Padmasambhava's lips moved rapidly, reciting some unheard mantra. He looked calm, unmoved even as his robes began to catch fire.

Druk Dorji opened his eyes wide and stopped crying as water began to surround his knees. He jumped up, water now up to his ankles, and ran to his father.

Tshering Chime cursed, splashing the water with his feet.

The royal guards panicked and ran away, yelling, screaming. The water was almost up to their knees as the young Dorji pulled his irate father by the arm, urging him to follow behind the guards toward higher ground.

The pyre where Padmasambhava, Lady Tsogyal, and Tashi stood was now a steaming pile of floating embers, the fire consumed by the rising waters.

Tashi moved and flailed about, now as scared of the water as she was of the flames moments before.

The ropes that bound the three of them dissolved with a mist.

Tashi didn't know what to do with herself, panicked beyond measure. Lady Tsogyal embraced her gently.

Tashi calmed down.

Nearby, what was once the path leading to the palace was now submerged, trees jutting up from the surface of the water surrounded by floating brambles.

The young Druk Dorji and his father, Tshering Chime, waded waist-deep until they reached what was now the shoreline of a new lake.

Tshering Chime howled with anger, making fists, cursing unintelligibly.

Guru Padmasambhava, Yeshe Tsogyal, and Tashi were enveloped in a dazzling cocoon of multi-colored light. The three sat calmly in the lotus position atop a huge, bright blue lotus flower that floated on top of what was now a majestic lake.

The shimmering colors reflected off the water's surface, bouncing rainbow colors on the trees at the lake's edge.

Isabel's Apartment, Guest Bedroom
Present Day

A rainbow of light streaked across the otherwise dark ceiling.

Becky opened her eyes, blinking, looking up at the projection. She stretched, took a deep breath, sat up on the bed getting her bearings.

She noticed a shaft of sunlight bouncing off a prism-like glass frame on top of the dresser.

Becky jumped out of bed and grabbed the frame. It had a photo of the Torres family when Becky and Isabel were young girls.

Becky threw the frame inside one of the dresser drawers, opened the window shades, squinting from the bright sunlight. An idyllic beach stretched before her. Beautiful. Inviting.

Becky sprinted out of the bedroom.

Isabel was lying on the couch, face buried in her tablet device, browsing.

Becky waltzed in, saw a fresh cup of coffee on the corner table, and snatched it up.

«What's up?»

Isabel didn't lift her eyes from the tablet. «You're up, finally. Do you mind getting your own coffee this time? Or at least make me another one if you're gonna drink mine.»

«Jeez, what's up with you? Why so crabby?»

«Takes one to know one.»

«Okay, now I know something's up. What is it?»

Isabel dropped the tablet on her lap, glared at Becky. «I went to get your stuff at mom's.»

«Oh, oh.»

«Yeah, and she's still — I can't stand it! What is wrong with her?»

«Same as always. You want the short list or the long list?»

«I'm serious! I can't believe she's denying what happened or worse, she's blaming everyone but father.»

«You mean, she's blaming me.»

«I got out of there as fast as I could and left her rambling. But it hurts, Becky, I mean, I love mom, but, damn! This is way too much.»

«It's not the first time she does this, Isa. It just feels worse every time around, like nothing will ever change. I'm so tired of it, and I imagine you are too.»

Isabel fell silent.

«But I don't wanna sit around and mope about this shit all day. As long as I'm on the fucking island, we should go hit the beach! Do you have a bathing suit I can borrow?»

«One piece, bikini? Thong, solid, print, modest, flashy, which kind?»

«Silly me! I forgot I was asking the island's fashion queen.»

Isabel sprang up from the couch, suddenly excited. «To heck with coffee, let's get out the chardonnay and hit the waves!»

«Well, all right, that's more like it! Sisters' day out! Let's go.»

The Beach

Becky threw two large beach towels on the sand. Isabel placed a small ice cooler and a large tote bag brimming with beach accessories next to them.

Isabel looked fashionable with her wide-brimmed sun hat, designer bathing suit, brand-name sunglasses, and matching sarong. Becky looked like she just threw on two mismatched pieces she found in her sister's drawers.

Isabel sat down, opened the cooler, poured two glasses of white wine, and handed one to her sister.

Becky took a swig. «Mmm, thanks! Aren't you going in?»

«Nope, I'm just here for the sun.»

«I never got the point of going to the beach and not going into the water. Might as well stay on your balcony!»

«It's not the same thing.»

«Yeah, I bet! Fashion queens can't be seen on their balconies, right? Fuck that, I'm going in!»

«Enjoy! I can't guarantee there'll be any wine left when you return.»

«Bitch!»

«Don't you know it!»

They laughed as Becky ran toward the surf.

She dove into the water, swimming like a fish. For the first time, joy filled her face as she looked up at the sun, did a series of alternate swimming strokes, dove under and exploded back to the surface— looking completely comfortable in her element.

«God, I missed this!»

Becky swam farther away from the shore, leaned back, floated face up, closed her eyes, and relaxed, basking in the sun.

Tiny Caribbean Island
Early 19th Century

Night. The moon was full, intensely bright.

A large rowboat glided silently toward the shore, paddled by six men cowering inside. In the front, Federico Sáenz—forty-five, gaunt, with a full beard—looked anxiously toward the shore.

«There! I see it!» he whispered in Castilian, but with an accent from the Canary islands that was now evolving into something different in the new world.

On the beach, an oil lantern was raised twice, then turned off.

Back on the boat, Arturo—sixty-five, chubby, bald, with a goatee—lit up a lantern, raised it twice, turned it off.

The boat hit the shore. Federico, Arturo and the four other men jumped out into the water and pushed the boat inland.

Two figures rushed toward them from the darkness, helping the men drag and hide the boat underneath scraggly bushes. The group saluted each other using a peculiar hand gesture, then embraced warmly.

All eight men disappeared into the bushes.

The men climbed up a small hill on the western part of the island. It was a tough climb, dotted with thorny bushes and small trees and not much as far as solid ground was concerned.

When they reached a flat clearing they stopped.

Arturo held his oil lamp, creating twirling amber glows and shadows around Federico and the other six men. They were fixing aprons around their waists decorated with elaborate symbols.

Federico placed a fabric sash around his neck emblazoned with more symbols and a gold medallion.

These were Freemasons.

They stood forming a square, facing each other.

«We all solemnly swear that, in addition to our former obligations, we will forever conceal and never reveal any of the secret arts, parts, and points of the hidden mysteries that I am about to reveal.»

Sáenz looked around at the other Freemasons as each, one by one, put their right hand over their heart.

«We swear!» they said in unison.

«Gentlemen. What I am about to reveal is well beyond the mysteries of our order, it comes from a timeless and sacred tradition that I'm entrusting you to keep secret with my own life.»

Sáenz looked around at each of their ashen faces as the men nodded to show their commitment.

He turned around and walked toward a seemingly impenetrable wall of weather-beaten rock. He ran his free hand over the rock's jagged surface and closed his eyes, chanting softly.

«Om Ah Hung, Benzra Guru Jnanasagara bam ha ri ni sa siddhi Hum. Om Ah Hung, Benzra Guru Jnanasagara bam ha ri ni sa siddhi Hum.»

The men's eyes widened with awe.

Arturo raised his lantern to gaze upon the impossible: Out of the solid stone wall, blue flowers began to sprout, glowing slightly, followed by an almost perfectly symmetrical slab granite with a perfectly formed imprint of a woman's hand embedded in it. of , The slab oozed out of the rock as if the rock wall were giving birth to it.

It was yet another of the objects Yeshe Tsogyal hid for her disciples hundreds of years before.

Sáenz grabbed the granite slab, turned around and showed it to his companions, their mouths wide open in shock and awe.

Arturo and the other Freemasons bowed in reverence.

For an instant, behind the Freemasons, floating about in the shrubs, Arturo caught a fleeting vision, a glowing translucent figure, Yeshe Tsogyal.

A rustle of bushes startled the group, followed by a yell.

«Halt! By order of the colonial government, you are under arrest!»

अग्नि

Fire

14

Tiny Caribbean Island
Early 19th Century

Arturo ran toward Sáenz, shouting, «Run away, we will distract them!»

A small patrol of civil guards emerged from the bushes, rifles in hand. The Civil Guard Commander—thirty-five, bony, mustachioed—pointed his revolver at Arturo.

«Stop or you will be shot!»

Arturo spun around, covering Sáenz with his body. «Fuck you, long live our Island's freedom!»

Sáenz tried to push his compatriot away from him. «Arturo, no!»

It was too late.

Shots blasted out. Sáenz squatted, covered his head. A hail of bullets whizzed by his ears.

Arturo screamed and collapsed.

Sáenz snatched off his Freemason apron and waved it like a white flag over his head as he ducked further down.

«Stop! Don't shoot! We are unarmed! Our friend has been shot, please, for the love of God, don't shoot!»

The remaining Freemasons raised their hands. The Spanish civil guards surrounded them slowly, rifles still pointed at them.

The sound of crickets, frogs, and the very wind grew silent.

A booming, unearthly voice cut through the stillness.

«Lower your weapons!»

Druk Dorji—in his forties—stepped out of the darkness, dressed in the regalia of a Spanish Army Commander, an ornate sword sheathed on his belt. His oriental features completely at odds with this time and place. The civil guards lowered their weapons and stood at attention.

«I believe you have something in your possession that belongs to me,» Dorji commanded in perfect, old-world Castilian.

Sáenz glared at Dorji, tried hard to control his voice so as not to provoke any more violence and not reveal his own fear. «Under whose authority do you attack us? We have broken no laws!»

«No laws?» Dorji retorted, laughing cynically. «A forbidden masonic cult, meeting in secret, conspiring to overthrow his majesty's government? You will be executed for treason in due time, but before that, kindly hand me the object I speak of.»

«I have no idea what you are talking about, commander. We are just loyal Spanish subjects visiting friends.»

Dorji chortled. «Oh, I see, just a social gathering, here, on this islet of shit. Not many people live here, so, perhaps you would like to share with us whom exactly you were visiting here, Don Federico, and why, pray tell, you happened to be waving a Freemason's Grand Master apron.»

«If you know who I am, then you know my father, and he will make you answer for this affront! Who shall I tell him was brazen enough to shoot at his son and one of his son's friends?»

«Someone who has known you, and loathed your unholy lot for ages. I have grown so tired of hunting you swine but I swear, I will continue to do so until all of you rot in hell! Now hand over the Terma or I will cut the heads off of each one of your cult followers one by one!»

Druk Dorji pulled out his sword. It gleamed under the moonlight, reflecting its unholy shimmer on Sáenz's face.

«I beg you to let these men go, they know nothing of what you speak. They are all innocent!»

Dorji spun around. His sword sang as it sliced the throat of one of the Freemasons.

The Freemason's body collapsed like a rag doll, blood spraying from his neck onto the ground. The remaining Freemasons stared with terror. The civil guards looked at each other, taken aback, and raised their rifles.

Dorji wiped the blood off his blade on Arturo's shoulder, the blade swiping dangerously close to his trembling neck.

«You have cost the lives of two of your foolish followers. How many more must die before you comply?»

«Long live freedom!»

Ángel, another of the Freemasons, no more than twenty years old, rushed Dorji. The other Freemasons followed like a pack of wolves.

Sáenz ducked as shots blasted out from the civil guards' rifles, setting the night ablaze in a fury of gunfire.

The bullet-riddled bodies of the Freemasons collapsed all around Dorji's feet. A thick shroud of gun smoke blinded the civil guards.

Sáenz stealthily slid toward the bushes, still squatting, then, once he felt he was out of sight, he began running wildly, clutching the bundled granite slab, maneuvering through the thick branches.

«Fools, I did not give the order to fire! Look for Sáenz, do not let him escape with the object!»

«What is this object? What is it that we are looking for, commander?» One of the guards asked.

«You will know when you find it!»

The civil guards coughed and wheezed as they searched among the pile of bodies for Sáenz. They lit up some oil lamps but the light bounced off the thick smoke, blinding them even more.

Somehow, Federico Sáenz popped out of the bushes, out of the shadows, into the glaring moonlight, tripping on a few stones, hands first into the sand.

Finally the sand! That meant the shore, that meant his life.

He scrambled to his feet, scanning the shoreline for the boat. There it was, partially covered beneath palm fronds.

He ran towards it, removed the branches as fast as he could, wrapped the granite slab in his masonic apron, and threw it inside the boat.

He struggled to drag the boat toward the water. His legs kept getting buried deep into the sand as he applied all his strength—a Sisyphean task—but he managed to move it slowly.

The Spanish civil guards finished turning over the bodies of the dead Freemasons. Sáenz was nowhere to be found.

Dorji was livid, his face red with rage. «He's getting away! Quick, go to the beach, they must have a boat.»

The Civil Guard Commander, older than his troops, shouted at Dorji, «Which way, sire?»

«Idiot, to the north, that way.»

«Follow me!» The Civil Guard Commander ordered his troops.

The civil guards took off behind him, rushing into the thick bushes. Dorji scanned the area briefly, then followed.

Federico Sáenz had managed to get the boat into the water. He clambered onto it, exhausted, grabbed the oars and began to row, nearly out of strength, wincing with each effort.

The current began to help him move slowly away from the shore.

He looked back toward the beach. The Spanish civil guards came running out of the bushes, searching all around them under the moonlight.

«There! I see the boat, shoot, shoot!» The Commander shouted.

The civil guards took aim and started shooting.

Federico Sáenz ducked as some bullets whizzed by, others splashed in the water. But to no avail—he was too far for their range.

As the sound of gunfire subsided, Sáenz breathed deeply, lifted his head slowly and looked toward the receding shore.

The boat stopped with a thud.

Sáenz spun his head toward the bow. Druk Dorji was standing on the surface of the ocean as if the water were completely solid, the waves crashing around his legs with nothing to hold him up, an act attributed to the most holy of beings in the Christian scriptures Sáenz had studied all his life.

Dorji's body reflected the moonlight with an eerie luminosity. He raised his boot on the bow, pushing the boat slightly back.

Sáenz moved back, horrified at the supernatural power of his foe. He stared in wide-eyed shock as Dorji climbed into the boat as if nothing, his clothes completely dry, as was his expression.

Sáenz spun around, grabbed the bundled slab of granite, intent on jumping off the boat.

Dorji's sword sang as he sliced Sáenz's back.

Sáenz screamed in agony, the granite slab slid from his shaking hands and plopped into the boat, and he plunged face first into the inky ocean.

Sáenz turned his body around, splashing wildly, as he saw Dorji smiling, the granite slab with Yeshe Tsogyal's delicate hand imprinted on it now in his possession.

With what was left of his life, Federico Sáenz yelled at his assassin, «All life is precious!»

Sáenz sank, swallowing water, as his life ebbed away.

Isabel's Apartment – Beach
Present Day

Becky gasped, coughed, and spat sea water she had just swallowed. She splashed around, tried to stand, but she was too deep.

Her body sank for a moment, then erupted onto the surface, gasping, desperately treading water. She yelled, reached for her back, wincing in pain.

Becky looked toward the shore. It looked impossibly far away.

Isabel was running toward her followed by a middle-aged man. Both dove into the waves, swimming frenetically toward her.

Becky continued to contort her body, trying to swim toward the shore while writhing from the excruciating pain in her back. Her eyesight became cloudy. She began to lose it.

«Isa!»

Becky sank just as the middle-aged man reached her. He wrapped his powerful arms around her, lifted her to the surface.

Becky yelled in agony.

The middle-aged man spun around, wrapped Becky's arms around his chest so that Becky could hold on to him as he struggled to swim toward shore while carrying Becky on his back.

«Oh my God, Becky! Becky!» screamed Isabel as she finally reached them and helped the middle-aged man with Becky's weight by wrapping one of Becky's arms around her shoulder.

«My back! It burns!» cried Becky.

«I know, paddle with your legs,» answered the man, breathlessly.

Becky's eyes rolled up and back again, fighting to swim with whatever strength she had left.

The three of them swayed back and forth with the surf, struggling to swim against the tide.

The group finally reached the shore. They plopped into the sand, out of breath.

That's when Isabel first noticed the bright red inflamed welt across Becky's back that looked exactly like the slash Dorji's sword left on Sáenz's back.

«Oh my God!»

«What?» replied Becky, wincing from the pain.

«Your back!»

The middle-aged man got up, tried to help Becky to her feet. Becky did her best but lost control and fell back on her knees.

«Can you crawl on all fours?» he asked.

Becky nodded and slowly crawled away from the surf until she reached her towel and tumbled face down on it with a heavy sigh.

Isabel ran to the ice cooler. «Let me put some ice on—»

«No!» Becky cried, «Don't! Jellyfish sting! Ice will make it worse! Use wet sand!»

Becky somehow managed to summon her will, remembering the natural healing lessons from her friend and mentor, Sylvia Chang.

The middle-aged man ran back near the waves, grabbed a mound of wet sand and returned to Becky.

«Got it! Do you want me to—»

«Yes, spread it on me! But, first, if you can, check to see if there are any tentacles.»

The middle-aged man got as close as he could to Becky's swollen welt, surveyed it carefully, then, convinced there was nothing to remove, gently packed some of the wet sand on Becky's back.

Becky shrieked.

Isabel jumped towards her neighbor. «Stop, you're hurting her!»

«No, that's fine! I just... please... Watch my breathing. Get vinegar, please.»

The middle-aged man sprinted toward the apartment building.

«Stay with her, I'll get it, and I'll call 911.»

«Okay, please hurry back, Fede!»

«Wait! What did you just call him?» Becky turned her head up, then winced as she bent her back.

«'Fede,' that's short for Federico, my neighbor.»

Becky's face contorted into a tearful, agonizing grimace.

«What? Federico? No way! No! No!»

She let out a guttural wail with what was left of her energy.

«Becky! What's wrong?»

Becky's eyes rolled up as she passed out.

Isabel's apartment, guest Bedroom

Becky lay face down on the bed, feet against the headboard, the red welt glistening with some ointment.

Isabel walked in.

«Doctor says to keep you on Benadryl, no need to go to the hospital unless your breathing gets worse or you get dizzy or get nauseous.»

«It hurts like shit!»

«I can't imagine. She said you knew what you were doing, when you asked for sand and vinegar. She says to just take it easy for a while.»

«Thank you, sis.»

«Sure, no problem. Do you need anything else?»

«No, Isa, listen. I really mean it. Thank you for everything. For saving my life today, for looking out for me.»

«C'mon I really didn't—»

«Yes. You did. Thank you! And please thank Federico too.»

«Yeah. I'm gonna have to take him out to dinner for this one!»

«Please wait 'till I'm well, so I can go with you both.»

Isabel smiled slightly.

A mobile phone rang. Isabel looked around, found it.

«It's Sylvia. Is that your boss?»

«Oh, yeah, please, let me have it. And, could you get me some water?»

«Sure.»

«Thanks, sis. Again.»

Isabel handed Becky her phone and left the room.

Becky switched to a video call. Sylvia Chang appeared on the mobile phone screen.

«Jesus! You look like a train wreck!»

«Yeah, that's about right.»

«You okay? What's wrong?»

«Jellyfish sting. Bad.»

«What? Seriously? How bad?»

«Could be worse. No serious symptoms or anything like that, but it hurts like a motherfucker!»

«Oh my, I'm so sorry! I was gonna ask when you planned on coming back, but now?»

«Yeah, I ain't sitting on a plane seat anytime soon, sorry.»

«Don't be, sweetie, the important thing is to take care of yourself. How's it going with your family and all that other stuff?»

Becky paused, took a deep breath. «You were right about, you know...»

«What?»

«About my father. It was worse than you or I thought, much worse.»

«Oh, my God, Becky, I'm so sorry!»

«Yeah, part of it came out by accident and then, with Soto, well it just came flooding out.»

Sylvia nodded, frowned. «That's a lot to handle. I can't even imagine! Are you going to keep seeing him?»

«Yeah, yeah. I kinda like how he works. Gonna see him again as soon as I can get my ass off this bed.»

«Good, good. It's important that you handle all this with a lot of support. He knows his stuff. But, more importantly, he's a good person. Would you like to talk to me about it?»

Becky buried her head face down on the bed, then up again. «Not now, Syl. I don't wanna get into it right now. It's been a really shitty day.»

«Of course, sweetie, I understand. Whenever you feel up to it, and if you don't feel comfortable talking about it with me, that's fine too.»

«I will, I promise, when I'm better. Thank you, Syl. For everything.»

«Don't get all sentimental on me. Just holler if you need anything.»

«You could send me some pastrami. There's no good pastrami here.»

Sylvia smiled. «Didn't you go vegan a couple of months ago?»

«Nothing like a good jellyfish sting to make you go back to beef!»

Sylvia laughed. «Yeah, I bet! Listen, I've got a client coming in, but please, keep me posted and let me know if you want to talk or anything, okay?»

«Of course, Syl. Always! Love you!»

Sylvia winked and the phone's screen went dark.

Becky stared at it for a few seconds. She turned around slowly, painfully, to face the head of the bed. She dropped the phone on the nightstand, stretched her hand to open the drawer, wincing in pain, fished out her bottle of pills, and took two pills out.

Isabel walked in, sat on the bed and gave Becky the water.

Becky gulped down her pills, craned her neck to look at her sister. She grabbed Isabel's hand and squeezed it tightly, smiling.

Isabel blushed and smiled, eyes watery.

15

Soto's Office
Present Day

S oto fidgeted with his laptop. There was a knock on the door. He lifted his eyes from the screen.

«Yes, come in!»

Becky—large dark sunglasses covering the bags under her eyes—walked in, dragging her feet. As she turned around to close the door, her backless blouse revealed a clear, shiny gel covering her jellyfish sting. The red mark was still visible but no longer swollen.

Becky spun around.

«What happened there?»

«You wouldn't believe it.»

«Try me.»

«Jellyfish sting.»

«Seriously?»

«Told ya.»

«Ouch! Are you alright? I mean—»

«I'm here, so I must be, more or less.»

Becky turned a chair backward and straddled it.

«What happened to your travel plans?»

«I ain't sitting on no plane for four and a half hours with this on my back, so I asked my sister if I could stay with her for a while.»

Soto nodded and smiled slightly. «I'm glad, I mean, not that you got stung, but that you're staying.»

Becky averted his gaze, slightly embarrassed. «Actually, to be honest, I wanted to stay anyway, before this happened. I was feeling good being with her, going to the beach together, you know, having a good time. God knows I hadn't been to the beach in ages, and then, well, this motherfucking thing happens to me, you know? On top of everything else! Talk about my fucking karma! Why am I being punished like this?»

«Karma has nothing to do with punishment. It's just the law of cause and effect. Karma is completely neutral, no judgement. We're the ones that give it a good or bad connotation.»

«Well, it sure as shit doesn't feel neutral to me! I must've done some really nasty shit in my previous life!»

«Yes, but you have also done a lot of positive things as well. We all have, over countless lives.»

Soto smiled warmly. Becky managed to relax a bit.

«At any rate, I'm glad you've decided to stay, and I thank you for wanting to continue working with me.»

«Well, yeah, I've been meaning to tell you, about my nightmares, there's something I've been meaning to ask.»

«Of course, what is it?»

Becky remained pensive for a few beats. «Well, how can I explain this? I thought that whatever is happening to me when I'm sleeping, you know, would show up in my dreams, but now, I feel stupid for saying this, but it kinda' feels like it's the other way around, like what happens in the dream becomes real for me.»

«Can you give me an example?»

Becky pointed at the wound on her back. «Here's a perfect example! I was asleep on the beach, out in the water, and I'm dreaming of the same bad guy as usual, and just as he cuts someone's back with a sword...» She paused, her look drifting, her eyes beginning to water. She shivered. «I felt it, at that very moment, as if it was happening to me, and that woke me up. With this on my back!»

Soto leaned forward, enthralled.

«And it's not the first time. Not by a long shot! I've dreamt of being shot by arrows, of drowning, of being on fire, and every time, I wake up and I'm either bleeding, I mean, you know, not bleeding like cut or anything but, you know, like my period starts then and there, or I begin to drown in the bathtub, or, I... I'm worried I might be crazy or losing it, and my body may be reacting, I don't know.»

Becky trembled.

«Well, if I may, the first thing is you are not crazy. We don't have any notion of time when we're asleep so it's quite possible that whatever is happening to your body while you're sleeping shows up in your dream, like when you're dreaming you have to go to the bathroom and, well, you wake up and you really have to go. In a way you're lucky this happens because it wakes you up before you're really hurt.»

«So, what then? I should feel happy about having these horrible dreams?!»

«Well, not happy but maybe fortunate. By what you've told me, you've woken up right before drowning a couple of times. So, that's been fortunate. There are so many things science has yet to uncover about our minds, bodies, and souls that there's room for many possibilities. To know which came first, the wound from your dreams or the one from the jellyfish, I would need some time to consult your natal chart and study, perhaps even ask my teacher to step in.»

«So, you're saying it could be more than just a dream or what?»

«I'm saying I don't discard any possibility until I seriously study it. Did you mention you had a good dream the other night? What was that one about?»

Becky relaxed a bit, wiped her eyes. «Yeah, there were a couple of, I don't know, wizards, gods, whatever. One of them, a woman, I've seen many times before. Come to think of it, she's been there as many times as the bad guy.»

«What's she like?»

«Oriental, white, glowing skin, long hair, beautiful to look at. Ooh, my, my hairs stood on end when I said that, isn't that funny?»

Soto smiled, holding back his excitement.

«So she's with this other, you know, powerful god-like guy, and they offer to help a king get rid of demons that are making him sick and ruining the kingdom. So in return, the king offers them his daughter, the princess, which is kind of fucked up if you think about it. So, they take the princess under their wing, get rid of the demons but then they get trapped by this nasty witch.»

«Was this witch the same bad guy from your previous nightmares?»

«Actually, no.» Becky paused to think. «Well, yes and no, the usual bad guy was there, but he was like, younger than usual, and following orders from this older guy. I'm not sure, but for some reason, I think this old guy was the bad guy's father! Am I making any sense or did I lose you? I'm rambling!»

«I'm right with you. You were saying this old man gave the bad guy, the one you've dreamed about for years, some orders. What were the orders?»

«To burn them all alive! The couple, the gods or whatever they are, and the king's daughter, the princess! I swear, I could feel the flames!»

«So did you see yourself as one of the people in the fire or just witnessing it all from the outside?»

Becky stopped. Paused to recollect. «Mostly from the outside, but, now that you mention it, sometimes I feel like I was the king's daughter, the princess.» Becky frowned. «Wow! I hadn't stopped to think about that. That's wild! Do you think the dreams are related to me and my own father? My sister kinda hinted that it could be possible. I told her to shove it.»

«What do you think?»

«I can see where this asshole king giving away his daughter just to save his own ass is like something my mother and father would do to us. And then the old man being pissed that his plans for his son were ruined is, I dunno, maybe.»

«What were the plans the old man had for his son?»

Becky paused again, remembering. «I think he expected him to marry the princess! Then the king fucked him up by giving her away to those other two. Wow! I forgot that part! That's really fucked up, but I'm not sure how it relates to me.»

«Well, dreams are metaphorical, symbolic, so it's probably no coincidence there's so much happening there that has to do with fathers, daughters, and sons.»

«One thing that's curious to me is that there were two different dreams that carried over the same characters, the same places and I guess at the same time, like one long dream in two parts. I mean, how could I pick up the same dream, continue the same story, on two different nights? That's weird!»

«So on a scale of one to ten, how do you feel about your nightmares right now, one being 'you're okay with them,' ten being 'they're still impossible to live with.'»

«I think they're at a seven.»

«Very well. How about your feelings about what your father did to you and your mother's response? One being, 'I feel fine,' ten being, 'I can't even live with it.'»

Becky took longer to think. Tears welled up. «I think an eight. Eight and a half.»

«Maybe a nine?»

«Yeah, definitely a nine.»

«So, how about dealing with that issue first and then we can get back to the dreams? Would that work for you?»

Becky sighed heavily. «Yeah, fine, perfect, I get it.»

«I'm going to ask you some questions and make some statements that may be uncomfortable or even shocking to you. They are not meant to be the truth about what you're experiencing but they may be an alternate way of looking at what happened to you. I just ask that you have an open mind and allow for the possibility of a different reality or point of view.»

Becky gave him a quizzical look. «Yeah, well, I can try, whatever.»

Soto took a deep breath, smiled, and sat back on his chair. «Very well. Let me start by asking you, who gave you your life?»

«My parents, of course, it's just one of them turned out to be a sick rapist, and the other one is an enabling asshole, so, fuck 'em!»

«How does it feel when I say that, the fact that they were rapists or assholes doesn't take away from the fact that they gave you your life?»

Becky shifted in her seat, crossed her arms, incredulous. «Yeah, so?»

«Would you consider that being alive is valuable to you?»

«It's a fucked up life, so I don't really know how to answer that.»

«Would you still consider ending it?»

Becky bolted up in her seat, a frown on her face, ready to pounce, then looked down, tears beginning to well up. «When I was a teen, you know that. But not anymore! I don't want to end it, I just hate having been born! I feel like I belong on another planet. I just keep telling myself, 'I wanna go home,' but I don't even know where that home is. I sure as hell feel I don't belong here.»

«Ok. Let's try this. Close your eyes and breathe deeply. Try to relax and be present, at this moment.»

A skeptical expression flashed in Becky's face, then she finally relented, closed her eyes, and inhaled.

«Now, to be clear, right now we are going to be working at the soul level, not the physical. So when I mention members of your family, I want you to visualize their souls, perfect, untarnished, and not the physical interactions you've had with them in this life, OK?»

Becky furrowed her brow, but kept her eyes closed. «That's tough, but I'll do my best.»

«I want you to imagine your mother's soul standing behind your left shoulder.»

Becky frowned.

«And visualize your father's soul behind your right shoulder.»

She grimaced but kept her eyes closed, playing along.

«Remember, this is their soul, not their physical being. And behind your mother's left shoulder, her mom, your maternal grandmother, and behind her right shoulder, her father, your maternal grandfather. Same thing with your father. His mother behind his left shoulder and his father behind his right shoulder. And your great grandparents are behind them in the same positions, and so on. It doesn't matter if you knew them or even knew what they looked like. Just visualize this huge group of people fanning out behind you, generation after generation.»

Becky's eyes darted about under closed lids.

«Now imagine that some great force, greater than all of us, whatever you wish to call it: 'God,' 'Supreme Wisdom,' 'Divine Light,' whatever works for you. That great entity chose exactly all those people to pass life on to you. Imagine all they went through: Their hardships, their joys, fears, tragedies, losses, and their loves, achievements, and all their wonderful gifts too, all of that flowing, for untold years, toward you. They are all here now, with you, supporting you at this very moment. And we honor them for what they were, as givers of life.»

Soto opened his drawer, pulled out a red, transparent plexiglass rectangular piece, about two inches (or about 5 centimeters) tall, and quietly placed it on his desk.

«Now, I'm going to ask you to breathe deeply, and open your eyes whenever you feel comfortable and look at the desk in front of you.»

Becky took a deep breath, opened her eyes slowly, and immediately cringed, her eyes avoiding the piece.

«I can't. I don't know why. It feels, I don't know, horrible, disgusting.»

«Can you say: It is almost impossible for me to see you. I find you horrible and disgusting.»

«You mean, say it out loud?»

Soto nodded.

«It's impossible for me to see you, I find you horrible and disgusting.» Becky still avoided looking at it.

«You caused me so much pain, I can't bring myself to see you.»

Tears escaped Becky's eyes.

«You caused me so much pain, I can't bring myself to see you.»

Becky slowly managed to look at the red piece.

«I can sorta look at it now, but I feel sick to my stomach.»

«Ok. Can you say to the piece, 'I see you and I respect you?'»

«It's tough to say that.»

«I know. Just try, see if you can.»

Becky swallowed hard. «I see you and I respect you.»

«'You are a part of me.'»

«You are a part of me.»

«How does it feel when you say that?»

«Still queasy, ugh!»

«So, repeat it, 'I see you and I respect you?'»

«I see you and I respect you.»

«'You are a part of me.'»

«You are a part of me.»

Becky's expression changed and became more peaceful.

«What about now? Has anything changed for you?»

«The feeling of sickness, it's much less, yeah. And I don't feel so weak, so disgusted.»

«Okay. Sit with that feeling for a while. If you need to repeat the sentences in silence, go ahead. Has anything changed when you look at the piece now?»

«Yeah. It doesn't seem so powerful now. Like it's become small, and I'm bigger.»

Soto got up, grabbed three colored rubber mats a square foot in size, and placed a blue one on the floor close to Becky. The two others, one brown and one pink, were placed three feet apart from each other, forming a triangle.

«I'm going to ask you to take your shoes off and stand on top of this blue mat when I tell you.»

Becky looked at him like he was crazy, shrugged, stood up, took off her shoes and stared blankly at the three mats.

«Very well. Close your eyes for a second. Inhale. Exhale. Take deep breaths. Allow yourself to connect with whatever comes up for you.»

Becky did as she was told.

«What's coming up is, I feel like an idiot doing this shit and I'm still pissed off at my family.»

«Perfect. Give those feelings a place inside you, they belong to you. Now, imagine that the blue mat is you, the pink one is your mom, and the brown one's your dad.»

Becky's expression became defiant and angry again.

«Yeah, brown, the color of shit!»

«Perfect, whatever you're feeling now has a place in your heart. Now, stand on top of the blue mat.»

Becky stood on the blue mat.

«Now, open your eyes, look at the mats in front of you, and imagine that you're looking at your mom and dad from where you're standing.»

Becky's gaze jumped back and forth between the pink and brown mats. Her eyes locked onto the brown mat, her expression unbridled anger.

«Allow yourself to feel whatever comes up, no matter what it is.»

«I wanna kill that motherfucker!»

Becky's expression gradually changed from anger to intense pain. She burst into tears, her body bent, shaking. She shut her eyes.

«Open your eyes, look at him and say, 'Father, what you did to me was too painful!'»

Becky opened her teary eyes. «No. It's too. I can't. No.»

«Can you say, 'It was so painful, I can't even say how painful it was?'»

Becky wrapped her arms around her chest, consoling herself. She closed her eyes, sobbing.

«It was so fucking painful, father!»

Soto nodded.

Becky's face and body seemed to jump back and forth from the fragility of a little girl to her anger as an adult.

«Open your eyes, it's important you have your eyes open for this, and say, 'Father, it was so painful for me, I can't even see you.'»

Becky squinted. «Dad, it was so painful for me, I can't even see you.»

«What's coming up for you now?»

«I kinda' wanna look now.»

«Ok, go ahead, when you can.»

Becky opened her eyes wider and focused on the brown mat.

«How does it feel when you look at him now?»

«It feels like... He's looking at me with shame, and regret.»

Becky's body began to relax. She slowly stopped crying.

«Now, can you look at them both and tell them, 'You gave me my life and that's all I need from you.'»

«You gave me my life and that's all I need from you.»

«The rest, everything that doesn't belong to me, I leave with you.»

«Everything that doesn't belong to me, I leave with you.»

«Stay with that for a second. Now, step out from your mat and sit on the floor with your mom and dad behind your back, facing the mat that represents you.»

Becky sat with the brown and pink mats behind her.

«I want you to look at the blue mat and tell me what comes up for you.»

Becky looked at the blue mat. Her eyes welled up with tears.

«I want to hold her.»

«So go ahead.»

Becky grabbed the blue mat and snuggled it.

«I want you to close your eyes and visualize that you are hugging little Becky, that little girl inside of you who got hurt. And as the adult Becky, tell her, 'I will always be here for you.'»

Becky began to sob. «I will always be here for you.»

«Say, 'no one understands your pain like I do. And nobody will ever love you as much as I do.'»

«No one understands your pain like I do. And nobody will ever love you as much as I do.»

«'I will always be here for you whenever you need me.'»

«I will always be here for you whenever you need me.»

«Now, imagine little Becky and your adult you, your mom and your dad becoming glowing spheres of light, pure souls, untainted by life. You can see that your mom and your dad were chosen by a higher, wiser force to pass life on to you. That's all that matters. And that deserves our honoring them, not loving them, just respecting that they were chosen by something higher than all of us, to pass life on to you!»

Soto paused. He closed his eyes, connecting with her.

«All life is precious, and it's the most important gift anyone can receive and pass on. We honor life and those who've passed it on by making the conscious decision to live life to our fullest capacity by accepting our parents and our ancestors exactly as they were, with their faults and mistakes, as well as their offenses, but also the great gifts and abilities they passed on to us. Because they also passed wonderful, positive things to us when they gave us our life. And who are we to judge them, whatever they went through that made them act as they did?»

Becky's body relaxed, her face lightened up.

«Now imagine these spheres of light all merge into one. Your dad, mom, the little you and your adult self, all becoming a single sphere. And that beautiful sphere continues to grow, until it envelops your sister, all of your ancestors, your friends, your neighborhood, your country, the whole world, the entire universe, everything becoming one within that sphere.»

Becky's face was transformed—beautiful, clear, in peace.

A faint glow began to emanate around Becky's body.

Soto opened his eyes wide, taken aback, speechless, frozen. He breathed deeply and regained his composure.

«Now, slowly, come back to the here and now, to my office. Taking deep breaths. Feeling your body, the floor, the air conditioning, the mat in your hands, feel present in the here and now. Take another deep breath and exhale with an 'aaah.'»

«Aaaah!»

«And, when you're ready, slowly open your eyes.»

Becky's luminescence gradually faded. She took another deep breath, opened her eyes, and stretched her arms.

«How're you feeling?»

Becky looked as if she was seeing the world for the first time. «Wow. Calm. Peaceful.»

«You don't know how glad that makes me.»

«I didn't expect this.»

«You took an extraordinary step today, I'm really happy for you.»

Becky's eyes drifted to the faded poster of Kurma, the half-man half-turtle god. She trembled slightly and smiled softly.

«This is all so new to me. I mean, I've done rebirthing, reiki, Santería, ayahuasca, you name it.

Like I've been to a spiritual shopping center. But this. This is a whole other level.»

«Perhaps the time was ripe for you to gain a new understanding at this very moment.»

«I wanna learn from you. How you did what you just did, about all these characters on your walls, you know, like the turtle man.»

Soto smiled. «It would be my pleasure to teach you, but it's not exactly like going to a regular school. You would have to study tons of texts, even learn new languages, but, more importantly, you would have to do a lot of work and practice a great many techniques that may seem, well, weird to you.»

Becky's speech was more steady, more settled than usual. Her gaze shifted from the poster to Soto.

«When I set my mind to do something, there's no stopping me. I want to learn. And I will practice, so, please. I'll ask Sylvia for some time off. I'm sure she'll understand. And I'll ask my sister to not throw my ass out of her house just yet.»

Soto helped Becky get up. Still dazed, Becky stumbled onto Soto, their faces inches from each other.

«Thank you, thank you so much!»

Becky hugged him.

Soto was caught off guard, raised his hands avoiding contact, then, finally, he patted her softly on her shoulders, avoiding the wound on her back.

16

Bhutan, Tshering Chime's House
8th Century

A few primitive-looking alchemy instruments were strewn all over the dark cavernous space, lit only with butter lamps.

Tshering Chime frantically filled cylindrical containers made of bamboo with liquids from large vats, then loaded them into a large trunk along with some of his devices, bunches of scrolls wrapped in leather, and other materials.

Druk Dorji—fifteen years old—rushed in, his innocent face red with anger, yelling at his father in Dzongkha, his native tongue

«I am not going with you, father! I will stay and fight for Tashi's love!»

Tshering Chime stopped abruptly, dashed to inches from Dorji's face and grabbed him by the shoulders. Chime's eyes turned an eerie blood red.

Dorji recoiled, shaking with fear in the clutches of his enraged father.

«You will listen to me now if it is the last thing you ever do! That devil's whore is gone! Do you really think she loved you?»

Dorji nodded, naively.

«Then I have been a terrible father for raising such a fool! I had the king promise her to you under one of my most powerful spells until those devilish usurpers arrived and broke it! She will never be yours now! This forsaken land, this putrid kingdom will never be yours or mine! So you will obey me now!»

Dorji was lost in anger and confusion, recoiling back away from his father's clutch..

His father intercepted him, grabbed him by the shoulders again, more strongly, buried his eyes in his son's with eerie intensity.

«We are going to be persecuted, hunted down by the king. You will travel through the mountains to the country up North. You will get to know a most wise and powerful man, Drenpa Namkha. He will teach more than I myself know. Learn from him, respect him, and become his devoted disciple. If you do as he says, you will become so powerful none of this will matter: Not this land, not this wench, nothing. You will have the entire world at your feet!»

«What are you going to do?»

Chime's expression softened for the briefest moment as he hugged his son, then pulled back and faced him sternly once more.

«I will hunt down these usurpers and finish them off before they finish all that we believe in. That is my destiny and I must face it alone. Now, you must go and you must devote yourself to learning the ancient ways of Bön, our true religion. You must promise me to master its powers while I am gone.»

«When will I hear from you again?»

Tshering Chime's expression became melancholic, eyes down.

«When I have fulfilled my destiny, you will receive word. Now go! Pack only what is essential. Your destination is very far and the travel extremely perilous. The king of the empire to the North has also fallen under the spell of these deviant wizards and he too is hunting our kind. Follow your guide's orders to the letter, he is already waiting for you outside!»

Young Dorji looked dazed, puzzled. He hugged his father briskly and darted off.

Chime looked at his son for a beat then continued packing.

Bhutan/Tibet Border, Forest

The wall of moss-covered trees surrounded by ferns and dense foliage seemed impenetrable. The trail was almost impossible to discern, especially because of the light fog that floated around it. It seemed as if the forest did everything it could to keep humans away from it.

The Guide—seventy-five, thin, stringy, tough as a log—glided through the rough terrain like he was born in these mountains.

Young Druk Dorji was having a much rougher time. He stumbled, slipped, got entangled in the thicket and fell in the mud. The Guide had to constantly come back with an impatient scowl on his face to help his hapless teenage traveler.

«Please! We need to stop! We have been walking up this mountain the entire day and it is getting dark!»

«Soon. After we cross the river.»

«River? I cannot hear any river!»

«Soon.»

Tibet, River

The sun was beginning to hide behind the Himalayan peaks.

The Guide and young Dorji reached the end of the forest. The wall of trees opened up to a grassy meadow dotted by stones and wildflowers at the edge of a river.

«How far is the bridge?»

The Guide shook his head with derision, reached the riverbank, tested the depth with his stick and slipped into the water about knee deep.

Dorji froze behind him, immobile. The Guide looked back.

«What are you waiting for?»

«I am waiting for a bridge!»

«No bridge! You cross right now, before it gets darker. There are bears and tigers. Hurry!»

Dorji looked all around, scared out of his wits.

«Wait, if there are bears and tigers, why did we not encounter any in the forest?»

«Could be good Karma. Or maybe it was not dinner time yet!»

Dorji didn't need any other prompting. He quickly reached the water's edge trying to follow The Guide's exact steps.

It was even more treacherous and slippery than the forest, and young Dorji kept losing his balance, having to almost bend over to keep from falling.

The Guide continued his walk as if nothing, the water almost to his waist, the current becoming stronger.

Dorji did his best to raise his belongings above the water and maintain his balance until he fell, plunging face first into the icy waters.

His belongings slipped from his hands and drifted away in the current.

«Wait! My things!»

«Leave them. You do not need them.»

Dorji cursed and punched the water, then resumed his wobbly path behind the guide.

The Guide reached the other shore and waited impatiently for Dorji, who was now drenched to the bones, cold and angry.

The Guide reached out with his hand to help Dorji out of the water, but the youngster rejected his help, climbing to the shore by himself, and slipping face first into the mud, exhausted.

«I hope you are satisfied.»

«Why would I be?»

«Forget it! Where are we going to rest?»

«Go find us some dry wood.»

«How about you finding it yourself? You are working for me!»

«Who told you this?»

«My father said you were my guide!»

The Guide laughed heartily. «So, according to you, a guide is a servant? A slave for you? You are a funny child. Now hurry and get the wood if you do not want to freeze!»

«You will freeze too!»

«Will I? Are you sure of that?»

Dorji noticed that The Guide was completely dry, with no hint that he'd just crossed a river waist-deep in water. His clothes were made of light fabrics and yet he looked completely warm, unfazed, and totally comfortable.

The sun was almost gone. Dorji began to shiver.

«Wood will be harder to find in complete darkness, so hurry.»

Dorji got up and began to scramble, eyes squinting in the ever darker wooded areas, testing fallen branches for dryness and collecting the ones that seemed suitable.

The Guide had been collecting stones and clearing a patch of grass for the fireplace.

Dorji reached him and threw the branches to the ground. The Guide scowled at his imprudent ward.

Dorji plopped to the ground, exhausted.

The Guide arranged the wood into a proper pile, closed his eyes, lips trembling slightly as if chanting soundlessly.

Flames erupted in the wood pile.

Dorji jumped back, terrified.

«What? How did you do that? Who are you?»

The Guide shook his head with contempt. «I am your guide.»

Dorji looked at the thin aging man up and down with puzzlement. Then his expression changed to understanding.

«You! You are Drenpa Namkha!»

The Guide indeed was Drenpa Namkha—wise sage, wizard, beholden to the Bön traditions. He scowled at his imprudent disciple.

«I have been called worse than that.»

Dorji immediately lay face down on the ground, hands extended toward his guru in prostration.

«I apologize, wise guru, for my disrespect. I hope you forgive me.»

«I hope in the future you will learn to see beneath the surface of what lies in front of you before you act. Now, get close to the fire.»

«Yes, master! I'm sorry, master!»

Dorji scrambled to sit near the fire like an obedient puppy.

«Oh, shut up already, you are making an ass of yourself.»

«I... I apologize, master.»

«Here, put something dry on.»

Dorji's eyes bulged with shock as Namkha threw him the bag of belongings he thought were lost in the river. They were bone dry.

Dorji opened the bag, found a coat and covered himself.

«Now, eat this and just sit there and stare at the fire.»

Namkha offered Dorji something moist, dark, moldy, putrid.

Dorji did as he was told, chewing the nasty substance, wincing, arching with disgust. But he managed to finish it.

He looked at the fire, squinting, furrowing his brow.

«What do you see?»

«I see fire. Flames. Wood.»

«No! Go beneath the surface. Get inside the flames, embrace them.»

«Embrace them?»

«Fire is not an element. Fire is a living entity, with its own consciousness. Look beneath the illusion and see it dancing, smiling at you, enticing you.»

Dorji's eyes were laser-focused on the fire. The flames reflected off his dark pupils. His pupils began to dilate. He smiled, an intoxicated smile.

«Yes. Do you see it now?»

Dorji laughed uncontrollably under the influence of something.

«She... She's beautiful!»

«Yes.»

«I love her!»

«Yes. But, be careful. She is very seductive, but can be treacherous. You must learn to respect her before you harness her power. Go too fast and sparks will fly, yes, but she will vanish and her energy will fizzle out. Take her energy slowly but always give it back.»

«How can I give it back?»

«You have your own fire within. You really do not need her. So, when she offers her energy, take it. But when she cannot offer it, give her some of your own as an offering. This is how you find balance with the entities of nature. Knowing that you are one and the same, you will never feel cold, or heat, you will no longer need food or drink. You will get everything you need from thin air!»

Young Dorji's mind was lost in a stupor, quite visibly hallucinating. He leaned over, got closer to the fire. With a weird smile, he grabbed a lit ember, recoiled, dropped it, yelled when he got burned, then laughed.

«You see? She entices, she beguiles, and then, when you least expect it, she bites you. You must reach out to her tenderly, slowly, finding her rhythm. Then she will be yours.»

Dorji concentrated on the flames once more, this time less intensely, more relaxed, his body swaying slightly as if dancing with the fire.

Tibet, Cave

A veil of smoke floated inside the cavernous darkness. The flames made the rock walls seem to dance.

Druk Dorji—fifteen—sat in the lotus position facing the fireplace, eyes half open, hands facing upward on his thighs.

The sound of the crackling fire and the cicadas got louder, affecting Dorji's concentration. He blinked, rubbed his eyes and tried to concentrate despite the high pitched noise.

His breathing became slower, calmer.

The hoot of an owl broke his focus. Again, he blinked, sighed, cracked his neck, breathed deeply and began to calm down once more.

He felt he was getting closer and closer to the flames. Dorji smiled.

«She loves me...»

Tashi's face flirted among the flames, beautiful, sparkling.

Dorji's eyes widened. He took a deep breath, grabbed his chest.

Tashi seemed to step out of the flames and sat with her back to the fire, facing Dorji.

Dorji breathed rapidly, sweat pouring from his forehead. He reached out to touch her, but she vanished like vapor.

Dorji got on all fours and angrily pounded the floor.

«This is useless! I cannot do this!»

Drenpa Namkha's voice echoed inside the cavern.

«Controlling one's mind is the most difficult task there is. Your mind is what confines you and binds you to this illusion we call existence. It may take a lifetime to master.»

Dorji sprang up, desperately looking all around him.

«I do not have a lifetime for this nonsense! I must get back to my father to help him take back what is rightfully ours, I need to find—»

«To find your precious princess? Ha, ha ha, my poor boy!»

«Do not mock me, old man! I will offer you all my respect, but there is no need for you to insult me!»

Namkha appeared like the mist from the darkness, his eyes a dark, eerie red, his expression intense, his voice booming.

«Your petty mind is an insult to all creation! Your existence is no more meaningful than a monkey's turd! How dare you question me, you fool?»

The fire burst with a loud crack. Sparks exploded toward Dorji's back, burning him.

Dorji yelped, frightened, threw himself face down on the ground, and crawled toward Namkha's feet in supplication.

«I am sorry, master, I did not mean to—»

Namkha kicked dust on Dorji's face, making him close his eyes.

«Quiet! There is no master! I am not here, and you are not lying there!»

Tibet, River

Dorji opened his eyes. He was lying face down on the grass next to the river bank, the bonfire dying in front of him.

Namkha walked out of the darkness toward the bonfire holding a bunch of dry branches, and threw them into the bonfire. Sparks flew.

«Wait! I... We were in a cave just now, you and I, on a mountaintop!»

«Oh, so you have seen this cave. Good for you. That happens to be our next stop. That cavern will hide us from the king's guards. We'll depart for there at first light.»

«But, how did I see that?»

«When you let go of your stupid mind, you can see anything and everything. Today, tomorrow, it is all one and the same.»

«Wait, I remember, you gave me something, some potent herb! You tricked me, I imagined all that!»

«No, you obstinate yak, I freed your mind for a brief moment so you could see what it feels like. But what we discovered instead is your dangerous attachment to this girl.»

Dorji sat up, still somewhat dizzy.

«You can't possibly understand my love for her!»

Namkha laughed. «What you don't understand is that while you sit here dreaming of her young bosom, she is well on the way to breaking free of her own mind! What, do you think she has been dreaming of you all this time? No, you monkey's ass, she has been learning siddhi from her teachers.»

«Siddhi?»

Namkha raised his eyebrows, shook his head with derision.

«Yes, yes, siddhi, extraordinary powers and supernatural abilities! These witches that your king sent for, they recognized her as a Tulku, a spiritual master reincarnated that has to be reminded of who she is. That is likely what she has been learning from them while you waste your time sulking about her beautiful behind! Now tell me, what on Earth made you fall in love with this child? How did you even meet if she is a guarded princess?»

Dorji slowly sat up, wiping some grass from his arms.

«I was in the forest around the palace looking for some mushrooms my father wanted. I heard this giggling, like the song of a most beautiful bird.»

Dorji's mind wafted away like the smoke from the bonfire, towards a distant memory that still burned like a bright flame in his heart.

Bhutan, Woods Near Raja's Palace
A Few Years Before

A slightly younger and far more innocent Druk Dorji was on all fours, covered in mud to the hilt, foraging for mushrooms, throwing his finds in a burlap bag.

He spun around at the sound of giggling.

Tashi Chidren stood there, her skin and hair radiant under the sunlight. She was surrounded by three maidens.

Dorji sprang up and bowed devoutly, head down, but never taking his eyes off the princess. The maidens laughed at him. He didn't shift his gaze for a second.

Tashi smiled but didn't laugh.

«What is your name?»

«My name is Druk Dorji, I am the son of his majesty's high priest, Tshering Chime!»

«Druk means 'thunder dragon,' and Dorji means 'diamond,' something indestructible, irresistible. Are you really irresistible, young boy?»

The maidens giggled playfully.

Dorji bowed down further, embarrassed, but kept looking at her, mesmerized.

Tashi glided delicately to the river's edge, removed a scarf from her neck, soaked it in the water, and returned to the dazed young Dorji.

She squeezed the water from the scarf over his muddy hands.

Dorji opened his hands to receive the water like a baptism, completely enthralled.

Tashi handed him the scarf, smiling. He took it, still bowing, wiped his face with it and tried to hand it back.

Tashi shook her head and smiled, turned around and walked away with the giggling maidens in tow.

Dorji pressed the scarf to his heart, eyes watering.

Tibet, River

Young Dorji's eyes were filled with tears as he looked down on the ground, the fleeting memories far too intense to ignore.

Drenpa Namkha squatted in front of him, laughing.

Dorji woke up from his reverie and scowled at his teacher.

«I fell in love with her right then and there! And we continued to see each other in secret around the palace every time we could. We barely spoke to each other but I could see in her eyes that she loved me and I love her back!»

Namkha laughed again, falling back onto the grass.

«You do not understand, you silly fool! She is a reborn Siddha! A powerful being in the process of reawakening! Of course you saw love in her eyes for you, but it was the same love she has for the trees, for the grass, a worm, a fly, even for a monkey's turd like you! This is not the romantic love you dream about, this is something else!»

Dorji was as miffed as he was confused.

«Now, if you are willing to shut your mouth, to listen, to learn, to practice, you may master your mind, really master it! If you do this, you will no longer need to conquer her, you will not want to, because the entire universe will be yours!»

«I understand, master, but I do not want the universe, I just want her!»

«Oh, shut up already, you are more annoying than a yak's ass! Time to sleep, we leave at dawn!»

Namkha formed a mudra, a specific gesture with his hand.

Dorji's eyes went white. He collapsed instantly, sound asleep.

Dawn

Druk Dorji's eyes opened as the tip of the mountains began to glow with sunshine. The light around the riverbank was still muted, bluish, with a heavy mist floating over the grass.

Dorji looked around, finding his bearings. He saw Drenpa Namkha on his knees in front of the fire, palms up, eyes closed.

Dorji sat up quietly, trying not to disturb him.

The flames began to grow in a spiral in front of Namkha.

Dorji covered his face and moved back, protecting himself from the intense heat. The column of flames became brighter, higher.

Dorji got low on the ground at a safe distance.

Namkha—eyes closed—grabbed a bunch of yellow scrolls wrapped in leather from his side, stood up, and walked into the column of fire. His entire body was engulfed in flames but not burning.

Dorji sprang up, grabbed one of the drinking gourds from the campsite, ran over to the water's edge, filled it, and ran back to Namkha.

But the heat was too intense. Dorji couldn't get close.

Namkha lifted the scrolls. They were unaffected by the flames. Then, miraculously, the scrolls vanished into thin air leaving Namkha's hands completely empty.

Namkha walked out of the fire column, clothes smoking but not burning, completely unfazed and unharmed. The column of flames lost its height and intensity until the fireplace became a mere pile of smoldering ash, no flames at all.

Namkha breathed deeply, stretched like he was just waking up from a deep sleep, and opened his eyes. He noticed Dorji standing there with the water-filled gourd in his hands and laughed.

He moved toward Dorji as if nothing had happened.

Dorji looked at him, open jawed, and threw the water gourd to the ground.

«Get your things, we have to leave.»

«Master, what did I just witness?»

«Something you were not prepared to witness yet. However, given that all things happen exactly when they are meant to happen, then, perhaps you were meant to see it now. I just hid some very important texts for safekeeping.»

«Safekeeping? Where are they now?»

Namkha sighed impatiently. «Yes, yes, I needed to protect these writings from the persecution of our enemies. In centuries to come, when it is the proper time, maybe you will come back to this place and retrieve these scrolls and their knowledge. Now, hurry, get your things, we must go!»

17

Tibet, Cave Entrance

Well-hidden on the edge of a mountain, surrounded by scraggly bushes, the dark entrance loomed large. Hundreds of feet below, the moon shone on a vast valley huddled between immense mountain ranges.

This was a veritable fortress.

As the young Druk Dorji and Drenpa Namkha walked inside, Dorji's eyes opened wide in shock—this was the same cave he had seen in his hallucination the night before.

«Master. This... This is the cave I saw back in the river—»

«I know. Find dry branches, we must light a fire or you will freeze. Be careful outside, we do not want you to plunge down the mountain. We must rest. You begin your teaching before dawn breaks tomorrow.»

Dorji stepped out into the darkness, walking slowly, carefully, trying to find suitable wooden branches for the fire. Stopping once or twice to survey the imposing mountains that enveloped him and the moonlit valley below.

Druk Dorji's training began.

The years in the cave became a blur of discipline and discovery.

In the beginning, Dorji sat surrounded by piles of yellow scrolls, devouring texts with rapt concentration. Namkha circled him like a predator, firing questions, forcing debates, never satisfied with surface understanding.

Time passed.

Meditation became his crucible. Deep in lotus position, breath controlled, mind quieting—until Namkha appeared behind him with a spin drum, banging away mercilessly. The young man's eyes would snap open, annoyed. His master would only laugh.

More years slipped by.

Complex yoga positions tested the limits of his body. Contortions that should have been impossible became daily practice. When he failed to hold a pose, Namkha's derisive head shake said everything, a thin branch smacking into Dorji's behind said even more.

By his mid-thirties, the lessons moved beyond the cave. They walked the mountain brush together, Namkha teaching him to identify plant species, fruits, mushrooms, roots, and herbs. Once, Dorji paused to take in the breathtaking valley below—the beauty of it, the vastness.

Namkha's walking stick cracked against his head.

The meditation deepened. Late in his thirties, Namkha could bang his drum behind Dorji for hours without breaking his student's concentration. The world around him would lose focus, darkening, until nothing remained but his silhouette, fully immersed in noth-ingness.

By his early forties, the practices had become second nature. He paced the cave endlessly, Japa mala prayer beads clicking in his hands, lips moving with silent mantras.

One evening, while Namkha dozed by the bonfire, Dorji allowed himself a smile. He formed a mudra with his fingers.

The flames intensified until the cave filled with blazing light, sparks flying toward his sleeping master.

Namkha yawned awake, unimpressed. With a casual gesture of his own, wind exploded through the cave—snuffing the flames, kicking up dust, driving Dorji backward.

The old master laughed at the frustration on his student's face.

Twenty years had passed.

Dorji—well in his forties, looking almost exactly as he'd appeared in Becky's dreams so many times before—stood in front of a rustic wood table overflowing with jars, tubes, fiery crucibles, and smoldering alchemy contraptions.

Dorji gingerly handled large tongs, pouring molten mercury into one of the fiery vats. He covered the vat. He waved the smoke away from his face, coughing, put the tongs down, and wrote something on a piece of parchment.

Drenpa Namkha entered the cave carrying a sack full of herbs.

«Mmm, nothing like the smell of quicksilver in the morning! Now, listen, this is where things get slightly complicated. You need the pressure to build up, but not too much or it may explode. Too much time to cool and it becomes too thick and poisonous, too warm and—»

«Yes, I understand, master, too warm and it may burn my entrails. I swear, someday I will find a way to make it easier to get it exactly right with none of this guessing or your admonishments!»

«Very well, since they are your entrails I should not care. If you burn and die, I will simply dance over your dead body. But, it would be a great inconvenience to have to carry you to the charnel grounds. Or maybe I could just drag you outside and let the vultures have a feast!.»

Dorji rolled up his eyes, shook his head, smiling—more than used to years of his master's sarcastic needling.

«Thank you, master. You are always so kind and understanding with me.»

«Do you understand why thinking in terms of a lifetime is meaningless?»

«Yes, master. If I can extend my life at will, it makes no sense for me to measure time in a traditional fashion, for I become eternal.»

«Yes, but be very careful, this magic does not make you immortal, it only extends your life, as long as you use it properly.»

«Of course. I understand, master.»

Dorji touched the distilling receptacle with the back of his hand, checking the temperature. He closed his eyes and took a waft of the steam coming out of the device.«I can tell from the odor that the potion is ready.»

«Are you sure?»

«Yes. I have developed an evolved sense of smell thanks to your teachings, master.»

«Very well. But are you willing to risk your life based on your nose?»

Dorji looked at his master, pursed his lips and breathed deeply. He placed a cup under the device's spigot and opened a valve. Out poured a pale, shiny fluid, steaming slightly.

He closed the spigot, shook the cup, and—looking straight into his master's eyes—drank from it.

Dorji's face contorted with disgust. He arched with nausea, got dizzy, lost his balance, and fell to the ground.

Namkha laughed loudly.

«This is not funny, master!» Dorji choked out.

«Of course it is! You continue to be arrogant! You think you have achieved mastery but you are nothing but a newborn baby stumbling on his first steps!»

«You have been saying that for years, master. I am tired of it! I am no longer a child, I am a man!»

«A man who has just been born today, at this very moment. And perhaps now you are finally ready to begin your real teachings.»

Dorji got up gingerly, exhausted and frustrated.

«What? What do you mean, begin? What have we been doing for the past twenty years cloistered in this dreadful cavern?»

«Learning how to learn. Learning to keep your mouth shut and listen. Learning not to trust what you see with your lying eyes. Now you are ready to be truly awakened. But before we begin, I am afraid I have to give you some unfortunate news.»

«What is it, master?»

«Your father is dead.»

Dorji stared at his master in disbelief, thinking it was another of Namkha's sarcastic jabs.

«I would rather you not joke about that. If this is one of your jests, I do not think it is funny at all.»

«I am sorry, but this is true. He was killed while trying to destroy the Buddhist sorcerer's consort and her disciples.»

Dorji straightened up and leaned back against the cave's wall, palms flat against the cold granite surface.

«Where?»

«In the mountains of your country, in the cave where her master defeated the spirits that your father called upon to protect your kingdom. That is the place where the she-devil chose to teach her disciples.»

«When did this happen?»

«Seven years ago.»

Dorji was livid. Like a flash he pounced on Namkha, nearly toppling the table with all the flaming devices, grabbing Namkha by the throat.

«Seven years? How could you? I should kill you right now for hiding this from me, you old bastard!»

Namkha remained completely cool, unfazed, as Dorji squeezed his throat. Namkha expertly grabbed Dorji's wrists and placed his bony old fingers in a specific muscle, making Dorji's arms flail and drop to their sides involuntarily.

Dorji's anger intensified, along with his frustration. He shook and gyrated his body, unable to move his arms. The ire in his look was beyond compare.

«Stop! Unleash me! How dare you!»

«This is precisely why I waited so long to tell you. I respect your anger and your pain. But do not forget that all this time I have been trying to teach you to control your emotions. Emotions are the chains that trap your deluded mind. You have studied this for years and yet, you still do not comprehend. That, my dear son, is the difference between knowledge and practice. That is why your training is just beginning.»

Dorji clenched his jaw, his entire body in a knot. He banged his body against the stone wall trying to regain use of his arms. He might as well be wearing a straightjacket.

«You should not have waited so long to tell me. I... I could have saved him! We could have done something!»

«And that is why your father entrusted your life to me. He knew you would try to save him only to be destroyed like he was. He begged me to protect you and to teach you how to become much more powerful than he ever was.»

Tears of pain and anger streamed down Dorji's reddened cheeks.

«I swear, I will destroy them all!»

«I respect that. But you cannot overcome their powers unless you have absolute control over your mind and body, over all the elements, over nature herself. That is the only way to defeat them. If you achieve that, you will become so powerful that the entire world will tremble beneath your feet!»

«Teach me! Teach me everything old man! I swear I will not sleep, I will not eat, every living breath will be devoted to learning how to disembowel them! They took my beloved Tashi, banished us from our land, and then killed my father! They deserve to be destroyed!»

Namkha became sullen. He dropped his head and closed his eyes.

«What is it?»

«Your princess was there. She was among those disciples your father meant to kill. And it was she who defeated him.»

Dorji's face darkened. His entire soul was about to burst. His eyes became a fierce, terrifying blood red. His entire body began to emanate a thin, intense glow.

He fell to the ground on his knees, shaking.

The light streaming into the cave from the outside world dimmed as ominous black clouds shrouded the valley in darkness. The cave began to shake and tremble. Fissures opened on the rock walls. Dust poured down on Namkha. He stepped cautiously away from Dorji.

The veins on Dorji's face swelled up and he raised his hands in ire as he let loose a horrific roar that boomed out of the cave and echoed through the dark valley.

His scream became an explosive clap of thunder.

वायु

Air

18

Bhutan, Eternity-Field Foundation Library
Present Day

The two-story, stained-glass Kalachakra Mandala towered over the space, dramatically illuminated for maximum impact.

The library's reading tables had been cleared away and replaced with a large stage featuring a wide, throne-like seat at its center. Floor chairs with back supports were arranged in a semi-circle facing the stage.

Large video screens and banners flanked the stage, each displaying the logo of the Eternity-Field Foundation and the conference title: *HIDDEN TREASURES OF BUDDHISM*.

Throngs of participants from all over the world mingled throughout the space. Some stood enthralled by the architecture, others greeted each other with warm recognition.

Off to one side, a Bhutanese woman—sixty years old—minded a table selling books and merchandise. At the other end, an interpreter's booth housed a young Bhutanese man handing out headphones.

Dr. Krishnaa Bhat moved through the crowd, greeting participants who bowed and saluted her with reverence, recognizing her renown. She smiled and returned their gestures with warmth and humility.

A booming voice rang from the loudspeakers in English.

«This is your last call. Our presentation is about to commence.»

The participants rushed to fill their seats as the library's lights slowly dimmed.

«Please get comfortable, and if you prefer, in the lotus position for the opening meditation.»

A beat.

«We invite you to close your eyes, breathe deeply, and repeat the following prayer in your mind, in silence.»

The sound of a gong enveloped the space. Soft music began.

«In the palace of the unborn, unceasing, and changeless, Secret Yogini, you realized non-arising. Supplications to you, Vajra Queen! Please grant your blessings for the collapse of the dualistic mind's delusion! Supplications at your lotus feet, Yeshe Tsogyal!»

The participants—men and women of wide variety in age, ethnicity, and color—concentrated with eyes closed.

«Please grant your blessings for the actualization of the enlightened intent of the three wisdom bodies! In all lifetimes, may I and all beings be lovingly cared for by the Guru Dakini. Not entering the wrong paths of an incorrect mind and never separating from you, may enlightenment be attained in this lifetime.»

The gong sounded. The soft music faded out.

«Please open your eyes and meet our host, the exalted Guru, Druk Dorji.»

Druk Dorji sat on the chair atop the stage, framed by dramatic, theatrical lighting that created a saintly effect.

«It is an honor for the Eternity-Field Foundation and myself to welcome all of you as our guests for this transcendent journey of self-discovery with many days of learning, meditation, and growth.»

His English was perfect, marked by a slight British accent.

Most participants clasped their hands together and bowed. As Dorji spoke, his eyes drifted many times to Dr. Bhat. Every time their eyes locked, he nodded and smiled slightly.

«As you know, the oldest school of Tibetan Buddhism is the Nyingma, founded by the great sage, Guru Padmasambhava, between the seventh and eighth centuries. During that time, and later on, in the ninth century, he also visited Bhutan. Guru Padmasambhava is considered a Buddha, a fully enlightened being.»

On the video screens, a painting of Padmasambhava appeared—the same one hanging in Soto's office.

«The Nyingma school of Buddhism is known for its Terma tradition, the belief that Guru Padmasambhava hid Treasures of Knowledge throughout the world.»

Images of Terma treasures and places of discovery worldwide flashed across the screens.

«The tradition is for these objects to be discovered by his disciples when they reincarnate centuries later. This is predicted to happen whenever and wherever they are needed in order to unveil the most profound teachings of the buddhist canon so that all sentient beings can achieve liberation. With these objects, the disciples not only regain their ancient knowledge but also unleash their incredible spiritual and siddhi powers.»

Dorji paused for effect.

«However, recent research has shown, and this may be controversial in some quarters, that the person actually responsible for distributing and hiding these objects was not actually Guru Padmasambhava as many in this tradition believe, but rather his most important disciple and principal consort, the Lady Yeshe Tsogyal.»

A murmur rippled through the crowd.

«Lady Tsogyal is recognized as the first Tibetan person to have attained liberation and enlightenment. The first Tibetan to have achieved the awakened state. In other words, she was and is a powerful Buddha in her own right. She was, and is in the words of Guru Padmasambhava himself, his equal in power and wisdom.»

A painting of Yeshe Tsogyal appeared on screen in her Dakini form, enlightened, surrounded by her eleven disciples.

«She had eleven disciples to whom she imparted the most advanced tantric Buddhist teachings about the powers within our bodies, our minds, and our undying spirit. After imparting these teachings to them, Lady Tsogyal hid eleven knowledge treasures, known as *Terma*, all over the world. Eleven objects, one for each of her eleven disciples.»

An image of the objects stolen by Dorji—hidden in his vault—flashed across the screens.

«Mind you, she did this in the eighth and ninth centuries, so she quite naturally did not do so by traveling by horse or carriage.»

Participants chuckled. Dorji smiled, enjoying the spotlight.

An image appeared of Lady Tsogyal flying on the clouds above mountain peaks.

«This tradition establishes that, when and where it is necessary for humanity, Lady Tsogyal wills one of her disciples to be reborn so he or she may uncover their given *Terma* treasure. When they find it, they instantly remember their teachings, skills, wisdom, and powers to help all beings achieve enlightenment. That is what I was reborn to accomplish. It is my destiny, and the very reason for this Foundation: To help the entire world heal.»

The participants applauded. Dorji bowed modestly.

On cue, Bhatua entered the stage carrying an object covered with a silk cloak.

«It is with the greatest humility that I now share with you a Terma Treasure I was entrusted by Yeshe Tsogyal to uncover in this day and age for the enlightenment and salvation of all sentient beings.»

Bhatua bowed before Dorji in reverence.

Dorji rose from his chair and lifted the silk cloak with all the flair of a circus magician, unveiling a plexiglass cube containing the wooden chest he'd stolen from Wa'a-Mama-ci back in the late nineteenth century.

The participants erupted in applause, straining their necks to catch a glimpse of the Terma treasure.

«My assistant will pass it around. I trust you will be careful with it.»

Music swelled through the loudspeakers as Bhatua carefully descended from the stage, walking in front of each participant with the plexiglass case.

The participants appeared enthralled, gleaming with excitement. Some bowed, others clasped their hands in prayer, some even dropped to their knees.

Dorji's eyes locked onto Dr. Bhat's and, for a flash, they glowed red.

She straightened up, startled, and looked around to see if anyone else noticed.

«We are humbled that you traveled from all over the world to share this day with us, and I hope you will join us in the garden tomorrow morning for our first day of formal meditation.»

The participants applauded excitedly.

Dorji stepped down from the stage and walked away quickly, avoiding the crowd.

On the video screens, aerial footage of the vast Eternity-Field Foundation complex alternated with faces of its current disciples and teachers —a Hollywood-quality production edited with music and narration.

The narration from the video echoed within the library. «Here at the Eternity-Field Foundation we offer you a unique, immersive study and meditation program with our learned scholars. Your presence is always welcome and your financial contribution, no matter how small, is always humbly accepted and put to the noblest of uses for our most sacred cause. Thank you for your support.»

Participants began to mingle and chat with each other. Others waited in line to buy merchandise from the Bhutanese woman. Mohammed stood guard discretely near her table.

The video continued, its sound volume decreasing slightly.

A voice rang out through the sound system. «Tomorrow's meditation will commence promptly at seven in the morning in the gardens. Breakfast will be available from five thirty AM. Thank you all and have a nice rest of the evening.»

The volume of the video's music came back up.

Dr. Bhat chatted with some of the participants, then strolled over to the library's seemingly endless bookshelves. They were cordoned off with signs that read, «Please do not touch.»

One book in particular caught her eye—the one with the title, «The Golden Eye of Buddha.»

She unlatched one of the velvet ropes from its stanchion and moved toward it. She reached out to touch it.

«I would rather you didn't touch that particular volume. It is an extremely rare first edition. In all honesty, it is the only one.»

Dr. Bhat jumped and shuddered, startled. She turned around to find Druk Dorji standing right behind her.

«I should know. I am the author. It would be my honor to offer you an autographed copy if you wish. I have many in storage. It was not a best-seller by any means, but it has a profound sentimental value for me as my first publication.»

Dorji offered a warm smile and bowed with apparent humility.

«I admit it is a weakness to have attachments to anything, as you well know, but I am still working on detaching myself from this particular piece of work.»

He gave a slight wink and smiled.

Dr. Bhat, embarrassed, struggled to hook the rope back on its stanchion.

«What, if I may ask, is your name, madam?»

«My name is Doctor Krishnaa Bhat. Please accept my most sincere apologies. I was just so intrigued with its exquisite design that I wished to see it closely. I never meant to pull it off the shelf.»

«Of course not. Please, allow me.»

Dorji took the velvet rope from Dr. Bhat's hands and hooked it back on its stanchion. He closed his eyes for an instant.

«Dr. Bhat, founder of the Institute for Human Consciousness and

Yoga Studies in India? Is it really you? I'm most impressed with your work!»

«You flatter me. I would never have imagined our humble organization would be of interest to a person of your stature.»

«My stature?» He laughed. «Oh, no, Doctor, please, you are the one that is flattering me. I am but a humble servant of Buddha dharma, nothing more.»

«I have to say, you have built quite an extraordinary institution, with international reach.»

«What you see is nothing more than the result of the many benefactors we have been blessed with for many years. However, as I mentioned before, these structures are of no importance to a practitioner of Buddha's teachings. So, in that sense, this institute, grandiose as it may seem to the uninitiated, is only a mere mirage, a mere reflection of the true wisdom that is being harvested within its walls.»

Dr. Bhat nodded and bowed slightly in reverence.

«Spoken like a true lineage holder, Guru Dorji. I'm very honored you invited me to this event.»

«It is my honor to have you here, and you have my word regarding the signed copy of my book. I'm looking forward to having you join us for tomorrow's morning meditation. I will have it for you by then.»

«Of course. Much obliged, Guru Dorji. Thank you. Namasté.»

«Namasté.»

They smiled as each clasped their hands in the traditional Namasté gesture.

Dorji left. Dr. Bhat glanced at «The Golden Eye of Buddha.»

Dr. Bhat's Room

The room was ample and well appointed, elegant without being too luxurious—more hotel room than school dorm.

Dr. Bhat sat on the bed in the lotus position, struggling to make out Soto's voice on her mobile phone among all the dropouts and hissing from the poor signal. She put the phone on speaker and placed it beside her.

«Hello? Hello? Can you not hear me?»

«*Got you! Signal's bad, but go on.*»

«I was saying, he is a fascinating person, and the Foundation he has built is truly remarkable.»

«*But?*»

«There is something odd that makes me uneasy.»

«*What is it?*»

«I cannot pinpoint what it is exactly. Perhaps his demeanor.»

«*His what? I didn't get that?*»

«The way he presents himself! His humility appears a bit forced, almost like it takes him too much effort to maintain his ego in check.»

«*So you don't feel comfortable sharing my client's information.*»

«Not quite yet. The workshop is just beginning, so I am going to be here for a week at least. Perhaps my mind will change.»

«*What did you make of her chart?*»

The phone's signal broke down.

«Her what? Can you repeat that?»

«*Her natal chart, did you get a chance to look it over?*»

«It shows all the auspicious signs, I agree. But, as you mentioned, she is suffering some very difficult times at present, and there may be worse to come. If what we think is indeed true, it may be complicated. Will you see her again?»

«Yes! She's shown a remarkable interest in learning buddha dharma! We're starting her lessons right away!»

«That's good! But, let things flow. Please be extremely careful, tread slowly. And please, when you do see her again, do not bring up what we think until we can be certain.»

«Of course not. I understand.»

«Let us speak again tomorrow night at the same time if you can. Perhaps we can communicate the other way.»

«What? I didn't get that! Did I hear you say, 'the other way?'»

A series of beeps sounded on Dr. Bhat's phone as the signal failed.

She shook her head, disappointed, and looked at the phone's screen. There were no bars on the signal indicator.

Dr. Bhat got up, fanning her face with her hands from the heat. She went to the air conditioner controls: 32 degrees Celsius or almost 90 Fahrenheit. She fiddled with the controls but nothing happened.

She moved to the vents, put her hand over them, shook her head. She tried to open the windows—they were locked.

Finally she went into the bathroom and threw some water on her face, wet a towel, put it on the back of her neck, and sat on the bed, back straight, calming herself.

Alchemy Lab

Druk Dorji studied his wall of security monitors, displaying images of the interiors of the guests' quarters.

On one of the screens: Dr. Bhat sitting on her bed.

Dorji's lips twisted into an evil grin.

19

Puerto Rico, Torres Law Firm, Ana Ramos' Office
Present Day

Ana Ramos worked intently on her laptop, surrounded by piles of legal briefs, a yellow legal pad, and some thick hard-bound books. The decoration was sparse save for framed degrees and awards on the walls and a photo of when she was sworn in.

The phone rang. She picked up, eyes still on her laptop.

«Good morning, sir, how are you?»

She stopped eyeing the laptop, her gaze concerned, body taut.

«Of course, pardon me. Right now? Do I need to bring anything? Sure thing, I will be right over.»

Ana finished typing a sentence or two, closed the laptop's lid, put on her blazer, and left her office.

Law Firm Boardroom

When Ana Ramos walked into the large room, the shades were half drawn over the panoramic windows that overlooked the city.

Her smile turned into puzzlement as she saw the people sitting at the end of the long oak conference table: Wilfredo Cruz, Octavio Marxuach, Ivette Duprey—all in their mid-seventies, all Presiding Partners of the Torres Law Firm. Socorro Vega, sixty-three, a portly, fake-blonde stenographer,sat rigidly off to a corner with a recording device and her note-taking machine.

In a flash, Ana's puzzlement turned into serious concern. Her body stiffened, straightening her back more than usual, while maintaining a cool, collected professional demeanor.

«Good morning, everyone.»

«Good morning, Miss Ramos. For the record, Senior Counsel Ana Ramos, Presiding Partners, Octavio Marxuach, Ivette Duprey, and myself, Wilfredo Cruz, are present.»

«This is going into a record? May I ask what this is about?»

«Please take a seat.»

Ana paused for a second, trying to read the partners' faces, then sat at the far end of the table, miles away from them.

«Mrs. Evelyn Torres, the widow of our esteemed, recently departed, founding partner, has brought to our attention the possibility of a conflict of interest on your part which could be considered a serious breach of professional ethics and most definitely a violation of your contract with this firm.»

«I can absolutely guarantee that everything pertaining to the Torres estate has been handled with the utmost diligence, transparency, and rectitude.»

«Yes, I have personally assured Mrs. Torres that this is true, although the firm will have to absorb the cost of an independent audit of the entire process in order to assuage any doubt the widow might have of this firm's due diligence.»

Cruz shifted in his seat and adjusted his tie.

«This, however, does not address the issue of your possible ethical violation, an issue that could cause you considerable professional harm if it were to be formally brought to the attention of the state Bar Association.»

Ana buried her eyes on Cruz, hiding her boiling anger.

Cruz looked at the other partners and cleared his throat.

«Socorro, could you please pause the recording?»

Socorro Vega turned off the recording machinery.

«Off the record, it seems you have been engaged in an intimate relationship with Mrs. Torres' eldest daughter. That, Miss Ramos, is a very serious allegation and cause for immediate dismissal.»

Ana's face went red. Her breathing stopped. The walls seemed to be closing in around her. Under the table, she buried her glossy fingernails into her thighs.

«With all due respect, sir I—»

Cruz raised his hand. That was all he needed to do to stop her.

He looked back at Socorro Vega and nodded his head. She turned on the recording device and set her hands on her machine.

«For the record, there is no need for explanations at this time. According to our bylaws and your contract, any formal accusation or substantiated allegation of conduct considered untoward is sufficient for us to initiate an internal investigation, especially if said alleged conduct could involve ethical violations.»

«Excuse me, sir, are you saying I am now formally under investigation?»

«If you will please allow me to finish?»

«Yes, of course, I apologize.»

«The partners and I have discussed this issue thoroughly and, given your exemplary record with this firm, we would like to avoid going in that direction. It has taken us an immense effort to convince Mrs. Torres to accept our proposed course of action in order to avoid any prolonged proceedings and unnecessary harm to all parties.»

«And what exactly is this 'proposed course of action she accepted?'»

Cruz frowned, annoyed by Ana's questions. He would much rather move things swiftly along.

Ana's jaw was clenched with anger.

«We propose to terminate your employment effective immediately, with a very generous severance package in consideration of your excellent record with this firm. We would prefer to resolve this in a quiet and discreet manner to save you and the firm from any unnecessary stress and discomfort.»

Ana placed her hands on the table slowly, coldly, controlled.

«Discomfort? Pardon me? You do realize my employment falls into not one but two legally protected classes, right?»

«With all due respect, counselor, bringing up issues of diversity in this current political climate may not be in your best interest. What would be in your best interest is to accept our very generous package, as well as our extremely positive letters of recommendation so we can all move on with the dignity and respect you and this firm are entitled to.»

Ana clicked her fingernails on top of the table—a slightly jarring staccato that belied her anger and frustration.

She took one good look at the partners one last time and rose, fixing her clothes, hair, straightening up with dignity.

«Thank you for the opportunity to work here, I will always be grateful for that. For the record, given what I have recently come to learn of Mr. Torres' personal life, I am no longer proud of having worked for him. In fact, I am very ashamed. Please send the severance package to my attorneys. I will leave their contact information with my assistant. Sorry, former assistant. Have a good day.»

And with that she walked out of the room, her body straight as an arrow—dignified, defiant, proud—and shut the door.

Isabel's Apartment, Living Room

Becky entered the apartment carrying some groceries and dropped the keys on a console table near the front door.

Isabel was pacing fast back and forth—angry, crying, frazzled, like she'd just been shot out of a cannon. Her hair was a mess in every direction, dark circles under her eyes.

Ana came out of the kitchen holding two wine glasses, standing in front of Isabel waiting for her to take one.

«Oh my God, what happened to you? What's going on? You look like a zombie!» Becky said.

«Would you like some wine?»

«Sure, why not?»

«What the hell, Ana? Come on! You have to sue them!» Isabel interrupted angrily.

«Please, tell me what's going on.»

«Your mother really outdid herself!» Isabel continued, furiously.

«Oh, so now she's my mother. What'd she do now?»

«She had Ana fired.»

«What? Seriously? Ana, is it true?»

Ana answered very calmly. «Actually, it wasn't your mother's fault. I screwed things up badly.»

«I kinda' find that hard to believe, especially if mother was involved.» Becky replied.

«That's exactly what I'm saying!»

«No, Isa, I've been trying to explain this to you. I shouldn't have taken on the case of your family's estate. It was a gross ethical breach on my part and it could've gotten me disbarred.»

«I still don't get it.» Becky asked.

«Your mother somehow found out about the two of us and ratted her out to her bosses, so they fired her!»

«Oh shit.»

«Yes, but, in all fairness, it was wrong for me to take on your family's case since there was an obvious conflict of interest.» Ana said.

Isabel was still livid. «But you did nothing wrong! You never did anything to favor me!»

«I know, but in the legal world, the mere appearance of impropriety was reason enough to have recused myself.»

«So, why didn't you?» Isabel asked, frustrated.

Ana stopped to take a sip of wine.

«I would've needed to explain why, in detail. I couldn't just say I didn't want to for a vague, personal reason, especially since I was on the partner track. This case was a great vote of confidence, like a rite of passage. I was the one chosen to handle the financial affairs of the firm's founder.»

Ana looked at Isabel lovingly.

«I felt it wasn't the time or place to tell them I was in love with you, the founder's daughter, let alone engaged in a relationship with you. We weren't ready to make it public, and the moment I shared that information with the partners, that would have made it very public.»

Isabel shook her head, holding back tears.

«You should've asked me.»

«You're right. I was selfish and I acted stupidly. I seriously regret that. I should have asked you. I am so sorry!»

Isabel dried her tears, smiled, and took her wine.

«I love you and I kept us a secret for too long! I was a coward, and once again, I let my mother control my life. I am the one that's sorry!»

«Oh, sweetie, please, don't be, this is all on me.»

«Well, at least the pussy's out of the bag, pardon the expression.»

«You asshole, this is serious!»

Ana smiled.

«She's right, there's no need to hide anymore, at least as far as your mother is concerned.»

«Oh so now that mother knows, we can all go out shopping together and play foursomes at her golf club!»

«Foursome? That sounds kinky, ha, ha, ha!» Becky added, throwing fuel into the fire.

«You are such a jerk! This isn't funny! First, there's what she did to you, and now what she did to me, to us. She's gone too far, I can't stand it! She's driving such a horrible wedge between us, and to go so far as to hurt Ana this way too.»

«Hey, she's not hurting me. If anything, I feel free now. I'm getting a heck of a financial package and they can't afford to say anything negative about me because it would only blow back against them. So I'm of a mind to take some much deserved time off, preferably with you. Then, I know there are quite a few great law offices out there that would kill to have me on their roster. Care for a glass, Becky?»

«Yeah, please, what the hell. Let's celebrate your coming-out party!»

Ana moved into the kitchen.

Isabel downed the last of her wineglass in one gulp.

«Make it two!»

Becky moved close to her and hugged her sister.

«Come on, the two of you are made of steel! This is a good thing. No more hiding, no more bullshit, and if mother wants to keep burning her bridges, fuck it. In the end, she's the one that's gonna end up alone.»

«I know, I know. But, it still hurts. After all we've been through, I hoped there was a way to heal the family, to bring us all back together. Now I look back and I feel like an idiot. I know that's never going to happen.»

Becky smiled and hugged her again.

«I'm here sis, and so's Ana, so you're not alone. Not by a long shot. You, Ana, and I are your family.»

Ana returned with the wine. Isabel and Becky grabbed theirs.

«What shall we toast to?»

«To the pussies being let out of the bag!»

Isabel covered her face, embarrassed, shaking her head.

«For chrissakes, Becky!»

Ana laughed. «I love it! Here's to us pussies being out of the bag!»

They all laughed, clinked their glasses, then guzzled the wine.

Tibet, Cavern 8th Century

Druk Dorji knelt on the ground in front of a bonfire, his expression as intense as the flames that reflected off his jet-black eyes.

In front of him a human skull filled with a shimmering, red liquid, reflected the flames.

He lifted the skull with both hands towards his waiting lips. He gulped the liquid down. Sweat poured down his brow as he tilted the skull more and more, emptying it. Some of the thick red liquid trickled down the corner of his mouth, his face, neck, and chest.

When he finished, he set the skull down beside him.

Drenpa Namkha moved toward him carrying a ceramic bowl. His lips moved rhythmically, reciting some unintelligible mantra. He placed the bowl in front of Dorji.

Inside lay bloody cow livers, half a raw fish, and a moldy piece of bread.

Dorji concentrated on the flames in front of him as he chewed the bread, gnawed on the fish—swallowing it, bones and all—then gobbled the livers.

The sweat on his body became more profuse. His body became unstable. He landed on the ground, face moving in all directions, dizzy.

«What? What was in the liquid, Master?»

«The end of you. The end of us.»

«What do you mean?»

«I can no longer help you. You are lost in your passions, your attachments, your hatred. Useless!»

Dorji looked at Namkha, dazed, confused.

«We must destroy your body. That is the only way. You have to die now!»

«What? No! You poisoned me?»

Dorji tried to get up, but he stumbled, fell, retched.

«This was all a waste.»

«No! Please! I do not understand! What... What more do you want me to do?»

Dorji began to shake uncontrollably.

Namkha walked out of the cave.

Dorji's world began to spiral—the flames enveloping him, the shadows dancing freakishly around him as he vomited.

Namkha returned, dragging and pushing a young woman. Her arms were bound behind her, her screams muffled beneath a sack that covered her face.

Namkha cut her binds and shoved her to the ground. She landed on all fours, facing the fire. She tried to rise but Namkha placed his foot flat on her back holding her down. She relented.

Dorji wiped the sweat off his eyes and crawled toward her on all fours until he was right in front of her face.

Namkha uncovered her face.

It was Tashi, older, her eyes contorted with horror.

Dorji's eyes widened. He pulled back, shocked.

«This ends now! Take her!» Namkha screamed. «Go on, consummate your love! Do it!»

«No! Not this way!»

«This is the only way! Before you die! Before she dies!»

«No!»

«You take her or I will!»

Namkha raised Tashi's robe, exposing her behind.

Dorji found the strength to get on his feet and pounced toward the old man, shoving him away.

Namkha locked eyes with his disciple, eyes ablaze, smiling devilishly.

Dorji spun around and fell on his knees behind Tashi. He raised his robe, closed his tear-filled eyes and assaulted the young woman viciously from behind as she screamed.

As Dorji's body began to tremble, Namkha rushed forward, knife in hand, and sliced Tashi's neck.

Blood sprayed on Dorji's horrified face.

Namkha laughed, a horrifying, devilish laugh that boomed and bounced off the cavern walls.

The young woman's body fell writhing on the ground.

Her face was Becky's, contorted in a horrible scream!.

Isabel's Apartment, Guest Bedroom
Present Day

Becky screamed until she practically lost her voice. She sat up with a jump, heaving, breathless.

There was a knock on the door.

«Becky? Are you alright? Open up!»

Becky looked around, disoriented. She lifted up her bedsheets—bathed in sweat. She twisted around, threw her feet over the side, tried to get up, slipped, and fell.

Another knock.

«Becky?»

Becky got up, holding on to the bed and the wall. She moved to the door and opened it, squinting from the glare of daylight.

«What happened? I heard you... Oh my God! You were screaming like crazy!»

Isabel noticed Becky's shirt was completely drenched in sweat. She entered the room, opened the dresser, found a clean shirt, and helped her sister change, throwing the sweaty one on the floor.

She helped Becky sit back down on the bed.

Becky touched her throat, coughing, and began to cry.

Isabel sat next to her, hugging her. Becky cuddled into her sister's embrace.

«That's good. Just let it all out. I've got you. You're safe with me.»

Becky sobbed and squeezed her sister, rocking back and forth.

20

Soto's Office

Soto looked at Becky from behind his desk sympathetically.

Becky was completely still—haggard, disheveled, frozen. Dry tears encrusted on her cheeks.

Soto handed her a box of tissues and smiled slightly, speaking softly.

«Do you feel you can describe it?»

Becky shook her head and closed her eyes briefly.

«That's perfectly fine. Can you tell me why this one felt worse than the others?»

«I just want this to stop.»

«I understand. What if I can teach you to have lucid dreams?»

Becky stared at him blankly.

«What if I taught you how to be aware that you're dreaming? You could be in control of what's going on, make conscious decisions. You could feel unafraid knowing it's all an illusion.»

«Are you serious? Is that possible?»

«It takes practice, but, yes, it is.»

Becky squinted at him, pursing her lips incredulously.

Soto got up and pulled some books from his shelves.

«We will go over the steps before you leave today. And I'm also going to get you started on some of my books on Buddhist traditions, including ones on meditation and yoga. As you put these things into practice it will help a lot with your dreams.»

«By reading books?»

«No. By practicing what they say. There's a reason this is called spiritual 'practice.' Studying these traditions is only a fraction of the process. You must engage in practice to enhance concentration, control your mind, and connect with your inner Self. It takes work.»

«You sound like Sylvia now, she's always banging me in the head 'cause I don't take time to meditate and shit. It always felt kinda' useless to me.»

«If you practice hard, until you can actually stop your mind from thinking, you experience the true nature of our non-dualistic reality. In other words, you realize that there is no 'You' that's separate from everything else, and that the cause of your suffering is your mind. Control 'it,' and you can ease your pain.»

Soto smiled broadly.

Becky looked away, her expression skeptical.

«After you study these, and practice, practice, practice we will go over some mantras that will help you also.»

«I've heard a whole bunch of those on YouTube and they all seem like a crock: 'mantra for money, for love, for success.' Bullshit.»

«I couldn't tell you about those. The ones you and I will practice will help you with your lucid dreaming, will help to calm you down, and even help you to dive deeply into the meaning behind these readings.»

«Why not start right now?»

«I will give you the instructions on lucid dreaming but for the mantras I prefer you to have some deeper understanding of the philosophy first. These should get you started.»

Becky reacted to the tall stack of books in front of her with a deep sigh.

«All these? Are you serious?»

«You said you wanted to learn this stuff. Are you really up for it?»

«I said I would, so, what the heck.»

Soto sat and typed on his laptop.

«I'm also sending you a list of people from my team that will be willing to help you. Feel free to contact them, give them my name, and start working with them as soon as you can. They're my dream team, forgive my pun.»

«Oh, God, astrologer and standup comic, just what I needed.»

Soto laughed warmly.

Becky finally let out a smile.

Bhutan, Eternity-Field Foundation Gardens

The sun began to rise over the Foundation's towering walls, bathing the lush green gardens inside in golden hues.

Everything was silent except for the occasional squawk of birds and the flutter of their wings. There was also the squeaky shriek of the golden langurs with their bright yellow fur as they played among the trees, their branches bursting with bright flowers.

Spring time in Bhutan in all its splendor.

Two dozen participants sat in an exquisitely landscaped courtyard facing Druk Dorji. His back was to them, as he faced two tapestries swaying slightly in the breeze. One was a likeness of Guru Padmasambhava, the other of Yeshe Tsogyal.

Most of the participants had their eyes slightly open, looking downward, deep in meditation.

Dr. Bhat sat in the lotus position among the group, eyes shut, shifting restlessly, furrowing her brow, fidgeting, unable to concentrate. She opened her eyes and looked around to see if anyone else was having the same problem.

Everyone else seemed enraptured.

She closed her eyes tightly. Sweat appeared on her brow. She opened her eyes.

Druk Dorji was in her face, nose to nose.

Dr. Bhat arched back, startled, and lifted her hands to push Dorji away.

Dorji wasn't there. He was still way out in front of the group, sitting as he was moments before in front of the tapestries.

Again, Dr. Bhat looked around at the others. Nothing. No reaction from anyone.

She dried her sweaty forehead with a silk handkerchief, took a deep breath, tried to control her breathing, and closed her eyes.

«Are you feeling well, doctor?»

Dorji's voice sounded eerie, distant, ethereal.

Dr. Bhat shivered and opened her eyes, looking from side to side. Dorji was still in his position.

Dr. Bhat stood up and walked softly toward the front, sidestepping the participants until she reached Dorji.

Bhatua appeared in front of her in a flash, his expression serious, ice cold, but respectful.

Dr. Bhat stopped cold in her tracks.

Dorji—eyes closed—raised a hand, signaling Bhatua. Bhatua bowed slightly, retreated a few steps, but remained close by.

«Are you feeling well, doctor?»

Dr. Bhat stared at Dorji, surprised. His eyes were still closed. He smiled.

«No need to be surprised, doctor Bhat, I have developed a very sensitive sense of smell, and your perfume is unmistakable.»

Dr. Bhat bowed her head slightly and whispered, «I apologize for the intrusion. I'm having considerable problems concentrating, controlling my mind. Which is very unusual in my case.»

«I see. Please, sit by me.»

Dr. Bhat sat facing him at an angle, avoiding being with her back to the tapestries. Dorji still had his eyes closed.

«Bhatua, would you be so kind as to bring doctor Bhat a cup of tsheringma tea?»

Bhatua nodded slightly and vanished as quickly as he'd appeared.

«You need not bother.»

«Oh, it is no bother at all, doctor. To the contrary, you are my most esteemed guest and it is my honor. The tea is grown by our disciples right here in these valleys. Finest quality, I can assure you.»

«I am sure it is, thank you. I have to ask, did you speak moments ago?»

«I have been in silent meditation, like yourself. No words have crossed my lips. Perhaps you have been visited.»

«Visited?»

«These mountains are steeped in powerful spirits. We have lived with them and respected their presence for years.»

«Are you speaking of elementals?»

«Oh, no, they are much more than that, far more powerful. Very hard to control. They can be playful at times. Other times, quite annoying.»

«Have you managed to control them?»

«Control? No. We tolerate one another. As long as we do not stand in their way, they do not seem to get in ours. But, as I said, they can be imprudent sometimes.»

Dorji opened his eyes for the first time. He stared right into her eyes, smiling slyly.

«Just let me know if they bother you again and I will see what I can do.»

Before Dr. Bhat could answer, Bhatua appeared out of nowhere with an elegant tray carrying a full tea service.

Dr. Bhat shifted uncomfortably from the sudden surprise.

Dorji got up lithely, like a dancer, and extended his hands toward Dr. Bhat.

«Please, join me for a walk.»

«What about the meditation practice?»

Dorji looked back at the participants, all lost in a trance.

«I think they can manage. Please.»

Dr. Bhat accepted his hand and got up.

They began walking down a path behind the tapestries with Bhatua behind them. They reached a set of patio furniture well hidden among the thicket.

Dorji invited Dr. Bhat to sit. Bhatua placed the tea tray on the center table, filled two cups, and darted away.

«Are you enjoying your experience?»

«Well, it has been very interesting so far, that is certain.»

«Why are you really here, Doctor?»

Dr. Bhat eyed Dorji up and down, smiling before answering.

«To learn more about the Terma tradition from a legitimate lineage holder, like the others here.»

«So you have never been exposed to a reincarnated disciple before now.»

«Not as far as I know.»

«And you have never come to suspect any person of being one of us.»

Dr. Bhat reached for her teacup and calmly took a sip.

«Hmm, you are so right. This tea is exquisite.»

Dorji eyed Dr. Bhat, smiling, enjoying her nonchalance.

«Well. Have you?»

«Respectfully, Guru Dorji, I don't understand the purpose of your insistent queries.»

«Oh, please, forgive me.» He laughed. «I am just curious! I ask the same questions of all our visitors, trying to ascertain whether they have any kind of link to the original disciples. I have spent my entire life dreaming of the possibility that there might be another one of us alive somewhere, in my time.»

«Yes, well, that would be amazing, I'm sure. Now, if you will excuse me, I would like to refresh before lunchtime if you do not mind.»

«Of course. By all means. I will send a pouch of our tea to your quarters. And, by the way, I must apologize.»

«For?»

«I completely forgot to bring you my book. I promise I will hand it to you at lunch.»

«Most gracious of you, thank you.»

Dr. Bhat nodded politely and walked away.

Isabel's Apartment, Guest Bedroom

The sun began to rise as Becky sat on her bed in the lotus position. Something in her appearance had clearly changed. She looked rested, well groomed, almost radiant.

On the bed next to her, a pile of books Soto had lent her lay open. Others had colored post-it notes peeking from between their pages. There was a letter-sized journal with her handwritten notes on it.

More books sat piled on both nightstands, and even on a chair in the corner. It looked like she was preparing for a bar exam or a doctoral thesis.

Becky's eyes were half open, slightly cross-eyed, focused on the space just in front of her. She took a slow, controlled breath.

SMASH!

The sound of a garbage truck dropping its container, followed by the annoying beep, beep, beep of it going in reverse.

Becky opened her eyes wide, annoyed. She shook her head, closed them, then resumed her attempt—eyes crossed, breathing slowly.

The buzz of a mosquito pulled her out of her concentration.Splat! Becky killed it.

«Shit! I shouldn't have done that. All life is precious but some of it is annoying as hell.»

Once again, she returned to her pose, concentrated, her breath calmed and controlled. She held that state for some time.

A door slammed, followed by children screaming somewhere in the hallways.

But Becky smiled, shaking her head slightly, still breathing calmly, letting it all flow.

Cars honked, police sirens wailed, and jet planes roared—all conspiring to distract her.

Becky tousled her hair as if exorcising a demon, shook her body, laughed, closed her eyes again, then opened them slightly, taking a very deep breath.

She exhaled with a resounding «Aaaaah!»

Her breathing calmed down. Her gaze wasn't focused on anything. Her stomach rose and lowered with a calm rhythm.

The noises began to fade. A slight smile slowly appeared on her face. We only heard her slow breaths.

The bedroom slowly became a blur—a fuzzy blotch of light and color with Becky floating in its center. Her body began to glow, her skin iridescent, translucent.

A knock on the door interrupted.

Everything in the bedroom zoomed back to reality along with Becky's normal body.

«Hello? May I come in?»

Becky shook her head and stretched her body. «Yeah, sure.»

Isabel casually walked in with two cups of coffee, looking for somewhere to place them.

«Sorry, your holiness, am I disturbing your enlightenment?»

«You are, actually.» Becky said, smiling wryly.

Isabel looked for some undisturbed surface to no avail. She looked at some of the book covers.

«Where should I put your coffee, on top of 'Sky Dancer' or on this one, 'Kurma,' what is he, a Ninja Turtle?'»

Becky reached out for her cup of coffee and blew on it. «Thanks!»

«You haven't spoken about your dreams for weeks. Are you sleeping well?»

«Like a baby.»

«Like a baby? You mean you wake up four times during the night crying because you peed yourself?»

They both laughed heartily.

«You jerk, I'm supposed to be the sarcastic one.»

«So how's the studying? My God, I've never seen you like this.»

Becky took a sip from her cup. She looked up at Isabel with a glint in her eye, holding back her excitement.

«I actually did it, Isa.»

«Did what?»

«I stopped thinking.»

«Yes, well, that's nothing new.»

Becky looked at Isabel straight in the eyes, with a more mature, controlled, and calm expression than we'd ever seen.

«I'm serious, Isabel. I actually stopped my thinking process. Gone, completely, it just stopped! And then everything just disappeared all around me, like there was nothing in my mind, no physical reality. I couldn't even feel my body, just pure calm and bliss. It was amazing, I can't describe it!»

Isabel surveyed her sister and smiled.

«You look good, sis. You really do. Much better than I've ever seen you. I'm glad you stayed here with me, and that you're doing all this.»

Isabel sipped her coffee.

«By the way, I heard your teacher's divorced. But I guess you probably know that at this point.»

«Wait, what? What's that got to do with anything?»

Isabel rubbed her temple, parodying mystical powers.

«Ooh! I can see it in your future. The two of you, all these months together, alone in his office.» Isabel made a «twilight zone» noise and then air quotes. «'Learning to meditate.'»

«You idiot! What the hell? You're crazy! I would never! I don't see him like that at all.»

«Aha, yeah, sure.»

Becky found her mobile phone buried somewhere among the books.

«Oh, my God, look at the time, I've gotta go!»

«But the sun's not even out yet! Must be the wedding bells ringing! Don't need to be a witch to see that coming. Ha, ha, ha!»

«Shut up with that! I'm not even seeing him that much, I'm working with people he recommended.»

Becky jumped out of bed.

Isabel planted a kiss on her forehead and started to sing the wedding march.

Becky threatened to throw a pillow. Isabel ran out of the room, laughing.

21

The transformation didn't happen all at once. It unfolded gradually, like a lotus opening to the sun—each practice, each lesson, each moment of surrender adding another petal.

On the beach, where palm trees dotted the grassy area and waves crashed nearby, Becky struggled through yoga positions she couldn't quite master yet.

Abadha—a fit woman in her late fifties—patiently corrected her form, her voice steady and encouraging.

As Becky's body strengthened and her mind quieted, the ancient teachings she'd been studying began to echo through her consciousness, no longer abstract philosophy but lived truth.

«The truth is that my life, all life, is inherently marked by suffering or dissatisfaction, physical pain and emotional distress.»

Inside the Holistic Energy Health Center, posters of human silhouettes with illustrations of chakras and channels of energy overlaid on them covered the walls.

Becky lay face down on a massage table while Leo—seventy years old, his long white hair tied in a ponytail—placed acupuncture needles along her body with practiced precision.

«The origin of my suffering is craving or attachment, specifically the desire for things to be or go my way... clinging to impermanent things, and an aversion to whatever is unpleasant.»

In Soto's office, Becky returned a stack of books so high she couldn't see where she was going.

Soto rushed to help her but the books went flying, landing scattered across the floor.

They both squatted to pick them up. Their hands accidentally touched.

Soto moved his hand away as if on a spring. Becky laughed.

«The way I can overcome suffering is by eliminating my cravings and attachments.»

In Isabel's apartment one evening, Becky sat on the sofa in lotus position, surrounded by Abadha, Krystal, and Iraida, both women from Abadha's yoga group.

They were all deep in meditation when Isabel walked in, all smiles, wine bottle in hand.

«This eradication of my cravings and desires is the key to my being able to achieve liberation from my cycle of suffering.»

Becky opened her eyes wide, looked at her sister, and shook her head with a bit of a scold.

Isabel frowned, raised her shoulders, and walked back quietly to the kitchen.

At the martial arts dojo, Becky practiced kickboxing with Ruby Camacho—fifty-five, a martial arts expert who appeared jovial and caring but demanding.

When Becky fell to her knees with exhaustion, Ruby clapped his hands and yelled at her with encouragement.

«My path to liberation involves cultivating wisdom, ethical conduct, and mental and physical discipline.»

Back at the beach, Becky ran vigorously on the hard sand where the waves broke, then turned toward the ocean and dove into the water, swimming like a champion.

In her room at Isabel's apartment, Becky wrote copious notes in her journal, surrounded by half a dozen open books.

She picked up one volume—*The Ocean of Theosophy*—turned the pages quickly, found what she was looking for, marked it with a Post-It note, then wrote something in her journal.

«Once I understand the nature of my suffering, its cause, and how to stop it, then I can begin to really understand the concepts of impermanence, non-self, and karma.»

She unburied another book from a huge pile and rummaged through the pages, stopping on one and reading intently.

She began to shiver. Her eyes reddened as tears welled up. She bit her lip, closed her eyes, and pressed the book to her chest.

The cover showed a Buddhist-style drawing of a woman and the title:

The Life and Visions of Yeshe Tsogyal.

Becky plopped back into her pillows, held up the book, and continued to read, shaking her head with wonder.

One night, she drove her sister's car slowly into the driveway of the Torres family home and stopped across from the front door.

«I need to gradually cultivate thoughts of kindness, compassion, non-judgment, avoiding thoughts of ill-will, anger, hatred, and harmful intent.»

Inside the car, Becky contemplated the entrance to what was once her home.

She reached for the ignition, about to turn off the motor, but retracted her hand at the last minute. She closed her eyes, shook her head, and drove away.

«So far, that's one of my most challenging obstacles.»

Back at the beach, Becky achieved an advanced yoga pose.

Abadha and the rest of the women applauded her. Becky jumped for joy.

«I practice speaking truthfully, kindly, and constructively, avoiding lies, gossip, and harsh language. Yeah, that last one has been another challenge.»

In Soto's office, Soto pointed to his laptop screen as Becky hunched over his shoulder.

She questioned certain aspects of the diagrams, pulled out one of Soto's own books to show him discrepancies.

«I refrain from harmful actions such as hurting or killing, not only humans, but any living thing.»

Soto grabbed the book, looked at the laptop, gave a deep sigh, agreed with her and smiled.

Becky jumped for joy and gave him a warm hug that lasted for a while.

This time Soto didn't pull away.

«There's not even the thought of stealing, corruption of any kind, and no sexual misconduct.»

At the Holistic Energy Health Center, Leo lay face down on the stretcher, patiently giving orders.

Becky found certain spots along his back and pressed her fingers against them.

Leo smiled approvingly and gave her the thumbs up.

«I must make a conscious, constant effort to abandon negative states of mind while cultivating positive ones.»

At the beach as morning broke, Becky stretched into a truly complex yoga pose to the amazement of Abadha and the other women.

She pulled out of the pose and looked at them, raising her shoulders as if it was nothing, then went on to do another even more complex one.

«I cultivate an awareness of my body, my feelings, and my thoughts, without analyzing or dwelling on any of those things.»

At the martial arts dojo, Becky sparred with her sensei, Ruby Camacho, dodging his attacks, counterpunching, kicking at lightning speed with seemingly little effort.

«I embrace life fully and take everything life throws at me without judgment, anger or rancor.»

In Isabel's apartment one evening, Becky sat in lotus position leading a meditation circle that now included not only Abadha, Krystal, and Iraida, but half a dozen more women from the yoga group.

Isabel and Ana were also engaged in the deep meditation practice.

«I develop single-pointed focus through meditation, leading to deeper states of awareness and insight.»

In her room, Becky shut a book closed. She breathed deeply and looked at the dozen books that surrounded her on her bed.

She shut her eyes for the briefest second, got up and out of bed, and began picking up the books one by one, piling them up on the floor.

«This is the Path to liberation. It is my Path now and forever.»

She took her journal and threw it across the room like a frisbee. Pages flew all over the place as she laughed, dancing with glee.

Torres Family Home

Becky entered the house looking radiant, renovated, her body fully erect with self-assuredness but without arrogance, her movements calm and fluid, unhurried but sure.

As she advanced toward the living room, she heard the distinct grating noise of the espresso machine.

«Hello? Mom, is that you?»

Evelyn Torres sprang out of the kitchen with a shocked look.

«Becky?»

Evelyn stopped dead in her tracks, stared at Becky, mouth agape with disbelief.

Becky smiled warmly.

«You... You look so different.»

«It's good to see you, mom. It's been a long time.»

There was a moment of pause as they both surveyed each other, Evelyn with visible trepidation, Becky with a warm, peaceful smile which made Evelyn's resistance soften slowly.

«Yes, yes, it has. Oh, I was just making some coffee. Would you like some?»

«I would love that, thank you.»

Evelyn, still slightly uneasy, walked to the kitchen. Becky followed.

In the kitchen, Evelyn's nerves betrayed her, she darted from the cupboards to the fridge, to the coffee machine, avoiding Becky's calm stare.

«You should've called. I could have been prepared.»

«I'm sorry about that, it was a spur of the moment thing. I didn't even know if I would find you here.»

«Where else would I be?»

Evelyn operated the noisy espresso machine.

When the noise subsided, Becky spoke warmly.

«I'm glad I found you. I really wanted to thank you in person.»

Evelyn handed the coffee cup to Becky, her gaze shifting everywhere, avoiding looking at her daughter directly. Evelyn's body tensed, expecting one of her daughter's usual caustic attacks.

«Oh? Thank me for what?»

«For giving me my life.»

Evelyn finally looked directly at Becky, confused, skeptical.

«How do you mean?»

«I've come to realize that something much greater than you and I chose you to pass life onto me. That's the greatest gift anyone could've given me, and I'm truly grateful!»

Evelyn turned away, fidgeting with the espresso machine, waving her hand above her head.

«Oh my God, you've joined a cult, haven't you? That's all we needed!»

Becky laughed warmly.

«No, mom, but what I have been doing is studying a lot, and meditating, and working with myself to become someone I love. And I just wanted to share that with you, make you a part of that process. You're always in my heart, mom, and I would like for us to move forward together, if you want that.»

Evelyn stopped what she was doing and held on to the edges of the kitchen counter, trembling. She closed her eyes as tears began to glide down her cheeks.

«I... I have been thinking a lot too. Trying to wrap my head around everything that happened... before. And, I know I was horrible to you, and to Isa too. I don't know why you would want me to be a part of your life after what I've done.»

Becky approached her mother slowly, smiling.

«It doesn't matter why. What matters is that I want us to be together, you and Isa, all of us. We might not be able to erase the past, but we don't have to be stuck in it if we don't want to. We can recognize it, know that it's there, a part of us always, and then, without resisting, just move forward.»

Becky was now right behind her mother. She placed her hand over Evelyn's shoulder.

Evelyn shivered as she slowly reached up and touched Becky's hand, squeezing it lightly.

Becky calmly, tenderly began to wrap her arms around her mother.

Evelyn broke down into sobs.

Becky embraced her tightly, her face snuggled against her mother's.

They began rocking back and forth softly in a silent, heartfelt lullaby.

Bhutan, The Cave
8th Century

The imposing mountains at the edge of the sky were buried in snow.

The entrance of the cave—the one seen so many times before in Becky's dreams,—was very difficult to discern between the blinding white and the jutting, greyish walls of rock.

A fresh set of small footprints led from the entrance up a familiar path, precariously near the edge of the precipice.

Tashi Chidren looked tiny and delicate below the walls of snowy granite. She maneuvered carefully, as far away from the edge as she could.

She found the familiar cascade that somehow refused to freeze and filled a small copper bowl with its water.

She turned back, careful not to slip and not to spill a drop of the precious liquid until she reached the cave entrance and navigated carefully towards its interior.

Tashi moved through the serpentine tunnel until she reached the large vaulted cave.

A chant echoed, growing louder as she approached the other ten disciples. They knelt and bathed in the light of butter lanterns, facing Yeshe Tsogyal.

Behind Lady Tsogyal, the imprint of Guru Padmasambhava's body—indented in stone—seemed to shake from the lamps' reflections.

«Om ah hum vajra guru pema sid-dhi hum... Om ah hum vajra guru pema sid-dhi hum... Om ah hum vajra guru pema sid-dhi hum.»

Tashi looked at Lady Tsogyal, bowed in reverence, and approached the disciples slowly.

Lady Tsogyal looked at each of her disciples, bowed her head and pointed to the small bowl in Tashi's hands.

One by one, still chanting, each disciple took the bowl from the young girl and drank heartily, returning it to her so the next one could partake, filling their parched throats.

The last of the disciples tilted the bowl over, drinking to what seemed to be the last drops, and handed the bowl back to Tashi.

She looked at the bowl, her eyes wide with disbelief—it was still as full as when she'd filled it at the cascade.

Tashi looked at Lady Tsogyal. Lady Tsogyal nodded, smiled and pointed at the bowl.

Tashi drank from it like there was no tomorrow. Still, when she finished, the bowl remained full.

Lady Tsogyal smiled sweetly at her and gestured for her to put the bowl down.

Tashi placed it on the ground. Lady Tsogyal signaled for Tashi to sit facing her. The young girl obliged, kneeling before her Guru in reverence.

As the chanting got louder, Lady Tsogyal looked behind Tashi, beyond her disciples, toward the cavern's entrance.

Becky was standing there, smiling, taking it all in with awe.

Yeshe Tsogyal smiled lovingly at Becky and gestured for her to get closer.

The disciples and Tashi had their backs to her. Becky's eyes began to well with tears.

«I recognize you, my great Guru!»

Becky moved closer, slowly, tentatively.

When she reached the circle of disciples, she knelt, bowing her head all the way to the ground.

When she lifted her head, she was kneeling right in front of Yeshe Tsogyal, exactly where Tashi had been seconds before, tears running down her face.

«I've missed you so much!»

Yeshe Tsogyal's eyes filled Becky's vision—loving, intense, all-seeing, eternal—burrowing into Becky's eyes.

Becky closed her eyes.

When she opened them, Tashi was sitting right in front of her, almost face to face, with her back to Lady Tsogyal.

Becky looked confused, disoriented, her attention shifting from Tashi to Lady Tsogyal.

Tashi extended both her hands toward Becky. Becky took Tashi's hands.

They both began to sway slightly to the rhythm of the chant.

Tashi's and Becky's eyes went blank, trembling. A glow began to appear around their bodies as they smiled with bliss.

The chant became louder. The glow of their bodies became blinding, lighting up the cave and all of the others inside.

Becky shifted her gaze to Yeshe Tsogyal, whose eyes were focused straight on her—intense, all-knowing, eternal, overwhelming.

Becky looked at her own body, glowing intensely, blindingly, her body becoming transparent, almost a phantasm.

Yeshe Tsogyal's mellifluous voice reached Becky's inner ears, her very soul, like a warm river, «The time has almost come for you to awaken, my dear shishya.»

The bright glow began to dissipate. Becky's body became solid once more.

Tashi's body was no longer there.

«Wait, my Guru, what do you mean?»

«You will know soon, when the time comes. You and I will meet again soon.»

Becky took a deep breath. A tear escaped her eyes.

Isabel's Apartment, Guest Bedroom Present Day

Becky opened her teary eyes with a gasp. She stared at the ceiling, calmed her breath, then slowly took in her surroundings. She closed her eyes for a second, breathed deeply, and smiled.

After a bit, she slowly got up, got dressed, and left the room.

22

Bhutan, Eternity-Field Foundation Dining Hall

The large space was a tasteful combination of historical Bhutanese design with a modern, minimalist, twist. The floor-to-ceiling windows, foggy with frost, offered a breath-taking view of the snow-covered valley below from any of the dozens of empty tables.

Dr. Krishnaa Bhat arrived, picked up a tray, plate and utensils at the buffet-style station, and helped herself to small portions of the steaming delicacies.

She placed her things on a table next to a window, grabbed a cloth napkin, wiped the condensation from the glass, and peered outside.

The structure jutted out over the edge of a steep cliff, hundreds of feet above the snow-covered valley.

Dr. Bhat sat, closed her eyes, took a deep breath, meditated briefly, opened her eyes and tasted her food.

She looked around the large hall. There was nobody in sight. She frowned slightly, looking a bit confused.

«Hello again, my dear doctor.»

Dr. Bhat jumped in her seat, scared, and turned around.

Dorji handed over a copy of *The Golden Eye of Buddha*, bound with a similar gilded spine as the one in the main library.

«Here is the book as I promised.»

Dr. Bhat was still shaken. She clutched at her Japa mala, the necklace of beads strung around her neck.

«You startled me, Guru Dorji.»

«Oh, forgive me. Go ahead, open the book. I have written a dedication.»

Dr. Bhat opened the book to the first pages and saw Dorji's dedication handwritten in Sanskrit.

«'To a new friendship I hope will be everlasting, sincerely, D.D.'»

Dorji pointed to one of the empty chairs next to hers. «May I join you?»

«Yes, of course, please.»

Dorji sat too close to her. Dr. Bhat pushed her seat back slightly.

«I find you uniquely intriguing.»

«Really? How so?»

«I feel that you came here for much more than to simply participate in a conference. After all, you are well versed in the Terma treasure traditions, so, I believe there is more to your presence here than you are letting on.»

«Well, studying the traditions from books can only take one so far in understanding. But to meet a true Terton, a reincarnated disciple of Yeshe Tsogyal, well, how could I possibly pass up on that?»

Dorji eyed her up and down. «Yes, indeed. So, what have you learned so far?»

She measured Dorji's gaze before proceeding carefully.

«You can be quite beguiling, in a positive way I mean, but, even though I know the workshop is just beginning, I feel that you are holding things close to your heart.»

«Really? What do you mean?»

«I read your biography in the materials we received, and I researched as much as I could online prior to my arrival, but, like you said about me, I sense there is much more about you and your past than you are letting on.»

Dorji turned to look out toward the valley.

In the glass window he saw a reflection—a mirage, a flash of an ancient memory—of a cave bathed in hellish, flickering flames, of his body writhing and pushing, , violating the defenseless young woman with Tashi's likeness as Namkha ran toward them, knife in hand, and sliced her throat, blood spraying on Dorji's horrified face.

Dorji's hands almost touched the window as his gaze moved away from it and returned to look at Dr. Bhat straight in the eyes.

«You are a well-educated person, Dr. Bhat, so you know how much our past can chain our ego to this temporary existence, so, why dwell on it?»

«I was hoping that learning from your own journey to free yourself from those chains would serve as a guiding light for me.»

Dorji smiled slightly at her wit, but his expression turned to something cold, more dark.

«You have come across someone other than I with the auspicious signs of a Terton, have you not? Another of Yeshe Tsogyal's disciples perhaps?»

Dr. Bhat frowned and shook her head. «What do you mean? I do not know about anyone else.»

«Come on, Dr. Bhat, don't take me for a fool. Your disciple, the one who practices astrology on that dreadful tropical island, he's met someone, has he not?»

«I don't know what on Earth you are talking about.»

Dr. Bhat broke into a sweat. Her face began to turn red. She looked down at her hands—they were shaking.

«I am not feeling comfortable, perhaps something I ate, so please, excuse me.»

Dorji leaned over. «You are very skilled, madam doctor, I can sense it. But you are no match for me.»

A trickle of blood came out of Dr. Bhat's nose.

She was struggling with all she had, body shaking, fists clenched. She grabbed the cloth napkin and wiped her bloody nose.

«I have grown tired of you resisting me, so please, spare yourself of unnecessary suffering and just give in and tell me what I need to know. I have waited far too long for you to finally open up to me. I have grown impatient!»

Dr. Bhat looked around the empty hall, and out the windows.

«What? What do you mean?»

«The workshop was months ago, in the spring. Do you not remember? It is winter now. Look around you. Most everyone is gone for the season to be with their families. There is almost no one here but you, a few trusted servants, and I. And, honestly, madam, I have grown sick of waiting.»

Dr. Bhat sprang up from her seat and took a few steps back.

«What? How dare you! I demand you release me at once!»

«My dear madam, the stars are aligned against you at this moment. You do not have the strength to resist me. There is nothing you can do but accept your fate and comply. So, if you do not wish to suffer a horrible fate, give me what I need.»

Dr. Bhat winced as if she'd been stabbed in the middle of her gut.

The blood continued to trickle from her nose. Her chest heaved, losing air.

She slid toward the windows with great effort, pressing her hands against the cold glass.

The words spilled out of her mouth uncontrollably, against her will. «August 10th, 1991... one forty five A.M., city of Guaynabo.»

She began to choke and cough.

«There, there, you see? It is so much easier for you to obey.»

Dr. Bhat's pain appeared to recede. The blood stopped flowing from her nose.

Still shaking, she leaned against the glass, panting.

Dorji closed his eyes.

«Well, well, I see she is a woman. She suffered great difficulties with her father. Naughty, naughty boy, her father. So sad. She is, indeed, the one disciple I have been waiting for, but she is not quite awakened yet. Odd that she would trust a man, your disciple, to be her guru after having been violated and betrayed by so many men.»

Dr. Bhat, still breathing heavily, turned her head toward him.

«You... You calculated her natal chart off the top of your head?»

Dorji smiled cynically. «I have had quite a bit of time to hone my astrological skills, madam.»

Dorji opened his glowing, red eyes and stared at Dr. Bhat coldly, evil seeping from his pores.

«I must meet this young woman in person soon but her exact location escapes me for some reason.»

Dr. Bhat began shaking. Another trickle of blood oozed out of her nose, reaching her lips. She wiped it off.

«What about your astrological skills? I don't know where she lives! Find her yourself!»

Dorji smiled devilishly. «Once again, I have underestimated your strength, madam. You were clever to erase your disciple's number from your mobile phone so I cannot trace him that way.»

«You are not really one of the disciples, are you? You are something else! You are a fraud, an imposter!»

«Such pontificating. We are all imposters one way or another.»

«Stop this! I demand my release!»

«Now, now, calm down. I need you to do something for me.»

Dorji gestured and Bhatua, stealthy as ever, appeared. He grabbed Dr. Bhat by the arms and dragged her away.

She was too debilitated to resist.

Puerto Rico, Soto's Office

Soto sat on the floor in the lotus position with his back to the low console table with Dr. Krishnaa Bhat's photo on it.

The lights were off, with only the flicker of two candles making the shadows quiver.

The wavy, translucent astral body of Dr. Bhat slowly materialized. Soto's astral body soon appeared next to his physical one, two blurry apparitions communicating with each other.

Their lips didn't move but they could feel their own ethereal voices inside their minds.

«My dear shishya. It has been awhile.»

«Yes, months. I was worried. I called your office. They are also worried.»

«I know, I apologize. I will let them know I am fine.»

«Where are you?»

«I am still at Guru Dorji's Foundation. He invited me to stay longer to study with him directly.»

«That's wonderful! Have you mentioned my client's case to him?»

«Oh yes! He has confirmed our assessment. She is indeed one of Yeshe Tsogyal's reincarnated disciples close to her awakening!»

«That's wonderful news! Her progress in Dharma practice is enormous, that would explain it!»

«Keep working with her, but do not reveal this information to her yet. Guru Dorji is interested in meeting her in person and giving her the initiation ritual personally.»

«That would be amazing! I will keep this between us while I continue to support her practice.»

«Guru Dorji will be contacting you directly very soon, as soon as the stars are properly aligned for her ritual. I am honored to be a part of this revelation, shishya, bless you!»

«On the contrary, the honor is mine and I thank you! I'm looking forward to meeting Guru Dorji in person soon! Will you be coming with him? Will I see you too?»

«I am afraid not, my dear shishya. I have decided to remain here at the Foundation working on more advanced practices that may take months or even years to master.»

«Wow, that's a surprise! I hope everything goes well for you.»

«We will keep in touch, shishya, one way or the other. You have gotten so much better at this. See you!»

Dr. Bhat's astral body vanished into a wisp of vapor. Soto's astral body dissolved into nothingness.

The physical Soto opened his eyes with a wide, excited smile, jumped up, turned on the lights and blew out the candles.

Bhutan, Eternity-Field Foundation, Dr. Bhat's Quarters

A disheveled, raggedy Dr. Bhat cowered, shivering, sliding back on her bed, pressing against the wall.

Druk Dorji, with Bhatua by his side, stood in front of her.

«Thank you. That was very well done, madam. Administering the girl's initiation personally will afford me much more power over her to take possession of her Terma treasure.»

«What will you do to me after you get everything you want?»

«I was hoping you would join me once I achieve my Mava Marga initiation, the culmination of the left hand practice. My control over all matter, living, and dead will then be complete. Why waste a life if it can serve me?»

«The only powers I serve are those based on compassion.»

«Compassion? Thanks to your beloved Guru Padmasambhava and his whore, Lady Tsogyal, our own Gods turned against us! Our priests were banished from the king's side, thrown out onto the streets, hunted like animals, hated and reviled by the very people they had protected for centuries! Where was their compassion then?»

«Your father was one of the king's priests? I am so sorry it turned out that way. It was his Karma.»

«Karma? That devil and his whore consort put our kingdom under their spell! First they stole my birthright and then they cast a spell on the woman I loved and made her kill my own father!»

«That is impossible! Guru Padmasambhava and Lady Tsogyal would never do such a thing. Their entire souls were devoted to respecting life, all life, above everything else! For them all life is precious!»

«Well, dear madam, they sure as hell did not respect my father's life! And I have made each and every one of their disciples pay for it for hundreds of years. Only one remains, soon to be mine, soon to die in his name.»

Dorji's eyes glowed a fiery red, his expression pure, unadulterated hatred.

Dr. Bhat's nose started pouring blood as she yelled with pain and fainted, plopping down on the bed.

Puerto Rico, Soto's Office

Becky strutted in, very excited. She ran over to Soto and hugged him warmly.

He was taken aback, slightly embarrassed, but smiled.

«I did it! I can't believe it! I've been able to stop my mind for longer than I ever imagined, I mean, completely! I'm controlling my dreams, so, thank you, thank you! You are unbelievable!»

«Don't thank me, you're just seeing the results of your discipline and commitment during these months.»

«And modest too. Ha, ha, ha! You're a great teacher, so stop resisting and accept the praise!»

Soto laughed. «Okay, you got me! Praise accepted, *señorita*. I'm a great teacher, thank you! Speaking of which, please sit your posterior on the floor and let's get right to it.»

Becky opened a yoga mat and sat on the floor like a giddy schoolgirl.

Soto sat facing her. They both assumed the lotus position and took deep breaths.

«Today I have a new mantra for you to learn and practice.»

Becky nodded quietly.

Soto placed a piece of paper in front of her with the words in Sanskrit as well as phonetic English.

Soto pulled out his japa mala, the prayer beads. Becky had hers around her neck. She pulled hers out.

«Oh, here we go. Listen carefully.»

«Hung orgyen yul gyi nubjang tsam. Pema gesar dongpo la. Yatsen chok gi ngödrub nyé. Pema jungné shyé su drak. Khor du khandro mangpö kor. Khyé kyi jesu dak drub kyi. Jingyi lab chir shek his sun. Guru pema siddhi hung.»

Becky practically jumped on the phrases without pause, without even reading them, almost as if she knew them by heart.

«Hung orgyen yul gyi nubjang tsam. Pema gesar dongpo la. Yatsen chok gi ngödrub nyé. Pema jungné shyé su drak. Khor du khandro mangpö kor. Khyé kyi jesu dak drub kyi. Jingyi lab chir shek his sun. Guru pema siddhi hung.»

Soto was stunned. He stopped and looked at her, wide eyed.

«What? Did I screw up?» She asked with a quizzical expression.

«No, no, just the opposite, it was perfect! Did you get this from any of the books?»

«No. First time I see it. Why?»

«You just picked it up immediately.»

«It didn't seem so hard.»

«Very good, let's continue together.»

Bhutan, Cavern 8th Century

The disciples' chant echoed throughout the walls and vaulted ceiling, reverberating deep within their bodies and very souls.

It was the same mantra Soto and Becky were reciting.

«Hung orgyen yul gyi nubjang tsam. Pema gesar dongpo la. Yatsen chok gi ngödrub nyé. Pema jungné shyé su drak. Khor du khandro mangpö kor. Khyé kyi jesu dak drub kyi. Jingyi lab chir shek his sun. Guru pema siddhi hung.»

On the granite wall, the indented silhouette of Guru Padmasambhava flickered like a kinctoscope thanks to the flames from butter lamps.

Tashi knelt before it, looking up at him, her face one of pure devotion, tears welling in her eyes.

Soto's Office
Present Day

Becky's tears were welling in her eyes as she opened them.

«Are you okay there? I lost you for a sec.»

Becky just nodded, deepened her breath to calm down, but her voice broke from pure, unfettered emotion.

«It took me months of reading. I mean, I absolutely devoured everything you gave me to read. Then I realized the true work is not in the books, any of it. Sure, they were the key to open the door, but they were really food for my mind, which is always hungry, starving, craving, unstoppable.»

Soto listened, trying to hold back his emotion, his awe.

«But the wonder of real spiritual work is about getting out of this head, to a state of no mind at all. No mind, no body, no passions, attachments, desires, nothing. And no book can teach you that. Now I understand what you told me months ago, about practicing. And I appreciate it immensely! You have been a great Guru. Thank you!»

Becky bowed before Soto as his eyes became watery.

He recomposed himself, smiling cheerfully.

«I have some great news! I was saving it for later, but now that you, well that you pulled the rug from under me, I want to share it!»

«Yes? What is it?»

«A very important Buddhist master is coming to the Island. I don't know exactly when yet, but I'm sure it will be soon.»

Soto paused and locked eyes with Becky.

«His name is Druk Dorji and he's a reincarnation of one of Yeshe Tsogyal's main disciples.»

«Of Lady Tsogyal? Oh my God! He's coming here? Seriously?»

«And he wants to meet you in person.»

Becky's eyes darted about, speechless for a moment. «Why me?»

«He knows of your amazing progress.»

Becky looked incredulous. «Oh my! Okay.»

«It's an incredible opportunity, and, who knows, they say we don't find our true Gurus, they find us!»

«Oh, my goodness! I don't know what to say!»

Soto smiled at her broadly. «Let's get back to work then!»

आकाश

Space

23

Bhutan, Mountain Path
8th Century

Nestled among immense, snowcapped peaks, partially hidden by billowy clouds, lay the mountain's imposing rocky wall—the wall that protected the narrow path Becky had dreamed about so many times before—a forbidding path meant only for the most daring or for the most devout. A line of pilgrims, women and men of all ages covered in thick furs, trudged gingerly up its treacherous curves, like snails slithering up the mountainside towards one particular cave..

Their slow, careful march was disturbed by a hooded figure moving at a quicker pace, zigzagging among the crowd, bumping into some, shoving others out of his way, sometimes pushing them precariously close to the edge of the precipice.

The pilgrims reacted to his impertinence with varying degrees of annoyance. Some yelled at him, others scowled, still others cowered back against the rock walls holding on for dear life.

But the hooded figure continued to scramble up the path at a feverish pace without concern for safety.

He reached the entrance to the cave we were now familiar with—the cave where it all began, where Guru Padmasambhava vanquished the demonic deities and Yeshe Tsogyal taught her disciples for years.

The cave entrance was now watched over by two royal guards armed with spears and swords.

The hooded figure slowed his pace, lowered his head, hid his face as he cut the line of pilgrims entering the cavern.

Inside The Cave

Butter lanterns flickered. A chant reverberated all around.

The chant was being sung by more than twenty pilgrims seated in concentric rings facing the imprint of Guru Padmasambhava.

"Om ah hum vajra guru pema sid-dhi hum."

Those just now entering found any place they could to sit and join the others.

The hooded figure slithered his way to a dark corner, shook off the snow as he removed his furry coat, revealing his face.

Druk Dorji.

His expression was livid as he looked at the growing crowd of pilgrims, upset by their willingness to bow down to what he considered a criminal entity.

He walked out of the shadows, pushing and shoving some pilgrims, his voice booming throughout the cavern walls.

«Listen to me, everyone, I demand to know what has become of Tashi Chidren, King Raja's daughter! Where can I find her? When will she be back? Answer me!»

The chanting stopped. The pilgrims stared at Dorji—some with shock, others with disbelief—but none of them moved.

«I said answer me, right now! Where is that whore hiding?»

A rumbling of voices rose from the crowd.

The king's guards entered the cave, spears in hand, moving swiftly toward Dorji, trying to avoid stepping on the seated pilgrims.

Dorji's eyes shone a bright, ominous red as he glared at the incoming guards. His body tensed. The veins on his face and neck popped out, seemingly about to burst.

A demon-like shriek exploded from Dorji's mouth.

The guards froze in their tracks. Blood began pouring from their eyes and noses as they yelled in horror.

Pilgrims jumped to their feet, screaming hysterically, bumping into each other, trampling others, running toward the exit.

The screaming stopped. All sound became muted, dead silent.

Then pilgrims and guards exploded in a million fragments of flesh and blood, their entrails flying in all directions.

Dorji's face was covered in blood, his expression absolute evil as he relished his unholy power.

The figure of Padmasambhava indented on the wall dripped with blood and guts.

Druk Dorji's deep-throated, demonic yell broke the silence.

Puerto Rico, Roberto Soto's Office
Present Day

Becky yelled as she opened her eyes and mouth, gasping for air, flinging her arms and legs as if battling an invisible enemy. She kicked the yoga mat beneath her as she scrambled back toward the wall, covering her face as she began to sob.

Soto sprang up from his yoga mat and knelt beside her. His voice was at once soft but firm, strong yet calming.

Her ashen face and his calming gaze were caught in the flicker of the candles atop Soto's altar—the only light in the room.

«Becky. Becky. You're here, safe, in my office. I'm here. I'm with you.»

Soto poked her back with one finger gently while placing another hand on her forehead.

«Hear my voice. You're in my office, Becky. It's all right, you're safe.»

Becky relaxed, uncovered her face, blinked, wiped her eyes. Their eyes locked.

Soto lowered one hand, patting her back gently.

Becky pulled him toward her, hugging him, snuggling on his shoulder until their faces touched.

Soto pulled away from her.

«What happened? Did you fall asleep?»

Becky nodded.

«Was it a bad one?»

Becky pulled him toward her and planted a deep, soulful kiss on his lips.

Soto's eyes grew wide. He pushed her away gently and got up, flustered.

«I...I'm sorry! That was so wrong!»Becky's face was a mass of confusion, her eyes pleading for answers.

«It's okay, I... I understand.»

«Do you?»

«We've worked closely together for months, and, with everything you've gone through, you're very vulnerable.»

Becky squinted, eyeing him, and brought her knees up to her chest.

Soto tried with all his might to remain detached, clinical.

«Remember you're working really hard to get rid of emotional and sensory attachments. The less you identify with your body and your mind, the closer you will be to reaching—»

«I get it, okay! But what if what I feel is something else? More profound. Not a mere desire but something more, a deep connection?»

«It's still a trap, an illusion.»

«So our philosophy admits no empathy, no love, no bonds.»

«Empathy toward every being with no discrimination, boundless love for all life, and, by definition, if you mention a bond, it means you are separating yourself from what you're bonding with, and that is the mirage, the lie. You know full well that your goal is that there is no you, and no me. No body, no mind, no duality, only pure awareness.»

Becky jumped up and ran to him, covering his mouth with her lips.

Soto recoiled, face red, and tried to pull away. His eyes began to water. He clenched his jaw and pushed her gently away, holding her by the arms.

Soto stammered, railed on like a locomotive, fighting against his own feelings and desires.

«Becky, no. I beg you. This is very difficult for me. I mean, you're like nobody I've ever met before. But this, what you're doing right now, not only does it go against everything you've learned but it's violating a huge ethical and moral boundary for me, for us both. The relationship between teacher and disciple is sacred to me and, believe me, keeping that distance with you has been a challenge for me, almost a test of my will! I'm human and I'm not invulnerable.»

«What if this is meant to be? What if it's something I need to go through? What if it's my karma?»

«Come on, Becky, don't try to rationalize this, please.»

Becky moved away from him. Tears escaped her eyes.

«You know I get the teachings. More than that, I'm living them, breathing them, you know that.»

«Yes, I do.»

«And I get it that the goal is to feel no attachments, no passion, no desires, complete mindlessness, to eradicate the illusion of duality. And I will get there, I know it!»

«I'm certain you will.»

Becky spun around and moved closer to Soto.

«But before I get there, I need to resolve something that's eating me inside. I want to have one experience, just once, of surrendering myself to love, willingly, completely, on my own terms, not forced by anyone, not against my wishes, not out of need or loneliness, just out of pure love, even if just for a moment, before that final step before I reach that level of nothingness we aspire to.»

Soto's eyes shifted all over the place, his face red with a cold sweat. He rubbed his hands against his legs nervously.

Becky got closer and closer with every word until she was in his face.

«And I want to have that experience with you, only you, because only you would understand how important this is for me. And I hope you appreciate what it means that I choose you to go through this.»

Soto was speechless, trembling, frozen, completely enthralled.

Becky moved even closer, her lips almost brushing his.

«So I ask you, will you be the one who helps me have this one final experience before I let go of everything?»

Soto closed his eyes, took a deep breath. When he opened them again, tears streamed down his face. He shook his head in silence, trying with all his might to resist the attraction

Becky was now practically inhaling his every breath.

«Please.»

They embraced, their lips melting in a kiss that was both tender and desperate. The candles flickered as they slowly lowered themselves to the floor, their silhouettes merging in the dancing shadows.

Isabel's Apartment, the Balcony

The dark vastness of the ocean swayed in the distance with the lights of tourist and cargo vessels blinking on the horizon. To the left and right, interminable rows of condos formed a wall separating the sea from the city.

Isabel sipped a drink as her hair flew back with the wind.

Ana Ramos entered the balcony, took in the air, and then snuggled lovingly with Isabel, planting kisses on her neck.

«Mmm. The only thing greater than this view is you.» Isabel said.

Ana hugged Isabel even more tightly. «I love it when you get poetic.»

Isabel turned around, kissed Ana passionately, then returned to her view of the ocean, wrapping Ana's arms around her waist.

«So, what've you been thinking?» Ana asked.

«I'm just taking in how much Becky's changed, you know? After everything she's gone through, she's really become a different person.»

«I think everything that's happened affected all of us. We've all changed for the better.»

«Yeah, even mother. My God, I can't even imagine how she managed to do that, you know, make peace with her. I don't know if I could've done that. Which makes me admire Becky so much more.»

«What about you and your mother?»

«I've come to make peace with her, learning not to blame myself for things out of my control. But it's all been thanks to Becky. She's been more helpful to me than any therapist.»

«So, what about us? When are you going to introduce me to your mother properly?»

Isabel turned around and looked Ana straight in the eyes.

«Please don't say 'it's about time.'»

Ana shrugged. Isabel smiled.

«I know you've put up with a lot. And I love you for that. But, you're right, it's about time.»

«Hey, I didn't say it.» Ana said, smiling.

«I know. Like I said, that's why I love you so much.»

Isabel kissed Ana on the lips gently.

«Becky's organizing some kind of spiritual workshop for a bunch of people at mom's house and we're invited.»

Ana laughed. «Oh my God, Isa, the word 'change' doesn't begin to describe what's happened to your family.»

«Our family, Ana. You're a part of it and I'm making it official to mom and the whole world that night.»

Ana stared at Isabel, blushing, eyes welling with tears.

«That's right, Ana, my love. I'm not hiding you, or us, anymore. I'm happy with you, whether the world likes it or—»

Ana's lips covered Isabel's. She locked her in a warm embrace.

They very slowly swung back and forth to the rhythm of the waves.

Ana finally came up for air, wiped her eyes and stared at Isabel lovingly.

«So, where's Becky been off to these days? I haven't seen her in a while. Is she staying with friends or what?»

Isabel winked and curled her lips in a funny, wicked smile.

«I get a feeling she's working hard with her teacher for extra credit.»

«You mean the astrologer? Really?»

«I don't know for sure, just call it my sixth sense.»

«Oh, so now you're the one developing spiritual powers?»

«Nah, call it female intuition.»

Ana laughed. «Well, if you're right, good for her! She deserves to be happy! I'm glad it's all working out for her.»

«I think it's working for all of us.»

«Yes, all of us!»

They embraced and kissed with caring, loving tenderness.

24

Torres Family Home,
Living Room

The furniture had been rearranged in a circle, leaving a large space in the center.

The women from Becky's yoga practice were there including Krystal and Iraida, their instructor Abadha, Leo the healer, Ruby Camacho the martial artist, Ana, Isabel, Evelyn, and Soto as well.

Everyone's eyes were closed.

Becky addressed the group with a gentle, self-assured tone.

«Behind your left shoulder is the soul of your mother, and behind your right shoulder, the soul of your father. It doesn't matter how they are or were in this life, what stands behind you now is their pure souls. And behind your mom's left shoulder, , your mom's mother, your maternal grandma. Her father, your maternal grandfather behind her right shoulder. Same thing with your father's parents, grandma behind his left shoulder, grandpa behind his right. It doesn't matter if you never knew them, if they're alive or not, what matters is their soul is there with you, always has been and always is. Keep breathing, deep breaths, in through your nose, out through your mouth.»

The group's bellies inhaled and exhaled in unison.

Becky paused for her words to sink in.

«Behind all of them, in the same order, your entire family system, eight generations back, no matter if you don't know what they looked like, your soul knows, and they're all here with you now, generation upon generation leading all the way up to you.»

The eyes of members of the group shifted behind closed eyelids.

«And behind all these people there's a bright light, all knowing, all loving, eternal, infinite. Call it God, the universal mind, the divine, whatever works for you. And that infinite, all knowing wisdom chose those people, exactly them, to pass life forward, for generations, until it reached you. Feel and see a cascade of bright water, flowing from that divine light through each and every one of those hearts, a river of life flowing all the way forward into you.»

Becky's eyes and breath shifted in unison with the group. She was at once leader and follower. Some in the group smiled, their bodies relaxed, transfixed.

«I want you to bow down, honoring all those ancestors who were chosen to pass life forward to you. And also, bow down to honor the families of all the other people here with you, fanning out behind them, generation upon generation.»

Most in the group bent at their waist, bowing in reverence.

«Take one last, very, very deep breath, hold it for a second, and blow it out with an 'aaaah.'»

The group inhaled and exhaled with a loud «Aaaah.»

Becky opened her eyes, adjusted to the light.

«When you're ready, open your eyes.»

One by one, the members of the group opened their eyes slowly—some with slight smiles on their faces, some still in a daze.

«Thank you for being here, for trusting me, and trusting this process.»

The group applauded with smiles on their faces.

«I want to take this opportunity to thank my sister Isabel for putting up with me during all these months.»

The group clapped. Isabel blushed.

«I also want to recognize the woman responsible for all of this. She brought me and my sister into this world. And, because of that, I honor you, Mom. Look at everything I'm creating with the life you gave me! Thank you!»

Becky walked briskly toward her mother and bowed down to her.

Evelyn burst into tears.

Becky signaled Isabel to join her. They both bowed down for their mother.

Evelyn stood up and hugged them both tightly as the group yelled and applauded.

After a long while, they released their hug. Isabel looked at her mother for a second, then scanned the room, took a deep breath, invoking all the bravery she could muster.

«I want to take this opportunity to introduce to you, and the world, my loving and beloved partner, Ana!»

The group whooped and cheered.

Isabel signaled Ana to join them. Ana approached the three gingerly.

Evelyn became tense, took a deep breath, shut her eyes.

Becky elbowed her gently. «Anger is a lonely place, mom, just try to love and accept Isabel as she is,» she whispered.

Ana reached them and locked arms with Isabel. The group applauded.

Evelyn ground her teeth and attempted a smile.

«Okay, everybody, there's goodies and drinks, with and without alcohol, thanks again, enjoy, and I hope you'll join me for another one of these sessions again soon!»

Some in the group applauded as they got up and began to mingle.

Abadha ran over and hugged Becky before joining others. Isabel and Ana went to the kitchen holding hands.

Becky invited Soto to come closer.

«Mom, I want you to meet someone very special to me. This is the head of the cult I joined.»

Evelyn's eyes widened.

Becky laughed. «I'm just teasing, mom! His name's Roberto Soto. He's been my therapist, astrologer, my teacher, and a very special friend.»

Becky looked lovingly into Soto's eyes. He smiled awkwardly and shook Evelyn's hand.

«Pleased to meet you. You have a wonderful daughter, Mrs. Torres, one of the most impressive learners I've had the honor of working with. Her progress has been incredible.»

«Most of the people here are part of his team, you know, experts in different disciplines, like Abadha the yoga teacher, and Leo, the one sitting there, he's a master of healing arts.»

Becky waved at Leo. He smiled and waved back.

«Roberto is going to host a very important Buddhist monk, well, more than important, he's the reincarnation of a disciple of Tibet's first enlightened master! This man's teacher, in a past life, was a princess who became a Buddha, a self-realized being, in her own lifetime.»

Becky almost stumbled over her own words with excitement. Evelyn looked unimpressed. Soto smiled with admiration.

Becky rambled on. «A female Buddha! Can you imagine? And she taught others, like this monk, how to become enlightened. This was back in the eighth century, you know, but he's been reborn now, and he remembers everything she taught him! Isn't that wild? He's coming all the way here from Tibet.»

«From Bhutan, actually.» Soto corrected her, softly.

«My bad, that's right, from Bhutan. He's coming here specifically to meet me and to give me a ritual of initiation into that Buddhist lineage! Isn't that fantastic?»

Evelyn nodded awkwardly.

«I would love to invite him, Roberto, Isabel, and Ana to have dinner with us here, if it's okay!»

Soto shook his head. «Hold on, Becky. It's perfectly fine if you don't wish to do that, Mrs. Torres, seriously.»

Evelyn shot an icy stare toward Becky. «I would have preferred you asked me in private, dear. But given that you've cornered me, I seem to have no choice now.»

«You do have a choice, Mrs. Torres.» Soto said, sincerely. «You can say no, and that would be perfectly fine with us. We'll just take him to a restaurant or anywhere else. No worries, really.»

«I'm sorry, mom, I got too excited. That was unfair of me. I really didn't mean to ambush you like that, it just came out. So, please, don't worry, we can do it at Isa's place or at a restaurant, but I would love for you to be there, to meet this person.»

Evelyn straightened her back, puffed her chest up like a peacock and wiped some invisible lint from her dress.

«It's perfectly fine. We can host all of you here, but you and Isa have to help me, I'm not going to be stuck doing all the preparations alone!»

Becky jumped with glee and hugged her mom.

«Oh, mom! Thank you, thank you! This is going to be great! I have to tell Isa! I'll be right back.»

Becky ran and disappeared to the kitchen.

Soto's eyebrows shot up, shaking his head, smiling.

«Are you really okay with this, Mrs. Torres? You don't have to do it if it makes you uncomfortable. She'll understand.»

«I'm trying very hard to understand all that's happened to her and to my other daughter. It's been a very difficult time for me, for all of us, and now, suddenly, everything seems to be moving very fast in a completely new direction.»

Soto looked at Evelyn with a pleasant, reassuring gaze.

«I imagine it has been difficult for you. All I can say is that the direction I've seen Becky take has been positive and healthy. And the changes she's made in her life have been profound and lasting.»

Evelyn stared at Soto, taking in his words. She began to relax.

«Mr. Soto, has anyone offered you something to drink?»

Soto smiled. «No, now that you mention it.»

«What can I get you, Mr. Soto?»

«Any kind of juice would be fine, or water if you don't have juice. And please, call me Roberto.»

«I will be right back with your juice, Don Roberto.»

Soto smiled as Evelyn walked away. She stopped and turned to him.

«And, Mr. Soto. Please don't do anything to hurt my child. I'm sure you know we've had our difficulties but I assure you, I love her and care for her very much.»

Soto's smile faded, replaced by surprise.

«Of course, but why would you say that?»

Evelyn locked eyes with him, her expression serious, stern.

«You're a smart, educated man, Don Roberto, but so am I. I'm sure you can figure it out.»

She turned around and kept walking, leaving Soto frazzled.

Soto's Apartment

Soto's face was frozen, staring blankly at the ceiling with concern and not a small amount of guilt. He slowly lifted his bedsheet, revealing his naked chest.

He looked to his side. Becky was deep in sleep.

He sat on the bed slowly, careful not to awaken her. He paused, head slung down, got up, and moved to the bathroom.

Soto shut the door behind him, turned on the light, squinted at the brightness, turned on the tap, and threw water on his face.

He dried himself with a hand towel and stared at the mirror, sighing deeply, nodding his head, furrowing his brow, tightening his jaw.

He threw the towel on the floor.

«What the hell am I doing?» he mumbled.

He closed his eyes for a bit, picked up the towel, placed it on the rack, turned off the light, and opened the door.

Soto tiptoed out of the bathroom, squinted in the darkness to look at Becky. She was still fast asleep.

He walked out of the bedroom, closing the door quietly.

In The Living Room

City lights and muted street noises spilled into the small, sparsely furnished space. The sound of liquid being poured into a glass from within Soto's kitchen added to the cacophony.

Soto walked out of the kitchen drinking from a glass of water, put it on the side table, and sat on the sofa in the lotus position, hands face up on his thighs, breathing deeply, eyes slightly open.

The sounds got louder, the lights brighter. Soto shook his head, stretched his arms and shifted his body. He tried again.

Police sirens, blinking lights, motorcycles roared.

Soto closed his eyes, cringing, started to break a sweat, got up, and went to the thermostat.

The thermostat screen read: *68°F/20°C, too cold for him to be sweating as he was*, he thought. He returned to the sofa, drank a sip of water, and assumed the lotus position.

A voice blasted from a police PA system, unintelligible. The roar of a truck's motor.

Soto wiped the sweat off his brow and shook his head.

The rhythmic thump, thump from a car blasting reggaeton.

Soto scrambled to the kitchen, came back with a dish towel, wiped his face and chest with it. He sipped more water. He returned to the lotus position.

A mobile phone rang from the bedroom.

Soto jumped up, tripped all over himself, and ran to the bedroom. He opened the door as quietly as he could and ran to the night table, but the mobile phone ringing had done its damage.

Becky shifted around in the bed, up on her elbows, half asleep. «What? What is it?» Becky asked, her voice hoarse.

Soto snatched the mobile phone and turned off the sound. On the mobile phone screen: *«Unknown Number.»* Soto disconnected the call. «Probably some telemarketer, I'm sorry, just go back to sleep.»

He leaned over the bed, kissed Becky gently on her cheek, and started to leave.

«Where you going?» She was still groggy.

«Living room, to meditate.»

«Want me to join?»

Soto smiled. «Nah, that's okay. You should rest.»

Becky didn't argue. She wrapped herself up like a cocoon.

The mobile phone started buzzing in Soto's hand.

On the mobile phone screen: «Unknown Number»

Soto tapped it off again, left the room, quietly closing the door behind him, went back to the couch, and placed the mobile phone next to the glass of water.

He sat in the lotus position and breathed deeply a number of times, trying to calm down.

The street noises rose. Outdoor lights flashed ceaselessly.

Soto began sweating profusely.

He grabbed the towel and wiped the sweat off, touched his forehead with the back of his hand checking for a fever, checked his pulse, got up and checked the air conditioning again.

He put his hand over the grille and leaned over it to get a blast of air on his face and body.

He returned to the couch, sat, assumed the meditation position, breathed deeply, stretched.

The mobile phone buzzed.

«Fuck!» he muttered.

Soto finally gave in, answered the phone.

There was a loud hiss on the earpiece.

«Hello?»

«*Hello! Is this Mister Roberto Soto?*»

«Yes, who's this?» Soto replied, annoyed at what was surely a spam sales call.

«*My name is Druk Dorji. I am so sorry to be calling at such a late hour.*»

Soto jumped to his feet.

«Oh! No, no! I should be apologizing to you for being rude! Please, forgive me, I thought this was a robocall or something like that. This is such an unexpected honor, Guruji! I honestly didn't expect you to call so late at night, or, I mean so early in the morning, or, whatever time it is over there!»

«*Please, don't worry. I know this is terribly unorthodox. I wanted to make sure you received my email with the flight information and that everything is in order.*»

«Yes! Yes, I did, thank you!»

«Are we still on schedule? As you recall, we must perform the ritual during the lunar eclipse.»

«Yes, yes, of course, everything is ready for your visit. Most of the arrangements have been made. As a matter of fact, her family has been kind enough to plan a dinner for us at their home.»

«That sounds delightful. It will be my honor.»

«Is that him?»

Soto looked up, startled to see Becky standing at the edge of the room wrapped up in the bedsheet. He placed a finger over his mouth, asking her to be quiet. She looked puzzled.

«Did I hear another voice?» Dorji's voice rang out.

Becky moved closer to the sofa, ignoring Soto's plea. «Is that you, Guru Dorji?»

«Yes! Rebecca, is that you?»

Soto tried to mute the mobile phone. Becky snatched it from him.

«Please call me Becky! I am so looking forward to meeting you, guruji, I'm really excited.»

«I am extremely delighted and honored to meet you. You must be very devoted to your studies to be working with your teacher at this early hour.»

Soto looked mortified and shot a panicked, wide-eyed stare at Becky. She just smiled, teasing.

«Yes, the work has been extremely hard, you know, and very demanding. I am quite exhausted!»

Soto's face went red, he felt Becky's sarcastic double entendres were completely out of place in such a serious context—This was not the place, sure as hell not the time.

«Well, I will not bother you anymore. I suggest you devote more time to

resting before I arrive. The initiation rituals are physically demanding, so, please, you two should go back to sleep.»

Soto, embarrassed, bumbled his words and scowled at Becky.

«Yes, I should get back to bed like you say, and Becky, you should get back to your place right away to sleep too. It's best you take a break from driving here every morning to study this early, from so far away, you know? Best to rest before his arrival.»

Becky struggled to hold back from laughing, amused at Soto's over-compensation.

«I will see both of you soon.»

The mobile phone speaker beeped as the call disconnected.

Becky burst out laughing, opened the bedsheet like a superhero's cape, jumped into the sofa next to Soto, wrapping them both under the sheet, and kissed him all over.

«This is serious. Not funny at all.» Soto scowled.

Still, Becky persisted in being playful, sarcastic. «Aw, are you upset?»

Soto angrily turned away from her.

«I'm sorry. My mistake.» Becky said, taken aback, suddenly realizing she'd gone too far.

«No. I'm the one that's sorry. The mistake was mine. All mine. I should've never allowed this to go this far. I'm really, really sorry.»

Becky nodded, got up, and walked briskly back to the bedroom.

Soto looked upset, crestfallen, depleted. He waited in the darkness, looking out the windows.

Becky came out of the bedroom, hastily clothed, knapsack slung over her shoulder. She went over to Soto, leaned over, planted a kiss on his forehead, and stood straight as an arrow.

«I can't tell you how grateful I am for everything you've done for me, especially this. I'm aware it was very difficult for you and you're probably right, it never should have happened. But please understand it was a breakthrough for me, a big one. I swear it will never happen again. You have my word on that. Never again. Bye.»

Soto nodded aimlessly.

Becky left, closing the door silently behind her.

Soto's eyes became teary.

25

Torres Residence

Isabel circled the dining room table, her fingers trailing along the pristine white tablecloth as she checked every detail.

Six place settings gleamed under the soft chandelier light, crystal glasses catching the warm glow. Everything had to be perfect.

Ana Ramos pushed through the kitchen door, two wine bottles cradled in her arms.

«Got a creamy chard and a Rioja,» she announced.

«I don't think these folks drink.» Isabel straightened a fork that was already perfectly aligned.

Ana's smile was mischievous. «You and I still do, I hope.»

Becky swept into the room, and Isabel stopped mid-adjustment. Her sister looked radiant—no, more than that: Serene. Like she was glowing from within.

«My goodness, you look gorgeous!» Ana set the bottles on the sideboard and stared.

Isabel nodded emphatically. «Doesn't she? Must be some weird mystical makeup routine she hides from us. She's become a real witch!»

They all laughed, the sound light and easy.

Becky wrapped Isabel in a fierce hug before planting a kiss on Ana's cheek. «Nothing to it. Frog's legs, cat's eyes, and the occasional ride on my broomstick. Thanks for all this, sis!»

Isabel's eyes sparkled with mischief. «So, are you announcing your engagement to Soto tonight?»

«Shut up you idiot.» Becky swatted her sister's arm. «Are you announcing yours to Ana?»

«Maybe, what do you think?» Isabel leaned over and kissed Ana on the lips. They both smiled into the kiss. Ana's cheeks flushed pink.

«I'll just put these on ice,» Ana said. She turned toward the kitchen and nearly collided with Evelyn Torres, who jumped back like she'd been startled by a ghost.

Becky rushed to her mother, pulling her into a long, tight embrace before dragging both Isabel and Evelyn into a group hug.

«Okay. Come on Beck,» Isabel protested, though she was still smiling. «I spent two hours doing my makeup and you're making me ruin it.»

All three women relaxed into each other's arms.

Becky took her mother's hand and led her around the table. «I think Isa has outdone herself, don't you think?»

«Hey, honestly, Ana helped me a lot,» Isabel admitted.

Evelyn's face softened as she took in the elegant table setting. «It all looks wonderful. And you look so beautiful, honey, and so happy. I'm so happy for you, for both of you.»

Ana returned from the kitchen, nodding respectfully at the older woman. «May I get you something to drink, Doña Evelyn?»

«Soda will be fine. Thank you, Ana.» Evelyn's voice carried the formal politeness she reserved for company.

The doorbell chimed through the house.

«I'll get it.» Isabel smoothed her dress. «Must be our guests.»

Evelyn settled at the head of the table while Becky bounced into the chair beside her, practically vibrating with excitement.

«My goodness, Becky,» Evelyn squeezed her daughter's hand. «You're acting like a debutante, almost like it's your *quinceañera.*»

Becky's laugh rang out like crystal bells.

Ana returned with the soda, placing it carefully before Evelyn. «Thank you, my dear,» Evelyn said.

Isabel's voice carried from the foyer, greeting the guests unintelligibly. She entered the dining room with Roberto Soto and a shadowy figure trailing behind them

«Mom, Ana, you already know Becky's mentor and good friend, Roberto Soto,» Isabel gestured gracefully, «and his special guest from Bhutan, eh, forgive me, I forgot his name.»

The figure behind them slithered out of the shadows—Druk Dorji. He was all smiles and charm, but something about him made Becky's skin crawl.

It was his face, completely new, yet somehow disconcertingly familiar. Her smile faltered. She gripped her chair's armrest.

«Hi, everyone,» Soto's voice carried warmth and genuine pleasure.

«My pleasure to see you all again, and may I present Guru, Druk Dorji.»

Becky kept her eyes fixed on the table, avoiding looking at the stranger directly.

«That's our mom, Evelyn Torres,» Isabel continued her introductions. «My little sister, Becky, and my partner, Ana Ramos.»

Druk Dorji glided to Evelyn and lifted her hand to his lips. «It is my honor to meet you, madam,» Dorji said with a silky voice in perfect Castilian.

He turned toward Becky, and she felt his attention like a weight pressing down on her. He bowed with practiced grace.«And it is a real honor to meet you, Becky, I'm looking forward to our work together.»

«Oh, my! Your Castilian is perfect! I can't detect any accent at all,» Evelyn interjected, completely seduced and enthralled by Dorji's charm.

Becky managed a nod but immediately shifted her gaze away from him.

«Please, have a seat,» Isabel gestured toward the chairs. «Is there anything I can get you to drink?»

Ana moved toward the sideboard. «We have some wine, soda and juice.»

Becky's head snapped up, her eyes flashing as she scowled at Ana. Ana looked confused by the sudden hostility. «They do not drink alcohol,» Becky said sharply.

Dorji's smile widened. «Wine will be perfect, thank you. Preferably red.»

Soto cleared his throat. «Any juice will be fine with me.»

«Wine and juice coming up!» Isabel's voice was perhaps a bit too bright. «Becky, what would you like to drink?»

Becky shook her head without looking up, tension radiating from her hunched shoulders.

Isabel caught Ana's eye and they both retreated to the kitchen. The silence stretched uncomfortably until Evelyn filled it.

«So, Mr. Dorji, is it?»

«It's... Guru Dorji, mom.» Becky's correction came out as a low growl.

Evelyn shot her daughter a sharp look before turning back to their guest. «Yes, Guru Dorji, I don't know much about your country, Bhutan. Can you tell me a little about it?»

Druk Dorji settled back in his chair, completely at ease. «Of course, madam. It is a most beautiful country, nestled in the very bosom of the Himalayas, with an amazing ancient culture filled with magic. It is a wondrous land for spiritual fulfillment.»

«Yes, it sounds wonderful.» Evelyn's voice carried genuine interest. «Must be very cold if it's all the way up in the Himalayas.»

«You would be surprised at how warm and inviting it can be.»

Ana returned with the wine and juice, serving their guests with practiced efficiency. Isabel followed with appetizers before settling beside Becky.

«Sure you don't want anything?» Isabel's voice was low, concerned. «Are you okay?»

Becky's jaw was clenched so tight her teeth hurt. She shook her head.

Druk Dorji lifted his wine glass, inhaling the bouquet like a true connoisseur. He took a sip, his expression thoughtful.

«Hmm. An excellent Rioja. My guess is a Castillo Marqués de Murrieta Reserve 2011, 2012, perhaps?»

Ana's jaw dropped. Evelyn's eyes went wide with surprise.

«My goodness!» Ana exclaimed. «How did you do that? You do know your wines!»

Evelyn leaned forward, intrigued. «I never would've thought you monks, you are a monk, right? Well, come to think of it, many of our Catholic monks drink a lot of wine.»

Becky's tension ratcheted up another notch. «We Buddhists are not supposed to.»

Druk Dorji's smile never wavered as he took another sip. «Well, it all depends on which school you belong to, what tradition, which practice.»

Soto shifted uncomfortably in his chair. «Guru Dorji is the reincarnation of a disciple of one of Buddhism's most revered and holy female figures, Lady Yeshe Tsogyal, Tibet's first enlightened being, a female Buddha.»

Evelyn's eyebrows rose. «Oh, I didn't know there was more than one Buddha, let alone a woman.»

«The word Buddha means 'awakened,'» Soto explained, his teacher's instincts taking over. «It means an individual who's attained spiritual enlightenment, who can see reality as it truly is.»

Becky fidgeted with her cutlery, the metal clinking against her plate.

«Tell me, Guru Dorji,» Evelyn leaned forward with genuine curiosity, «what is this initiation, I think she called it, that you're going to perform on Becky? Is this like a blessing?»

«I'm here to recognize her as another of Yeshe Tsogyal's reincarnated disciples and help awaken her powers—»

Soto cut him off with a nervous laugh, shooting Dorji a warning look. Becky noticed the exchange and frowned, her face going pale, her body beginning to tremble.

«Becky has put an enormous amount of effort into studying and practicing Buddhist traditions,» Soto said quickly, «and this ritual will be sort of like a blessing, yes.»

The pressure building inside Becky finally reached its breaking point. She sprang up from the table so suddenly her chair scraped against the floor.

«Excuse me for a moment.» She strode quickly toward the kitchen, her movements sharp and agitated.

Isabel was on her feet immediately. «I'm going to check on the food. Please feel free to ask Ana if you need a refill. I'll be right back.»

She followed Becky's path, leaving behind a table full of confused faces and uncomfortable silence.

26

In the Kitchen

Becky yanked open the refrigerator door and grabbed a beer, twisting off the cap with more force than necessary. She downed half the bottle in one long gulp.

Isabel appeared in the doorway. «Mind telling me what's wrong? Oh my God! Why are you drinking again?»

«I don't know how to explain it,» Becky lowered the bottle, her hands shaking slightly. «But I swear that guy is a fake, a liar. I know he wasn't there.»

«Wasn't where, what are you saying?» Isabel moved closer, her voice gentle but puzzled.

«In Bhutan. The female buddha he's talking about, Yeshe Tsogyal. He was never her disciple!»

Isabel stared at her sister and laughed, the sound sharp in the small kitchen.

«What's the fucking joke?» Becky's voice rose.

«Becky, for God's sake,» Isabel shook her head, «is this about that lady hiding things all over the world centuries ago for her students to find years later? Come on. Seriously? You don't really believe any of that, do you?»

Becky grabbed Isabel by both arms, her grip firm and desperate. «I'm dead serious, Isa. Somehow, don't ask me how or why, but I... I swear I've seen Yeshe Tsogyal and her disciples! I've seen her in my dreams. I've seen them all, for years, every night, for most of my life, Isa!»

Isabel searched her sister's face, looking for signs of a breakdown. «So now you're convinced you're what, a reincarnated goddess?»

«Not a goddess, just her disciple. Maybe. I... I don't know. It's weird. A gut feeling I have, hard to describe. I don't think I'm making this up. Somehow I know I'm not!» Becky's voice was steady, certain.

Isabel studied her sister with growing concern. Was this what a psychotic break looked like?

Becky noticed her sister's look and met her eyes with firmness. «I'm not crazy Isa, I swear,» Becky's grip tightened. «This is real, as real as it gets!»

«Ok, ok,» Isabel tried to keep her voice calm. «Assuming what you say is true, don't you think Soto would've said something by now? Shouldn't he have seen it in your horoscope or something? How come he hasn't told you anything about it?»

The question hit Becky like a physical blow. She stared at Isabel, the implications sinking in like stones dropped in deep water.

Without another word, she darted back toward the dining room, leaving Isabel alone and thoroughly confused.

Becky burst into the dining room and leaned down to whisper in Soto's ear. Dorji watched them with predatory interest.

«Can you come with me?» Her breath was hot against his ear. «I need to ask you a question.»

«Right now?» Soto looked uncomfortable.

«Yes right now. In private.»

He pushed back from the table reluctantly. «I'm sorry, Guru Dorji, Mrs. Torres, Ana, please excuse me.»

Dorji's smile was indulgent. «I understand. Go ahead. By all means, indulge Rebecca Torres. She deserves all your attention. After all that she has suffered in this life.»

Becky straightened like she'd been struck by lightning. She stared at Dorji, nausea rolling through her stomach. She looked away quickly, then whipped her head back to glare at Soto.

«What the fuck have you said to him?»

Soto jumped up, panic written across his face. «Nothing, I swear! Guru Dorji, Mrs. Torres, Ana, we'll be right back.»

Dorji's voice cut through the tension like a blade. «Sexually violated by so many men, beginning with your father. It must have been horrible indeed. Is that not so, Rebecca?»

The words hit the table like bombs.

«What?» Evelyn's voice cracked.

«What's he saying?» Ana pressed her hand to her mouth.

«Shut the fuck up!» Becky looked ready to lunge across the table.

Soto grabbed her arm, holding her back as she strained against him with pure rage.

Isabel walked in from the kitchen, oblivious to the explosion that had just occurred. «Dinner's almost ready! Hope you're all really hungry!»

Dorji's voice was silk over steel. «You must be very hungry for your awakening, Rebecca. You must be aching for it deep inside. Or has Soto been satiating that hunger with something else?»

«No, Guru please,» Soto's voice was desperate, «she doesn't know!»

Becky spun toward him. «Wait! I don't know what?»

«My goodness, Soto!» Dorji's tone was mockingly surprised. «You haven't told her? How could you not?»

«What's he talking about?» Becky's voice cracked like a whip. «What haven't you told me? Tell me!»

«Stop Guru, she isn't ready yet!» Soto pleaded.

«What Soto has not told you Rebecca,» Dorji's voice filled the room like poisonous gas, «is what I mentioned just moments ago before your precious teacher rudely interrupted me. You are one of us, Rebecca! You are one of Yeshe Tsogyal's original disciples!»

«Don't listen to this bullshit, Becky,» Isabel stepped forward protectively. «This has gone too far!»

Dorji's eyes began to glow with an inner red light. «Can you not feel it, my child? You know the truth, and you placed your trust on this man, this false teacher of yours. And now he's taken advantage of you, violated you like all the others before him.»

«Oh God, no! Stop this!» Ana backed away from the table.

«What is this, someone please tell me what's going on!» Evelyn's voice rose to near hysteria.

«Please, Guru, stop it, stop it!» Soto begged.

Becky's face went white as bone. She stumbled backward.

«Those nightmares you have suffered all your life are not dreams, my dear child, they are real.» Dorji's smile turned seductive and devilish, his eyes burning red. «They are memories and visions of those of us who studied with Yeshe Tsogyal, including you.»

Becky retreated, terror freezing her muscles as she felt herself being pulled into his hypnotic gaze. Soto reached for her. She shoved him away with surprising strength.

«Is it true?» Her voice was barely a whisper. «Did you know this all along and didn't say anything?»

«Didn't say what? I don't get it.» Evelyn looked around the table desperately.

«We weren't sure,» Soto's voice broke. «My teacher and I hadn't confirmed it. She asked me to keep it from you because if I'd told you, you'd thought we were crazy! You weren't ready for it!»

«So you did know, you son of a bitch!» Becky's scream filled the room. «How could you not tell me?»

«Somebody, please, I'm going crazy!» Evelyn gripped the edge of the table.

Ana moved toward Isabel, seeking safety in numbers.

«Wait a minute, mom!» Isabel's voice cut through the chaos. «Becky, please, do we have to do this now?»

«Yes, now!» Becky was beyond reason. «All this time you lied to me, just like my father and all the other fucking worthless men in my life, you asshole! You disgust me!»

She raised her hand to slap Soto. He recoiled, completely defenseless.

But at the last second, she stopped and pulled her hand back—he wasn't even worthy of a slap.

Dorji slammed both hands on the table with a sound like a gunshot. The utensils jumped and clattered.

«Enough of this nonsense!» His voice boomed through the room. «You've been chosen to uncover Terma treasure! I have waited countless years and traveled thousands of miles to find you. And now you must fulfill your destiny! You must be initiated by me during the eclipse!»

Becky doubled over, nausea hitting her in waves. She reached for the wall to keep from collapsing.

«My dear girl,» Dorji's voice turned sickeningly sweet, «rejoice in realizing your true identity, this is your destiny, come with me and be awakened!»

Becky straightened, finding strength in her anger. «Fuck you both!»

She turned to run, stumbling slightly.

Dorji shot out and grabbed her arm. For a moment their eyes locked. Becky recoiled at the sight of his bright red, gleaming eyes.

She twisted his wrist with a precise martial arts move, breaking his grip, and stormed toward her bedroom.

The slam of her door echoed through the house.

Dorji threw back his head and laughed, the sound cold and cruel. «She is quite the prize, is she not?»

Soto's face was pale with shock and anger. «Guru, with all due respect, the way you handled this was all horribly wrong, completely uncalled for!»

Dorji shrugged and finished his wine in one swallow. «Just being honest and straightforward, unlike you.»

Evelyn shot up from her chair, her body rigid with maternal fury. «Don't you ever touch my daughter again, do you hear me? I don't care who you are or what kind of voodoo you practice, I want you out of my house right now.»

Dorji lifted his hand, pointed it at Evelyn, her body involuntarily landed on her chair like a rag doll, her eyes filled with surprise and fear.

Dorji rose gracefully and bowed to the group. «Very well. Thank you for your hospitality. Roberto, are you coming with me?»

«No, I don't think so. I will contact you later.»

«Fine. You all have a pleasant evening. I will walk myself out. Just make sure Rebecca is set for our ritual. I will contact you with the details.»

Soto tried to hide his anger and disappointment.

Dorji turned and left them standing in the wreckage of what was supposed to be a perfect dinner.

Evelyn's trembling voice cut through the silence like a blade. «Mister Soto... I... I don't know what happened just now but... I believe you owe us an explanation.»

«Yes, I can understand that,» Soto's shoulders sagged with defeat, «but I would rather discuss this in Becky's presence if you don't mind.»

Evelyn's scowl could have melted steel. «I do mind! You better start talking!

«Hold on one second, mom, please! I'll go see if Becky's alright and if she wants to come back down. I think she deserves to be here to listen to this explanation too,» Isabel said, though her voice quivered, suggesting she was afraid of what those details might be.

27

Becky's Old Bedroom

Becky paced her childhood bedroom like a caged animal, her hands making brief, anxious contact with the artifacts of her past. She yanked open dresser drawers, searching for the old photo album, then slammed them shut. She threw open the closet and shoved her old clothes around on their hangers, her face a mask of fury and confusion.

The front door slammed somewhere below. She moved to the window and peered through the shades.

Mohammed held open the door of a massive black Lincoln Navigator. Dorji reached the vehicle but stopped, looking up directly at her window. His smile made her skin crawl.

Becky jerked back from the window, pressing her spine against the wall. She heard the SUV door slam and the vehicle pulling away.

A knock on her door made her jump.

«Becky?» Isabel's voice was soft, worried. «It's alright. He's gone. You can come out now.»

«What about Soto? I didn't see him leave.»

«No. He wants to talk to you.»

«Yeah, I bet he does!»

«Come on, Beck, I'm sure there's an explanation for all this.»

Becky shook her head, tears of rage and betrayal burning her eyes. One droplet escaped, trailing down her cheek.

«Please, Becky,» Isabel's voice carried a note of desperation. «I thought we were done with this talking through doors stuff.»

Despite everything, Becky smiled weakly. Her body relaxed slightly as she opened the door.

Isabel stood there with a puppy-dog expression that almost broke Becky's heart. Becky pulled her sister inside and held her tight.

«Fuck Soto! Fuck all of this!»

«Let's find out what he has to say,» Isabel rubbed her back soothingly. «I mean, I can't leave him alone downstairs with mom, she'll rip him to shreds.»

«He deserves it.»

«I know, but, come on, let's get this over with. We listen to his bullshit, we send him away, and move on. Come on, the food's getting cold.»

Becky looked at her sister with pure adoration, took a deep breath, and grabbed her hand. «Okay, let's do this. I'm hungry, and pissed off!»

They walked toward the dining room together, Becky drawing strength from her sister's presence.

The Dining Room

The scene that greeted them was like a war council. Evelyn sat with her arms crossed, studying Soto like a queen deciding how to execute a traitor. Soto paced nervously, wringing his hands. Ana sat at a safe distance, gulping wine.

When the sisters entered, everyone froze. Becky's eyes locked onto Soto with venomous intensity.

Soto broke the ice. «First of all, I want to apologize for all this—»

Isabel's eyes rolled back in her head. Her body went rigid, then began convulsing violently. Blood poured from her nose as her mouth twisted in agony. She toppled toward the floor.

Becky lunged forward, catching her sister's falling body, cushioning her impact even as Isabel's weight drove them both to the ground.

«Oh God, Isabel!» Becky's scream tore from her throat.

Soto dropped to his knees beside them. Ana jumped up, her eyes bulging with disbelief. Evelyn stood up, frozen, at the head of the table.

Soto touched Isabel's forehead and jerked his hand back in shock. «Mrs. Torres, I need you to call 911, right now! Ana, I need you to get some ice, she's burning up!»

Becky cradled Isabel's twitching head and torso, her own body absorbing the violent spasms. «Oh, my God, oh my God! Isa?»

Ana ran for the kitchen. Isabel's body went limp as her bladder released.

Evelyn moved slowly around the table, staring at her stricken daughter. «Isabel? Are you all right, honey?» Evelyn's voice was distant, shocked.

«Mrs. Torres, listen carefully,» Soto's voice cut through her daze like a whip. «I need you to call 911 right now! Now, Mrs. Torres, do it now!»

Evelyn snapped out of her trance and ran to make the call.

Isabel's back arched as she clawed at her throat, gasping for air. Her fingernails cut deep scratches in her chest as her entire upper body shook uncontrollably.

«Does she have any condition? Has this happened before?» Soto's naturopathic knowledge kicked in.

«No! Nothing! I don't—Oh God!» Becky held her sister tighter, trying to absorb the worst of the convulsions.

Blood began flowing from Isabel's mouth.

Ana returned with a bag of ice, her face white with shock. Soto placed it under Isabel's armpit and grabbed napkins to wipe the blood away.

«My God! What's wrong with her?» Ana's voice was barely a whisper.

Soto shook his head grimly. Becky fought back tears, trying to be strong as Isabel continued seizing in her arms.

Evelyn's voice echoed from the kitchen, shouting unintelligibly into the phone.

Then Isabel stopped breathing. Her eyes rolled back, showing only white.

Soto checked for a pulse at her neck and found nothing.

«I need you to get up,» he told Becky urgently. «We need to get her flat on the floor.»

Together they managed to slide Isabel's body onto the floor. Soto immediately began CPR, pushing hard on her chest, breathing into her lungs, getting her blood all over his mouth, then pushing her chest down again.

Nothing.

Evelyn returned from the kitchen. «Ambulance is coming—»

She froze at the sight before her: Becky on her knees crying desperately, Ana pressed against the wall in shock, Soto pounding on her daughter's chest.

Isabel suddenly gasped, spewing blood as her eyes fluttered open. She looked at Ana with love, then at Becky, trying to smile. Her lips moved but no words came.

«Fight, sis! Come on, stay with me!» Becky leaned over her.

Isabel's eyes rolled back again. Her spine arched violently as she vomited a gush of blood across Becky's face.

«Isa, my God!» Becky fell backward, wiping her sister's blood from her eyes.

Ana ran to Evelyn, wrapping her arms around the older woman and gently turning her away from the horror.

Isabel convulsed again. Soto stuffed a napkin in the corner of her mouth to prevent her from biting her tongue.

Becky got back on her knees, her face inches from her sister's. «Isa, Isabel, don't you dare leave me! Come on, fight, goddammit!»

Blood began trickling from Isabel's eyes.

Becky screamed.

Isabel's final scream was inhuman, a sound of pure agony. She convulsed one last time, vomiting more blood, bleeding from every opening in her head.

Becky and Soto tried to hold her, but suddenly Isabel's body went completely limp.

«No! No! NO!» Becky's voice broke.

Soto began CPR again, smashing his fists against Isabel's chest with desperate force.

Every phone in the house began ringing at once—landlines, mobile phones, all with different ringtones creating a cacophony of electronic noise.

They all jumped at the sudden sound.

«Could it be 911 calling back?» Evelyn's voice was small, confused.

«All phones at once?» Ana looked around in bewilderment. She ran to her mobile phone and answered. Her face went pale. All the ringtones stopped simultaneously.

Ana looked over at Becky with frightened eyes. «Becky? It's for you.»

Becky lifted her gaze from Isabel's still body. «What? Who?»

«It's him. The man who was just here.»

Becky shook her head in confusion. «What do you mean?»

«He wants to talk to you.»

Becky looked at Soto. He opened his eyes wide, shrugged helplessly, and continued trying to revive Isabel.

«Can you put it on speaker?»

Ana touched the screen.

Dorji's voice filled the room, booming and echoing with unnatural resonance.

«*Hello, Becky.*»

«Hello?»

«*So sorry about your sister.*»

Ana looked at Becky with growing alarm.

«What?»

«I apologize for what I did to her but it is necessary to make you aware of how serious I can be.»

The words hit Becky like physical blows. «What're you talking about? What the hell do you know about my sister?»

«I can end her life, painfully, right now, Rebecca, so listen carefully. I need you to meet me so we can complete your initiation ritual tonight, during the eclipse. Then, you can lead me to your terma treasure and we can avoid spilling any more blood. Do you understand?»

«Are you crazy? What the hell are you talking about? What ritual? My sister is dying, shut the fuck up!»

Becky jumped up and snatched the phone from Ana's hand. Evelyn stared at her daughter with horror.

«Silly girl. You think you can disconnect the call? Really?»

Becky looked through the sliding doors into the darkness, squinting, trying to see if he was out there spying on them. Nothing.

Isabel suddenly screamed in agony and grabbed her head. Blood gurgled from her eyes, nose, ears, and mouth. Soto pulled back, frightened, trying frantically to clean up the bleeding.

«I can end all your lives right now, little girl, do you understand me?»

Becky shivered, looking desperately between Ana and Soto. Evelyn's face went ashen as she collapsed into a chair, her fingernails digging into the tablecloth.

«I don't know what you're talking about! I don't know what you want from me. Leave us alone!»

Isabel screamed again, the sound horrible and inhuman. She convulsed, vomiting blood, more bleeding from her eyes, ears, and nose. Soto tried to hold her but her body went limp again.

«No, no, please stop!» Becky's voice cracked. «If you're really doing this, just stop it! I don't know what it is you want from me, I don't care, just tell me what you want, just please stop!»

«The ritual must be performed tonight, during the moon's eclipse. I will send for you. If you do not meet me there, everyone you love will die in a most unpleasant way. Do you understand?»

«Yes, yes! Okay, fine, come and get me, just stop this!»

The line went dead.

Becky stood in the sudden silence, shaking uncontrollably.

Ana held on to Evelyn. Evelyn rocked back and forth, terror etched in every line of her face.

Becky turned slowly toward Soto and Isabel.

Soto looked up at her, his face drained of color, tears streaming down his cheeks. «She's gone, Becky. I'm so sorry!» His voice broke completely.

He collapsed next to Isabel's body, defeated.

Becky felt the world tilt. She tried to hold onto the table but her legs gave out. She dropped to one knee, retching, but her stomach was empty.

She stared at Isabel's still form and let out a scream that seemed to come from the depths of her soul. She looked at Soto through a haze of grief and rage.

«This is all my fault, isn't it? All my fault! All my nightmares, they were real, weren't they? And you knew it all along!»

Soto closed his eyes and shook his head. «No. I... I wasn't sure. I still don't know for sure.»

Becky crawled to Isabel's side, her frilly white dress soaking up her sister's blood. «Isa... I'm... I'm so sorry, you're all I had, and I did this to you! I killed you, Isa, I killed you, it's all my fault! I gotta go, I have to leave! You all have to leave here, right now! He will kill all of you too... I have to leave you. You have to go! Go! Now, all of you!»

She struggled to her feet, dizzy and disoriented.

«What? Wait!» Evelyn's voice was desperate. «The ambulance is coming, you can't leave! You can't leave us! Don't go!»

«I'm sorry, I can't... I just, I just have to go now, I can't be here right now, I just can't, sorry!»

«Becky?» Ana let go of Evelyn and stepped forward. «You're in no condition to drive, and—»

«I have to go! And you should all leave before... He...Go, just go, right now, go hide, go!»

Soto slowly got to his feet and moved toward her. He reached out gently to touch her shoulder.

«You're in shock, Becky, you need to stop.»

Becky spun around and struck him with a lightning-fast martial arts chop that sent him crashing to the ground.

«Don't you dare touch me again. Ever!» Her voice was deadly quiet, ice cold. «If you care about me, get my family out of here now before he or his people come to get me. He shouldn't find you here. If this is all true, then we're all in danger. Get the hell out, as far away as you can! Please!»

She grabbed Isabel's car keys from the counter and left, disheveled and soaked in her sister's blood.

The front door slammed behind her like a gunshot.

In the distance, a siren wailed, growing closer.

Ana moved slowly to Isabel's bloodied body and began to cry uncontrollably. Evelyn covered her eyes, on the verge of shock, sobbing.

Soto picked himself up off the floor and touched Ana gently on the shoulder. «I... I hate to say this, but I think she's right. As soon as the ambulance arrives, we should get going. I'll figure out where we should go.»

Evelyn uncovered her face. «What are you talking about?»

«I'm afraid Becky might be right. We're all in danger if we stay here. We need to hide. Far away.»

Ana clutched Isabel's body tightly, rocking back and forth, sobbing uncontrollably.

The siren was almost at their door.

28

Secluded Beach

Isabel's car screeched to a halt where the pavement ended and the old dirt road began, surrounded by tall, scraggly bushes and palm trees. The sound of waves crashing echoed somewhere in the darkness ahead.

Becky killed the engine and stepped out into the pitch-black night. She stumbled through the bushes, tripping and falling until she cleared them and reached the sand.

She kicked off her shoes and threw them away, then walked barefoot across the beach until she collapsed to her knees facing the shore.

She sat in the sand and stared up at the sky. The moon had only a sliver of white remaining, the rest was a reddish shade of amber.

She laughed, the sound manic and broken, wrapping her arms around herself. «The fucking problem's me.»

Her bare toes dug into the sand as tears began to flow. «It's me. The problem is all me. It's always been me. Not mom, not dad, always me!»

She stood and walked slowly toward the ocean. The cold water shocked her feet but she didn't stop.

She looked up at the moon—the orb had become completely blood red.

She continued to trudge aimlessly towards the ocean. «It's always been me, Isa. Oh my God, Isa, what did I do to you?»

The waves crashed against her calves, then her thighs. She kept walking until they reached her waist.

«How could I bring you into my shit? How could I destroy the only one I love? The only one that ever love me?»

The waves reached her chest, lifting and dropping her like a toy. One wave smashed into her face.

Becky spat out saltwater and laughed hysterically, spinning and jumping in the surf. «All this time, I've been the whole fucking problem, the whole problem! Fucking everyone's life up! What the fuck, I even ended your life, Isa, I fucking killed you!»

The next wave submerged her completely.

Becky came up flailing, spitting water. She surfaced and looked up at the moon—it seemed larger, its eerie red glow a reminder of Dorji's evil eyes.

She shivered. «There's your fucking eclipse, you fuck! Shove it up your ass!»

Another massive wave covered her.

This time she didn't surface. She stopped fighting the ocean and let herself get dragged by the current, into the depths, into the darkness, into the void.

29

Bhutan, Cave Entrance 8th Century

The memory came to her like a vision painted in starlight.

Eight hundred years ago, high in the Himalayan mountains, Tashi Chidren lay dying in the snow. An arrow protruded from her belly, and the cold seeped through her bones.

The Old Man knelt beside her, offering what comfort he could.

The sound of approaching footsteps crunched through the snow. The Thugs arrived with swords drawn, murder in their eyes.

The Old Man raised his spear, ready to defend her with his life.

But something impossible happened.

The Thugs stopped dead in their tracks, their mouths falling open in wonder. They threw down their weapons and fell to their knees.

Behind them, Tshering Chime appeared, his face twisted with fury. «What the hell are you doing? Kill them!» he screamed in Dzongkha.

The Old Man kept his defenses up but looked back in amazement.

Tashi had risen. She pulled the arrow from her abdomen as if it were nothing more than a thorn and tossed it aside. Where there should have been a wound, there was only smooth, unblemished skin with a faint blue glow.

In the snow where her blood had fallen, blue flowers began to bloom.

Tashi's face was serene, touched with the slightest smile. She began to levitate, rising sixty centimeters into the air, floating toward the Thugs with otherworldly grace.

The Old Man bowed his head in reverence but kept his spear ready.

Tshering Chime went livid. He drew his enormous sword and lunged toward Tashi.

The Thugs leaped to their feet, grabbing him and wrestling the sword away before throwing him to the ground like a rag doll. One of them knelt before Tashi, offering Chime's weapon.

Tshering Chime's eyes glowed red with hatred as he glared at her. «You defiled our Gods, usurped my power, dishonored my family, so you and your kind must die, you whore!»

One of the Thugs struck him across the face.

Tashi shook her head sadly. She took the sword, raised it high above her head. Tshering Chime recoiled in fear, expecting to be struck. But instead, Tashi swung the sword away and hurled it toward the precipice.

«All life is precious,» she said in their native Dzongkha.

The Thugs looked on with even greater reverence, some weeping openly.

Tshering laughed diabolically and spat at Tashi's feet. The angry Thugs lifted him and carried him toward the edge of the abyss.

«No!» Tashi commanded. «All life is precious. None of us has the right to judge anyone!»

The Thugs released him.

Tshering looked at her with pure contempt. «I will die before I violate my beliefs and my family's honor!»

He bolted to the edge of the path and threw himself into the precipice.

Tashi closed her eyes, then faced the Thugs with infinite compassion. «I am sorry. But this was his karma. We must accept his destiny as it was meant to be. He will forever have a place within my heart.»

She glided slowly down to the ground. The Thugs prostrated themselves before her, their faces buried in the snow.

«Remember!» she told them gently. «All life is precious!»

Secluded Beach Present Day

The memory faded. Becky blinked and found herself back in the present, drowning in the dark ocean.

Becky was surrounded by complete darkness. A large bubble escaped from her mouth as she gurgled and tried to swim to the surface. But the surface was too far, too dark, impossible to reach.

Her eyes closed as another bubble rose from her lips. She slowly gave up swimming, out of energy, lost, defeated.

Then something massive bumped into her from below, pushing her upward at incredible speed.

Becky's eyes flew open as she blindly grabbed the edges of the object and held on for dear life. Her face burst through the surface, expelling water and coughing violently as she clutched whatever had lifted her.

The large, rubbery mass glided toward shore, carrying Becky on its back.

As the waves crashed harder near the beach, Becky slid off and found herself feeling sand beneath her feet. She struggled to stay up as the waves crashed around her legs.

Something, large and alive, brushed against her leg in the darkness. She stumbled back, slightly scared.

Then she saw it, slowly crawling out of the water, now visible under the bright, uneclipsed moon.

It was an enormous leatherback turtle—in Castilian, a *tinglar*, the largest species in the world. Nearly seven feet long, graceful and powerful in the water, she now struggled to drag herself on the sand with huge paddle-like flippers to reach her nesting ground.

The waves crashed around her ancient form.

Becky hobbled out of the water, crying and coughing, catching her breath. She saw other huge turtles emerging from the sea nearby, making their slow, majestic march to lay their eggs.

She stumbled and fell to her hands and knees beside her savior's massive head—noble, wise, powerful. A survivor like she was and savior like she would need to become.

A flash of understanding hit her: Kurma, Vishnu's incarnation, half-man, half-turtle.

She rolled onto her back, crying and laughing at once. «Kurma, you saved me, ha, ha, ha! Yeshe, my true Guru, I understand everything now, completely. All life is precious, starting with my own! Thank you! Kurma, thanks for saving me, for protecting life!»

She looked up at the moon. Only a sliver of darkness remained from the eclipse; the moon was almost completely clear, immense, and shining brightly.

Her eyes closed.

Everything went black.

Flashes of light, unintelligible voices, and faces swirled in the darkness.

Becky opened her eyes to see blurry silhouettes swirling above her. As her vision focused, she gasped.

Yeshe Tsogyal's radiant face hovered over her, surrounded by all the other disciples from Bhutan, all smiling with infinite love.

Becky's eyes opened wide as she smiled broadly.

Lady Tsogyal touched her forehead with gentle fingers. «This is your awakening, Becky. You were once born as Tashi, and born millions of other times before that. Now, in this lifetime, you must go to the aid of your loved ones, and confront your past, so you can restore balance, peace and harmony to this world.»

«Thank you, my Guru. I will protect them and I will confront this evil face to face, so I may share your teachings for the benefit of all humanity.»

A blinding white light filled her vision.

Becky closed her eyes, nodded, then reopened them.

A small flashlight waved back and forth, temporarily blinding her. Marta Allende, a woman in her fifties, leaned over her with the light, then turned it off to check Becky's pulse and touch her cheeks.

Becky reached up and touched Marta's face gently. The woman smiled.

Becky hugged her tightly, then suddenly sprang to her feet.

«Whoa, hold on!» Marta steadied her. «You look like you're in shock. I need you to relax!»

Becky smiled at her, then looked around at the faces of those who had found her, many wearing t-shirts or baseball caps identifying them as a group that protected turtle nests.

«Thank you. Thank you all! I'm all right. And thanks to all of you for taking care of these wonderful, majestic beings! All life is precious!»

She ran toward Isabel's car, leaving the flabbergasted group behind.

The sun was coming up, bathing the shoreline in reddish hues. Half a dozen of the huge turtles marched slowly up the sand to complete their ancient ritual of life.

30

Soto's Office

Roberto Soto sat cross-legged on the floor of his office, facing Dr. Krishnaa Bhat's photograph. He looked like he'd been through hell—his clothes bloodied, his hair disheveled, his eyes half-closed. Only two candles flickered in the darkness.

Soon his translucent astral body materialized close to his physical one.

The shimmering, mirage-like astral form of Dr. Bhat appeared across from him. Their lips didn't move as they communicated.

«Thank goodness I finally reached you!» Soto's voice echoed in the ethereal plane. «I need to warn you, Guru Dorji is a threat. I believe he's somehow responsible for the death of Becky's sister, and now he's hunting Becky down.»

«I know. He has been holding me prisoner for months.»

«What? What do you mean, prisoner?»

«Never mind that! Just listen to me carefully, shishya! This man is extremely powerful and evil. You and the girl are in terrible danger. She is one of the original disciples just like you suspected, but this man, this monster is not! He wants to kill her and steal her Terma treasure.»

«Now I get it! He was threatening to kill her family if she didn't allow him to initiate her during the lunar eclipse.»

«Do not let him do that by any means! Where is she? Is she safe?»

«I have no idea. I haven't been able to reach her after... After her sister's death. I've been busy making arrangements for her family to leave the country after she begged me to. Why does he want the Terma treasure so badly?»

«He has kept himself alive for more than a thousand years, probably using alchemy, stealing countless Terma treasures, and murdering the disciples for some sick vendetta. Becky is the only one left for him to kill in order to complete his Vama Marga initiation.»

«Vama Marga! The Left-Hand path?»

«Yes, as you know, it can lead to enlightenment for those who are strong-willed and pure of soul, but for the unrighteous, the evil, that practice leads to perversion, and this devil is the most grotesque result of it.»

«You said he hasn't completed his own initiation. What happens if he does?»

«If he completes it, he gains limitless power over life, death, the elements, everything, everyone.»

«Oh, shit, okay! So, what can I do?»

«I'm implanting a *dakshinachara* mantra in your mind. Repeat it from now on, constantly. I have been reciting it for days with many other Masters I have reached in the astral plane. This will help protect you both. Find the girl, and when you do, have her recite it too. Contact any close friends you or she may have, alert them, protect them however you can, have them hide as far away and be as isolated as possible. I know this is hard, but it is vital for their survival.»

«I will do everything I can, I promise! But how do we stop him?»

«This mantra will weaken him and disorient him, but only someone as powerful as she can defeat him.»

«Who?»

«Becky.»

«What? Are you serious?»

«My dear shishya, understand she is a Siddha, a Tulku, a powerful, enlightened being, trapped in a temporary, unawakened state. That's why this man is so anxious to control her! Once she's initiated, she will remember who she is, find her hidden treasure, regain all her spiritual powers, and then, she might be able to defeat him.»

«Might be?»

«Nothing is certain, my dear shishya, but let us hope for the best! That devil must not find her before that happens!»

«Wait. How will she be initiated?»

A pause stretched between them.

«I sense a higher power will intervene.»

«What about you?»

«Don't worry about me. Just take care of Becky and yourself. I will see you soon.»

The astral bodies faded away.

Soto opened his eyes, his lips moving slightly as he recited the protective mantra. He stood, grabbed his keys and mobile phone, blew out the candles, and left.

31

Torres Residence

The sliding glass doors exploded inward with a tremendous crash, sending a rain of glass flying across the Torres family living room. A wrought iron lawn chair bounced across the shiny tile floors.

Mohammed stepped through the destruction, the crunch of glass under his boots echoing in the empty space.

He moved methodically through the house until he found the dry pool of blood on the floor and walls of the dining room. He grabbed some of the leftovers from the top of the table, brushing some flies away and washed the food down with the wine from an open bottle.

After a loud burp, he disappeared deeper into the home and up the stairs, smashing doors and cursing loudly, unintelligibly, in some foreign language.

Isabel's Apartment

The front door flew open with a tremendous boom, sending splinters flying from the broken wooden frame in all directions.

Bhatua walked in with his hunting knife drawn, checking each empty room, the closets, under the beds. Convinced the space was completely empty, he spun around and left.

Soto's Office

The door collapsed, shredded like it was made of paper.

Mohammed stepped in followed by Bhatua. It took them only seconds to search the space.

Bhatua pulled out his mobile phone. He spoke in Dzongkha: «Empty too, guruji. What do you wish us to do?»

San Juan, Luxury Hotel

Druk Dorji's face was distorted with anger. He looked ancient, decrepit, practically a skeleton. He moved slowly, his strength and vitality drained away.

«Just get back here right now!» he screamed into the phone in Dzongkha.

He dropped the device and cursed.Dragging himself to the dining table, he opened a small valise and rummaged inside, pulling out a tiny stainless steel mason jar. He opened it and drank every drop of the liquid inside.

The transformation was as instantaneous as it was horrible to see—the wrinkles in his face, neck, and hands disappeared. His hair darkened, his muscles filled out, his vitality returned.

«Why can't I see that whore?» he muttered.

«You're looking in the wrong place.»

Becky's unearthly voice surrounded him, bouncing off the walls.

Dorji spun around, his eyes bulging with shock.

Becky's astral body was luminous, floating in mid-air, her presence filling the room with ethereal light. «I see you have reverted to your native tongue, Guru Dorji,» she spoke in flawless Dzongkha. «But you're not really a Guru, are you? You're really a Black Bön, a shaman, someone who strayed from the rightful path and became a witch.»

Dorji switched to English, his accent now slightly British. «Why you conceited little cunt! Whom do you think you are dealing with? You have tampered with forces way beyond your measly comprehension.»

His eyes glowed fiery red as he clenched his jaw, his lips moving to the rhythm of some dark mantra.

«Are you trying to hurt me? Good luck with that! You murdered my sister and you're hunting my family because you want my Terma treasure, right? Well, I have a proposition.»

Dorji released his tension, his eyes returning to normal as he tried to appear cool and in control. «How can you be here like this? When I saw you a few hours ago you were not initiated! It is not possible!»

«You of all people should know that everything is possible. Now, do you want the Terma treasure or not?»

«Of course, you stupid whore! Where is it?»

«It's back in your old neighborhood. Where this whole thing started.»

«Where do you mean?»

«Bhutan, in a cave I bet you remember really well, one where you horribly murdered dozens of innocent people for your petty fixation. I expect it will take you about three days to get here since you don't seem to have mastered the power of teleportation like I have. So, please hurry, I'm freezing my ass off!»

«What? You have the siddhi of teleportation?? Impossible!»

Becky's astral body vanished, leaving Dorji staring at empty air.

His face contorted into a mask of pure rage. His body shook and tensed, eyes glowing horrific red, veins popping from his neck and forehead. The very size of his body increased making the room appear claustrophobic.

A scream blasted from his core, booming throughout the hotel, followed by a loud, muted BANG!.

Glass windows and sliding doors exploded outward. A million shards flew in all directions.

Screams and fire alarms filled the night.

32

Dr. Krishnaa Bhat sat on her bed in the lotus position, breathing deeply. Plates of half-eaten food and soiled bedsheets showed the toll of months of captivity.

Becky's astral body materialized across from her, luminous and translucent.

Dr. Bhat gasped and opened her eyes wide in awe.

«It's so good to meet you, Dr. Bhat,» Becky's ethereal voice enveloped them. «My name is Becky.»

«It is an honor, blessed Yogini. My heart fills with joy to meet you!» Dr. Bhat jumped from the bed and fell to her knees, bowing deeply.

«No, no! Please. I don't deserve any of that. You do, for everything you've gone through to help me!»

«I bow to your limitless compassion.»

Becky's astral form nodded and smiled. Dr. Bhat stood.

«Dorji is flying back to Bhutan in a couple of days. I am meeting him at a cave in the mountains where he will attempt to steal my Terma treasure and murder me. So, I humbly ask if you can help me.»

«Anything you wish.»

«You told Roberto this guy has been alive a thousand years and you think it could be alchemy.»

«Yes, I believe so.»

«That means there is likely a lab of some kind where you're being held.»

«Yes. I have noticed very particular odors at times. Unmistakable, a mix of molten gold and mercury.»

«Can you get to it?»

«There are cameras and security guards all over the building.»

«I'll make sure that's no problem. You will be perfectly safe. Once you get there you'll know what I want you to do. I have projected the instructions into your mind. After you do this, you must pretend nothing has happened. Forgive me for asking that you tolerate more time in captivity. I will come get you after. Will you do this for me?»

«Of course. I trust you implicitly.»

«I thank you for your trust.» Becky's astral body extended her hands until they seemed to be holding Dr. Bhat's. «Now try to picture in your mind, with as much detail as possible, the corridors, the spaces where you will move, and the place where those odors are most prominent. All doors will open, the cameras will not see you, you will be invisible to everyone around you. I promise I will come to you soon, in person.»

Becky's astral body vanished.

Dr. Bhat sprang into action, splashing water on her face and putting on a light sweater. She ran to the door—it was unlocked.

She smiled, opened it carefully, and slipped out into the dark corridor.

33

Bhutan, Mountain Path

The barren snowcapped peaks of the Himalayas stretched endlessly, their paths seeming unchanged after thirteen centuries. The same treacherous mountain trail from so many of Becky's nightmares wound along sheer rock faces where one misstep meant a fall of thousands of meters.

Becky navigated the dangerous path with surprising ease. She had been here before, not only in her dreams, but also, as she finally understood, in one of her millions of previous incarnations.

Perhaps the most important one of all.

Clouds of condensation blew from her nose and mouth, yet she wore only a light sweater, jeans, and regular athletic shoes impervious to the cold.

Her lips moved silently, reciting the *dakshinachara* mantra.

She reached the waterfall where, thirteen hundred years ago, a young Tashi Chidren had fetched water for her spiritual teachers, Padmasambhava and Yeshe Tsogyal and later, for all her fellow disciples.

Becky closed her eyes, then, in a soft voice as flowing and crystalline as the waterfall itself,

«Om AhHung, Benzra Guru Jnanasagara bam ha ri ni sa siddhi Hum.»

The water shimmered with a blue glow as dozens of small blue flowers cascaded downward. She opened her eyes and plunged her hand into the freezing water.

When she pulled it out, she held the Phurba—the three-edged ritual dagger Lady Tsogyal had given her as Tashi centuries before.

She secured it in her belt and returned down the path towards the cave.

Mountain Trail

Four figures wrapped in thick furs struggled up the snowy, steep path toward the cave: Mohammed and Bhatua pushing and shoving a reluctant Dr. Bhat along, and Dorji some yards behind, puffing vapor like a dragon, breathless and struggling to keep up, his face creased, his thin goatee and eyebrows almost completely white, looking much older than usual

«There, guruji, I see her!» Bhatua called out in Dzongkha.

Dorji stopped and looked up at the plateau above them.

Becky stood calmly with her arms crossed, waiting.

The sight of her made Dorji's face contort with rage. He plunged his hand into his pocket, pulled out the tiny mason jar, and gulped its contents. His body surged, the lines in his face cleared, his beard and eyebrows grew darker, and he moved swiftly with renewed strength as he climbed recklessly, pushing his servants and Dr. Bhat aside.

Cave Plateau

Dorji and Becky faced each other once again but this time, she did not avoid his hypnotic stare, her body language and expression was one of confidence and fearlessness.

Bhatua and Mohammed arrived dragging the exhausted Dr. Bhat.

«Becky?» Dr. Bhat's voice was weak but hopeful.

«Why'd you have to bring her?» Becky demanded in English.

Dorji smiled coldly. «A guest for our grand celebration! This is such an important part of our journey I thought she should be here to share it with us, wouldn't you agree? Try anything and they will not hesitate to kill her.»

Bhatua unsheathed his commando knife and held it to Dr. Bhat's throat. Dr. Bhat winced.

Becky's eyes blazed. She tried to reassure Dr. Bhat, «Just do as he says! I'm really sorry! Everything will be alright!»

«Now, hand over the Terma treasure before I kill her, you whore!»

«So much anger.» Becky's voice was calm, almost sad. «The first time we saw each other, we were just a couple of innocent children. And I think you really fell in love with me.»

«What? What are you babbling about?»

Suddenly, thirteen-year-old Tashi Chidren stood in Becky's place.

Dorji's eyes widened in disbelief. «This can't be! What trick is this?»

Bhatua and Mohammed pulled back in fear. Dr. Bhat smiled, enthralled.

«I chose the path of enlightenment, of compassion, and non-arising,» Tashi said gently. «But you, my little thunder dragon, once pure and radiant like a diamond, turned your heart into a hard and cold piece of coal. You chose the path of pain, terror, and death.»

Dorji moved closer, examining her. «Tashi? No, it can't be!»

«How long did you hold onto my scarf, little dragon?»

Dorji's expression turned darker, malevolent. «My hatred towards you has boiled over for more than a thousand years and so has my resolve to kill you for murdering my father! You will die here today!»

«I am so sorry for your father's death. But I had nothing to do with it. He chose to kill himself, threw himself down this very precipice. A terrible decision, one that will cost him a lot of pain in his future lives. Such is the karma of killing oneself.»

«Enough! I know you're lying, he would never do that! I'm not falling for your lies! Hand over the treasure! I will show you just how serious I am! Bhatua, kill her, now!»

With a flashing motion, Bhatua cut Dr. Bhat's throat. Her eyes bulged as she clutched at her neck, blood spraying across the snow.

Tashi was Becky once more. She sprinted toward Dr. Bhat, shoving Dorji back with ease. He flew through the air like a rag doll.

Becky reached the thugs in a flash, pushing the massive Mohammed back as if he were a feather. He landed hard, his head striking a rock.

Becky knelt beside Dr. Bhat, closed her eyes, and placed her hands just above the wound without touching it.

Bhatua lunged with his dagger.

Becky spun around and looked him in the eye. «No!» she said in perfect Dzongkha. «All life is precious!»

Bhatua stopped dead, taking two steps back.

Becky's hands glowed with an eerie blue aura. Dr. Bhat's wound miraculously vanished. Where her blood had spattered, blue flowers sprouted from the snow.

Dr. Bhat sputtered, shook her head, and began to sit up.

Mohammed awakened to witness the impossible. He dropped to his knees in veneration. Bhatua threw his dagger away and fell to his knees as well.

Dorji struggled toward them, his steps short and wobbly, his body failing. «How are you doing this? How can you resist my power?»

Becky turned to face him, her expression peaceful.

She looked back at Dr. Bhat, who winked at her.

The memory came: Dr. Bhat entering the cavernous alchemy lab, surveying shelves of bottles, grabbing one and pouring its contents into the distilling contraption, sabotaging the mixture.

Dorji's trembling, old hands reached into his pocket, pulled out the vial with his potion, uncorked it and smelled. He closed his eyes briefly, knowingly, eyes that were now failing, almost blind. He knew right away–the potion had been tampered with.

«You could have chosen the path of virtue, the cessation of passions, and escaped the traps of the mind and body,» Becky said sadly. «You could have been a true guru, truly immortal.»

Dorji collapsed, his knees and hips cracking, brittle and devoid of strength. He stretched his bony hand toward her, helpless and weak, bursting into tears.

Becky knelt and touched his wrinkled face tenderly. «All life is precious, including yours. You will always have a place in my heart. Our souls will always be bonded. But our destinies are different. You will not stalk me any longer. Be in peace, my little thunder dragon.»

Dorji's teeth began falling out, his remaining hair dropping away, his skin sagging. «My... My love for you was too much... My hate more so.... It made me a monster... Forgive me!»

Becky held his hand. «I accept you exactly as you are, with all your darkness and light. I respect your destiny without judgement. Someday we may meet again. But for now, just rest in peace.»

Dorji's decaying body turned to dust, blowing into the wind and dissolving into the snow.

Becky rose and looked at Bhatua and Mohammed, still on their knees, shivering with cold and fear.

«And I'm sure you too are very anxious to hand yourselves in to the authorities for all your misdeeds,» she said in Dzongkha.

Both men nodded repeatedly.

«If you don't, I will find you and take you in myself.»

They nodded with even more fervor.

Becky smiled and went to Dr. Bhat, whose face glowed with awe. She took the older woman's hands.

«I would love for you to meet my family. They're waiting for me back in New York. Would you like to go with me?»

Dr. Bhat nodded, tears of joy in her eyes.

And just like that, they both vanished into thin air.

34

New York, Sylvia Chang's Apartment

In Sylvia's tiny New York apartment, Ana Ramos, Evelyn, and Soto huddled together, looking haggard and worn. They rubbed their hands together and crossed their arms against the cold.

Sylvia Chang handed out steaming mugs of hot cocoa.

A knock on the door made them all jump.

Soto moved protectively toward it, looked through the peephole, then immediately began unlatching the many locks.

Bright light flooded in as he opened the door.

Becky and Dr. Bhat stood in the hallway, looking exactly as they had moments before in the Himalayan cave, some of the snow from Bhutan still clinging to their shoes and clothes.

Soto stared in disbelief. Becky reached out and touched his cheek warmly, smiling and nodding. He remained frozen, transfixed.

Becky walked past him. Soto embraced his mentor and friend, Dr. Bhat, warmly.

In the living room, Evelyn stared at her daughter, tears welling in her eyes. They moved toward each other, embracing tightly as Evelyn broke into full sobs.

Everyone stood in profound, reverent silence.

Soto and Dr. Bhat joined them. Sylvia embraced Dr. Bhat as if they'd known each other forever. When they separated, Ana shook hands with Dr. Bhat, then hugged her as well.

Becky moved to Sylvia and embraced her tightly, her gratitude clearly visible.

Somehow, spontaneously, they ended up in a circle with joined hands, studying each other—some with questions in their eyes, Becky and Dr. Bhat with love.

Secluded Beach

It was sundown. The golden rays of the Caribbean sun bathed the beach in warm, reddish hues, the same secluded beach where Becky had been rescued by the turtle.

The group stood in a circle like they had before, holding hands, except for Becky, who carried an urn with Isabel's name clearly etched on the front, along with a bunch of bright blue flowers.

Becky walked solemnly toward the shore as the others watched. She waded into the ocean until she was thigh-deep, then opened the urn and spread the ashes into the water.

A single tear trickled down her cheek.

She closed her eyes, breathed deeply, then opened them to look up at the bright, immense, full moon that was beginning to rise on the horizon.

A slight, loving smile crossed her lips.

She dropped the flowers and watched the tide carry them away toward the horizon, where they would continue their eternal journey through the endless sea.

THE END

BRANDS AND TRADEMARKS MENTIONED IN THIS BOOK

All brands and trademarks mentioned in this book belong to their respective owners. None of them have sponsored or otherwise paid for this book's creation or distribution. If that ever changes in the future, we'll update this book to indicate that.

ABOUT THE AUTHOR

Ernesto Morales-Ramos has been a communications professional for more than 40 years, creating compelling content for Fortune 500 companies, political candidates, non-profit organizations, and individuals. He first became aware of his interest in the occult as a child when he asked his mother to buy him a book on witchcraft along with his first of many Tarot card decks. It was his close friend, José N. García, astrologer, Freemason, Vedic, and Buddhist scholar who first introduced Ernesto to the Nyingma Buddhist tradition of Terma treasures. Tibetan Lamas who have visited Ernesto's homeland have said there are Terma treasures waiting to be uncovered on the island - this became his inspiration for this novel. Ernesto is a practicing *Bert Hellinger Family Constellations* Facilitator, screenwriter, director, producer, video editor, and communications professor. He lives in his native Puerto Rico with his wonderful son, Ángel Gabriel.

www.ingramcontent.com/pod-product-compliance
Lightning Source LLC
Chambersburg PA
CBHW061116100726
47911CB00013B/561